D0558764

BOOK SALE
DAMAGE NOTED
Staining
7-19

The Available Wife

Part 2

Redford Branch Library
21200 Grand River
Detroit, MI 48219
313-481-1820

Carla
PENNINGTON

JAN -- 2012

RD

Life Changing Books in conjunction with Power Play Media
Published by Life Changing Books
P.O. Box 423 Brandywine, MD 20613

This novel is a work of fiction. Any references to real people, events, establishments, or locales are intended only to give the fiction a sense of reality and authenticity. Other names, characters, and incidents occurring in the work are either the product of the author's imagination or are used fictitiously, as are those fictionalized events and incidents that involve real persons. Any character that happens to share the name of a person who is an acquaintance of the author, past or present, is purely coincidental and is in no way intended to be an actual account involving that person.

Library of Congress Cataloging-in-Publication Data;

www.lifechangingbooks.net
13 Digit: 978-1934230350
10 Digit: 1934230359

Copyright © 2011

All rights reserved, including the rights to reproduce this book or portions thereof in any form whatsoever.

Acknowledgements

GOD, none of this would be possible without You walking by my side through the good and the bad. You gave me this gift to share with the world. I know You have more in store for me, so I will sit back and wait for Your sign. I look forward to my next journey.

My grandparents, Ollie and Rosie Brown, keep smiling down on me.

My Mama, Rosa Pennington Browne, there are no words to describe you because you are of your own world. I guess the saying is true…I get it from my mama! *laughing* You are my cheerleader, promoter, sponsor, advertiser, etc. and you do it all without hesitation. You've been by my side ever since you reentered my life. I'm happy that I have my mama back because no matter what I say or do, I need you. I'm so happy to have you as a mother and friend. You refuse to allow me to fail. You're my inspiration. You pulled yourself through the darkness and never looked back. You're living proof that anything is possible. I'll always be your lil' Womba. I love you, Mama!

My Daddy, Carl Pennington, thank you so much for being here for me. No words can express how much that means to me. I love you, Daddy!

My crumbsnatchers, looks like we'll be going to more Wrestlemania events! Kemyria, I'm so proud of you and can't wait for the day you graduate as a forensic scientist. I know we butt heads at times, but it's only because I love you, baby. You will always be my child so don't you ever forget that. Keep up the good work, future CSI. Kemberlyn, my quiet child, you remind me so much of me when I was a little girl because we both experience the middle child syndrome. (We need the most attention). People used to call me weird a lot because I was always in my own little world and I see you do the same. Baby, if someone calls you weird, thank them for the compliment because that means you're unique. Keep doing what you're doing, baby. Mama looks forward to you becoming that scientist that you're striving to be. I see the Nobel Peace Prize in your future. Jevon (Ju), I remember the day that I gave birth to you. I told everyone that you were going to give me a hard time because you were so impatient to enter into this world. I called it because you do give me a hard time. Baby, I love every headache that you give me because for some odd reason, those headaches always seem to go away because you always end up making me laugh. Keep at your gymnastics and baseball, sweetie because Mama is ready to go to the Olympics and sit in the sky boxes at your baseball games.

My big sister, Kimberly Pennington Saxton, I know you and I are not that mushy- mushy type but we're going to have to get over that for the moment. LOL! Kim, I love you dearly. I must really do since I named my kids after you. LOL! You've always been there for me even when I didn't want you to be. I cherish talking and laughing with you everyday. If only you knew how that makes me feel. You're my sister, no matter what, and I wouldn't have it any other way.

My brother Bryan, what makes you think our relationship would be any different from when we were younger? I will still whoop your a—! I love you, Chopper!!!

Uncle Boo Boo, Aunt Mary, Aunt Arby, Uncle Abraham, Aunt Linda Sue, Uncle Sonny, Aunt Lela and Uncle Jimmy, even a blind man can see how much all of you mean to me. You all have had a hand in raising me and keeping me on the straight and narrow path. Although I tried to veer off a few times, y'all were always there to pump my brakes and guide me back onto that path. I love you all and I hope I continue to make you proud. We are the real "Meet the Browns!" I'll holla!

Aaron Brown, I guess I could've tossed you up there with the aunts and uncles, huh? Everything I said above goes out to you, too but with a little extra! LOL! I love you, brousin'. Now, raise your glass… "I can feel it coming in the air tonight. Oh Lord!"

My girls, Rashunda, Krystal, Simetra, Valencia, Kim T. W., Kim B., Tennille, LaTonya, Ameila and Anna, you chicks have been rolling with me for years and I'm so happy to have you as my friends. This is a big moment in my life and I am happy to be sharing it with you ladies. Enough of that mushy mushy ish, right?? Pass the Verdi! Better yet, who's got the tequila??? This is party time and who better to party with than my girls! Raise your glasses, triques…Cheers!

My homies, Wesley "Chuckie," Tommie, Gemini, Commie, Herb, and Cedric, thanks a million for always having my back. Y'all are like my brothers from different mothers… and fathers for that matter. LOL! Thanks for always giving ish to me straight…no chaser! I love you guys! Hold up your beer bottles…Cheers!

Craig Warden, thank you for helping me with a few scenes in this sequel. *wink*

To my LCB family, it is an honor being part of this family and I appreciate this second opportunity that you've given me. Tressa, thanks for always having a lending ear whenever I had questions. I really appreciate all that you've done to put me on the map as a serious author. You're the truth! Leslie, it was easier this time around, huh? LOL! Seriously, I appreciate all that you've done. I'm so happy for unlimited text messages. LOL! Jackie D, Danette Majette, C.J. Hudson, Capone, Miss KP, J. Tremble, Tonya Ridley, Kendall Banks, Chris Renee and the rest of my LCB crew, I appreciate all you've done to make this an exciting and memorable moment in my life. Let's keep it moving! We're the best!

Thanks to all the test readers. You guys are truly appreciated.

Thanks to all the urban bookstores who support this genre; Urban Knowledge, Horizon Books, etc. You push these books like they were your own. Thanks a ton!

Ella Curry of Black Pearls Magazine, thank you so much for all you've done for me and my LCB family. You're a rare "pearl." It is a pleasure knowing you.

Shani Greene Dowdell, again, I appreciate the opportunity you gave me to be a part of the Mocha Chocolate anthologies. You've become an important person in my life. Thanks for your friendship.

Wanda Mays Noel of Wine About Books (ATL), thanks for the opportunity to be a part of your blog talk radio show.

Niyah Moore, I am so happy to have you as my friend. We will meet soon. I can't wait.

Dell Banks, thanks for all you've done.

Robert "Scooter" Myers, I don't know what to say to you. LOL! Thank you for all your support on and off the grid. Your friendship is greatly appreciated. I'm sure I'll see you soon.

Kiesha Bonham and "The Perfect 10 Bookclub" out of Birmingham, AL, it was an honor being a part of your meeting and I look forward to the next. Kiesha, thank you from the bottom of my heart.

Darryl and Johnita Evans (Legends Lounge), thank you sooooo much for your assistance in making my first book release party a huge success. I look forward to the second opportunity.

Joshlyn "J'Renee" Witherspoon, Ericka "Speakeasy" and Benjamin "Benjammin'" Emanuel, y'all made my book release party a hit! You can never know how much that meant to me. Thank you so much!

Andy and Sharon Stanfield, you were the ones who gave me my first opportunity to showcase my writing skills in my first book "FLING." Thank you so much for that experience.

To my Facebook and Twitter family as well as all of my

readers and fans, thank you soooooooooooo much for your support and making this dream possible. I promise you this, I will keep the heat coming.

Mattie T. Blount High School class of '94 and especially '95, y'all have shown me so much love and support. It is overwhelming. Raise your glasses and beer bottles......Leopards for life!

To anyone that I may have overlooked, please forgive me. It was not intentional. If I could thank you all, I would.

Again, I'm shouting out to my hometown, Prichard, AL. Your small town girl is doing big things. P.A. all day, baby!

Smooches,
Carla

Chapter 1

I stared across the long table watching the two impatient, male lawyers as they waited for me to make my next move. After giving them the evil eye for a few minutes, I turned to my own Jewish lawyer who was sitting beside me. He gave me a 'go ahead' nod. I didn't expect anything more or less from him since I'd already fattened his pockets. I just never knew I'd need him under the present circumstances.

The black pen trembled in my hand as I hesitated signing the papers. I sat in the same spot for what seemed like hours. I hoped that something dramatic would happen to stop me from signing the paperwork like a fire or hurricane. I could even deal with someone bursting in and shooting up the place. I knew the lawyers were getting agitated due to my delay, but I didn't give a damn. This was my life that I was signing over. My eyes began to welt up as I placed the tip of the pen on the signature line. I hesitated for a few more minutes after glancing at his name then frowned immediately. Mr. Alphonso Jamar Townes or "A.J." as he was known was about to own my legacy, Kingquole Records.

I was even more heated that A.J. wasn't present at the meeting. His lawyers gave a pathetic lie that he'd missed his flight from Vegas, and would be late. I wanted A.J. there to feel all the anger that I was giving his lawyers. When I read the line on the document stating that he wanted me completely off the label, I nearly had a panic attack. When I agreed to sell Kingquole Records to him, A.J. agreed to keep me on as Vice President. We'd verbally gone over the deal on countless occasions, but from the looks of it, that bastard had fucked me once again. I wanted desperately to say that the deal was off, but there was no way I could afford to run the company even if I hadn't agreed to sell. It was probably best that A.J. didn't show his face after all. If he had, the pen that was trembling in my hand would probably have ended up in the side of his neck. I was just that pissed.

With all the other events that had unfolded over the past six months, selling my dream label to A.J. was the icing on the cake. I was in so much debt from the label, the proceeds from the sale were going straight to my lawyer so he could distribute it amongst all the creditors. Being arrested for all the Kingston bullshit was just the beginning of my troubles. I still couldn't believe that Germaine had made me shoot him. Even worse, he'd left me holding the gun…literally. Germaine disappearing with my boys and knowing that my sister's bitch ass was sleeping with him and taking care of my sons didn't help the situation either. It irked me knowing that Jalisa was playing mommy to *my* kids.

"Ms. Wright?"

I broke away from my horrid thoughts when my lawyer called my name. "What?" I snapped while sniffling in the process. The tears I'd been forcing back were slowly leaking from my eyes.

"You need to sign the papers, so that…" my lawyer attempted to say.

"I'm going to sign them, damn it! Don't fucking rush me!" I barked. Now wasn't the time to rush me.

He adjusted the tie around his pencil neck as I gave him a stern 'don't fuck with me' look. He needed to shut up. The pen trembled in my hand again. My life was truly over. I had nothing. I had no one. I even had to let my artists out of their contracts because I no longer had the money to finance their projects. Not to mention, no one wanted to work with me anymore, so I couldn't even get any investors. I had more money going out than I had coming in. Truth be told, I had nothing coming in. All of it was going out to defense attorneys who were trying to keep me out of jail after I paid a hefty million dollar bond to get out. The rest I'd spent on paying a few private investigators to locate Germaine and my boys. I couldn't believe in the past six months his ass had yet to be found. Germaine wasn't that smart, so the fact that he'd managed to stay low key after all this time was puzzling to me. Even Jalisa hadn't surfaced. Spending money to find them hadn't come cheap so basically I, Niquole "Nikki" Wright, former CEO of Kingquole Records, was broke. My once luxurious life was now gone.

I wiped the tears from my eyes. I wanted A.J.'s lawyers to see the daggers I was shooting at them as if having to sell my label was their fault. Anyone associated with A.J. was on my shit list. One of the lawyers even had the audacity to check the time on his gold Presidential Rolex as if he had somewhere to be. That only made me prolong the signing for a few more minutes, even though I knew those bastards would stay there as long as it took.

I took a deep breath and mumbled the words, "I hate you, A.J.," before finally scribbling my name on the line. Afterwards I flung the papers toward his lawyers, slammed the pen down and ran out of the boardroom. I hated the fact that I'd agreed to have the meeting at A.J.'s lawyers office. I probably should've done it at Kingquole, so I could see my baby one last time.

As if my luck couldn't get any worse, when I was halfway to the elevator, I saw A.J. walking in my direction. He'd finally decided to show up. I assumed he was on his way to the meeting to see how things had gone. In my eyes, he didn't need to show his face to finish choking the life out of me because his lawyers had already done it.

I wanted to turn around and jet the other way as soon as

we made eye contact, but there was no where to go. The exit door leading to the stairwell was too far away.

Fuck it, I thought as he neared me with a smug ass smile on his face.

He gently grabbed me when I tried to walk past him as if he wasn't there.

"What in the hell do you want, A.J.?" I immediately tore into him after yanking away. He grabbed me again.

"Damn, Niquole. Don't be like that, baby," he replied as if he was truly sorry.

"How in the hell do you expect me to be, A.J.? I can't believe you want me completely off the label…the business that I built! You promised me…you promised that I could stay on as Vice President. How could you betray me like that? You know I needed the job for the money. You just took my life away from me, and now you don't even want me to be a part of it."

"Don't look at it like that, Niquole. You signing the company over to me was for the best especially with all the shit you got going on. How were you gonna keep it afloat with no money? You know you gotta have paper to be in this business, baby."

It's funny how he completely skated around the Vice President issue.

"Fuck you, A.J.! I don't need your smart ass comments right now."

"Niquole, I told you that I'm not changing the name of the label if that's what you're worried about. I can resurrect it. Kingquole Records is gonna be bigger than before. I'm not changing anything. *You* made Kingquole Records. I just want to make it greater and you know I can do it."

Hearing him talk about *my* label pissed me off even more. I yanked away and walked off only to be stopped again. This time, I was pushed into the ladies room.

"What in the hell are you doing, A.J.?" I watched this son-of-a-bitch lock the door, then back me into the wall. Those hungry, lustful eyes were the same as I'd always remembered them; gray and hypnotic. "What are you doing, A.J.?" I asked again while trying to push him off of me.

"Come on, Niquole. You know how we do." He stared into my eyes.

"*We* ain't doing this shit anymore, A.J.," I stressed while pulling his hand from under my shirt knowing good and damn well that I didn't want to.

"Niquole, you know this is what we do. We fight. We fuck," he continued while I tried to push him away. "You know you want this. Stop fighting."

"A.J., stop it!" I begged. "I hate you! I fucking hate you!"

"I know you do, baby. Show me how much you hate me," he whispered in my ear after making a second attempt under my shirt. This time, I didn't stop him. "I swear to you, baby, this is for the best. I'm doing this for us. This is the right thing and you know it," he continued.

"A.J., please stop," I pleaded knowing that I was on my way to giving in.

He needed to know just how pissed off I was at him for keeping my name off the label. My anger resurfaced. I pulled his hand from under my shirt again. I couldn't do this. Our fuck/hate relationship had taken a major turn this time. Before, he would steal my artists or I would blackmail him but now, him owning my label, and not bothering to keep me on as Vice President was too much for me.

"A.J., I can't do this! Stop!"

I shoved him, but he didn't give up. I knew he wouldn't anyway. Instead, he stared into my eyes. I turned away for fear his eyes would put me in a trance like they always did.

A.J. chuckled then stepped back up to me before pressing his lips against mine. "Niquole, no matter what we do to each other, you know you can never resist me," he whispered. "Baby, I know we've done some fucked up shit to each other in the past, but not this time. I promise…I'm gonna make Kingquole Records bigger than before. All I need you to do is sit back and watch. Trust me."

A.J. knew he had me with those words because business wise, he was the man. I knew he could take Kingquole Records much further than I could right now. At that moment, he lifted me off the floor and carried me over to the sink. He had such a fucking hold over me that I had to give in. All of a sudden, I found myself hopping off the sink then coming out of my jeans.

"That's a good girl," A.J. said as he pushed his pants and boxers to his ankles then turned me around.

I slapped my hands on top of the granite sink as A.J. pushed my shirt up and began kissing and sucking my back while groping my breasts and grinding my ass. His dick nestled snuggly inside the crease. I reached behind me and parted my ass cheeks so that he could grind a little harder. While he tended to my body, I stared at myself in the mirror and wondered what the hell I was doing. How long would we continue our fuck/hate relationship? Only time would tell.

"Mmmmmmm, Niquole, baby," he moaned in between pressing his lips against my skin.

Before I could respond, he quickly slipped on a condom, parted my pussy lips, then plunged inside of me. He felt bigger than I had remembered. I gripped the faucet trying to hold on for dear life. I damn near popped a nail that was in desperate need of a fill in as A.J. stroked me in the way he knew would send me over the edge. He jabbed…then rolled….jabbed….then rolled.

"A.J.!" I called out to him after dropping my head because I couldn't take it. However, he grabbed my head and lifted it back up so that I could see him in the mirror.

"Look at me while I fuck you," he growled seductively in my ear while staring at my reflection.

His Lamman Rucker looking ass knew just how to work me. He threw me for a loop when he lifted my right leg and placed it on top of the counter. This gave him easier and much better access inside my walls. Each strong, deep, long thrust he made lifted me off the floor. I was being handled…in a good way.

"Oooooh, A.J.….right there! Right there!"

"About to cum, baby?" he asked my reflection.

My facial expression answered for me. He reached around my thigh and fondled my clit as he pounded me. Each time I would lower my head or close my eyes, he demanded that I watch him fuck the shit outta me. Deciding to join in on the fun, I lifted my leg a little higher to help him knead my pussy as we boldly watched each other in the mirror. I could easily forget our drama whenever he was inside of me. I wanted him to live there if that was all it took to take the pain of losing my label away.

"Shit! Niquole! Fuck!"

"What?" I asked. It sounded like something was wrong.

"The fucking condom broke."

"We're good," I panted needing him to get back to what he was doing. "I got my tubes tied after Nathan was born," I assured.

He went right back to drilling me after that lie.

"Here we go, baby. I'm about to cum."

"Me, too," I concurred while rolling on his third leg. "Alphonsoooooooooooooooooo!" I sang loudly.

Seconds later, he pulled out and released on the floor. He knew not to trust me.

Chapter 2

"This is where I belong," I said, stretching underneath the plush comforter inside one of the ninth floor suites of The Four Seasons.

It felt like I was opening up some curtains when I swept my hair away from my face. My hair had grown so much over the past few months and I couldn't even afford to get it done like I used to. The weekly trips to the salon were gone. But it didn't matter. I could still give my twin, Kerry Washington, a run for her money.

Glancing at the clock on the nightstand, my eyes widened when I realized it was 1:15 p.m. I couldn't believe I'd slept that long. Then again great sex could put you in a coma-like state sometimes, especially A.J.'s dick. He and I had a wonderful night of drinking and chatting over Raspberry Ciroc followed by several rounds of explosive lovemaking. After that bathroom action, there was no way I was gonna pass up his offer to spend the night with him in a luxury hotel. There was nothing better than a plush down comforter, marble floors and room service. Damn, I couldn't imagine not being able to afford shit like this anymore.

"A.J.?" I called out to him.

When there was no answer, I assumed he'd stepped out. Turning over, I could hear the sounds of a rustling noise under the covers when I moved. Curious to know what it was, I pushed the covers away from my naked body. It was a Nieman Marcus bag with a note attached from A.J. I didn't even bother to look at the note first.

With a wide smile spread across my face, I eagerly emptied the bag. There was a pair of J Brand skinny jeans, an olive Alice + Olivia V-neck belted cardigan and a pair of black Chanel ballerina flats. I wasn't crazy about the shoes.

"Well, at least he tried...and remembered my sizes."

I snickered thinking that I could rock the cardigan with a pair of stilettos much better. However, I was in no predicament to be choosey especially since I was now wearing the same clothes over and over. Six months ago I didn't do repeats, but now I had no other choice. The only good thing was that my wardrobe still consisted of top designers, so I was grateful to still have a little bit of Niquole left. Thinking back to when A.J. and I were intertwined in a full blown affair a little over eight years ago, he treated me like a queen. Whatever I wanted, I got. Where ever I wanted to go, I went, but he fucked it all up when he wouldn't leave his wife for me. I shook those thoughts and finally read the note.

Niquole, thanks for last night but it was strictly business. Thanks for the label. Don't take the changes personal.

"Fuck you A.J.!" I said, throwing the note down. Was he trying to be funny?

If this outfit was considered some type of a peace offering, his ass had a long way to go to give me peace for taking my name off the label.

"Asshole," I spoke as if I was talking to him directly.

After easing out of the bed, I stared at the three-pack Trojan condom box that we'd gone through that was on the floor. All three condoms ended up in pieces. We hadn't had sex in a while, and I didn't have time to contract some damn STD. In the past, and in all the years we'd fooled around the one thing I loved about him was that he'd never passed anything off to me. I hoped like hell his ass was still clean.

Still cursing A.J. out, I walked into the restroom, then took a long, hot shower. Thoughts of Germaine appeared as they'd done so many times ever since he showed me his "tough" side after the night everything went down with me, him, Kingston and Jalisa. At first, I was rooting for Kingston to eliminate Germaine so that he and I could be together, but secretly, I wanted it to be the other way around. I was kind of turned on with Germaine's newfound manly ways. It was Kingston's fault that I felt that way especially after coming to grips that he really didn't give a shit about me. After he was shot, and Germaine and Jalisa fled the scene, I wanted to do the same, but still couldn't leave him there. I just knew he was dead until I noticed that he was still breathing. I rushed to the phone and called 911.

However, if I would've known I was going to be arrested, I would've ran and I definitely would've gotten rid of the gun even though I wasn't the one who actually pulled the trigger. Now, Kingston lay in the hospital in a coma, which was a good thing for me since my charges had been dropped from murder to attempted murder. Both charges were bullshit though.

I shouldn't have been the only one at the precinct being questioned like I was on an episode of *The First 48*. Germaine and Jalisa should've been right there with me since they were the ones who masterminded the shooting.

After finishing my shower, my mind quickly went back to the note that A.J. had left. What did he mean by last night was strictly business, and for me not to take the changes personal? Just like me, A.J. couldn't be trusted. Something wasn't right about this shit and it weighed heavily on my mind. I hurried into my clothes. For some reason, I felt the need to get to Kingquole. Quickly grabbing the shopping bag, I grabbed my purse, then headed out the door.

I laughed at the fact that I was now one of most talked about in the industry. It was embarrassing to build such a huge name and then, in the blink of an eye, have it tainted. All this negative shit that I was going through was all over the place; tabloids, internet, newspapers, magazines, blogs, etc. All of this because I wasn't on my game. All of this because of a man who didn't want me. All of this because of an assistant who played me. I was happy that bitch, Meagan, was dead. I probably could've saved her life by getting some help, but she shouldn't have stolen my money and fucked my man. There was one thing she must've forgotten before she decided to take her life. I'm Niquole "Nikki" Wright, so good riddance, bitch.

No sooner than Meagan disappeared, Johnathan and Nathan quickly trotted inside my thoughts. I had neglected them so much because of Kingston. Now, they were gone. I never thought I could miss the smell of baby piss and shit, crying and whining and early morning cartoons as much as I did now. Knowing that my bitch of a sister, Jalisa was taking care of them made me miss them even more. She had hers coming though. There was no way she was going to just up and take my life as if I never existed.

When I arrived at Kingquole Records several minutes later, I immediately slammed on brakes in the middle of the street. I couldn't believe my eyes. The new marquise that I'd just purchased one year prior was in a dumpster on the side of the building along with all of my office furniture. I could even see some files piled on top. To add insult to injury, a SOLD sign was plastered on the door surrounded by a second sign that read: **Another A.J. Townes Production coming soon.** There was also a scaffold out front as if the building was about to be remodeled. I quickly referenced the note that A.J. had left back in the room: *Strictly business*.

"That son-of-a-bitch lied to me! He *is* changing the name of my label! He's changing everything!" In a fit of rage, I began screaming and beating the steering wheel with both of my fists. "This is fucked up, A.J.! How could you do this shit to me?"

Now, I knew why he'd talked such a good game in that bathroom the day before. Everything he'd said about not changing Kingquole was all a fucking lie. He'd obviously said all that shit just to get in my pants. Once again, I'd been betrayed by A.J. Townes.

As a few horns blew for me to get out the way, I angrily pulled into the parking lot and parked in front of the building. I reached on the side of my seat for the trunk release and popped it. I hopped out of the car like a woman on a mission and grabbed the tire iron from the trunk. If I couldn't have Kingquole Records, A.J.'s ass wasn't going to have it either. Not in perfect condition anyway.

"Fuck you, A.J.!" I screamed before banging the tire iron against one of the windows. After two forceful swings, it finally shattered. "You've fucked me for the last time!" I burst another window. "You lying son-of-a-bitch!" I burst another. "This is mine! I built this shit!"

I began ripping the posters down of him and a few of the artists on his label. I then walked over to the scaffold and aggressively pushed and pulled trying to make it fall disregarding my own safety. When it wouldn't budge, I rushed back over to the windows. But before I could cause anymore damage, suddenly a hand stopped me from taking another swing. I turned to the interrupter.

"What the fuck are you doing? This is none of your business. Let me go!"

"It is my business since I work for A.J.," he spoke still gripping my arm.

Little did he know, his words went in one ear and out the other. By him working for A.J. only added fuel to my burning flame. I grabbed the tire iron with my left hand and tried to burst another window. Without warning, I was lifted in the air, then placed across the stranger's shoulder.

"Put me down, damn it!" I screamed and kicked. "You need to stay out of this shit!"

"Look, you need to calm down. Do you know how many people have driven by and saw what you were doing? I'm sure one of them has called the cops by now."

I calmed down as I thought about my current legal issues. He was right. I didn't need any more trouble. After carrying me to my car, he set me down. I tried to hurry into my car to get the hell out of dodge in case someone did call the cops, but he stopped me.

"What?" I barked.

"You shouldn't be driving since you're so angry."

"Look, I don't need your advice right now."

"Why don't you go have a drink with me then?"

"Have a drink with you? I don't know you," I snarled. Had he lost his damn mind? He wasn't about to abduct, rape and kill me.

"Well, have a drink with me and get to know me," he chuckled. "I'm Marko."

I stared him up and down. "Are you even old enough to drink?"

"Yes, I'm old enough," he chuckled again. "I'm twenty-three."

I looked at his young face that had a fresh pimple on his forehead. "It's too early for a drink."

"It's not too early. Plus, it looks like you're having a bad day."

"I am having a bad day. Your *boss* is a fucking asshole."

I stared at him when he didn't respond. He did seem like a nice guy. On top of that, he was a cutie. He could've easily passed for Lenny Kravitz's son. His jet black, tapered haircut, thin sideburns and goatee accentuated the butterscotch skin on his six foot two frame. The only minus I could find was his dark lips, which didn't go with the rest of his complexion. He was dressed in a pair of Rocawear jeans, hoodie, Nike boots and a long chain with a diamond encrusted pendant. I wasn't im-pressed with his style of clothes, but the necklace was a plus. I wondered if he had money.

"I think I'll pass, Marko," I replied before attempting to slide inside my car. I wasn't about to get caught with this young dude.

"Come on. Just one drink," he countered. "By the way, I told you my name now, what's yours pretty lady? That's the first step in getting to know someone."

This lil' young boy was trying to work his game.

"I'm Nikki," I replied.

"Nice to meet you, Nikki. So, what about that drink?"

"You're very eager about getting me to have a drink. Are you some kinda pervert who drugs women?"

"No, I'm not," he defended himself. "I just see someone who I like and would like to get to know better."

"Listen, I'm not some young chick who's easily flattered so you can save all those lines for someone else."

He smiled, showing a great set of teeth which was a plus. "Look, truth be told, I don't want to have lunch alone."

"Then why didn't you just say that instead of running around in circles?"

"I apologize, and I understand if you don't want to go. Hope your day gets better." As he was about to walk away, something made me stop him.

"If you try anything, trust me, you will regret it. You don't know what the hell I got in my purse," I threatened after reaching inside my car and picking up my bag. I still had the tire iron in my hand.

"I don't think I'd enjoy crossing you but in the meantime, I'll take that," Marko stated as he eased the tire iron from my hand. "I don't want you to whack me over the head," he joked. "I was actually on my way to Gravitas on Taft Street, but if that's not cool, we can go somewhere else."

Gravitas, I thought. I hadn't been to a nice restaurant in a while so I was happy with his suggestion. "Gravitas is fine." I smiled internally. After leading me to his smoke grey Range Rover, we drove off. The truck was another plus.

As we drove to the destination spot, we chatted a little, but I let him do most of the talking. He didn't need to know any of my business just yet. Letting men in so easily had always been my downfall. We were fifteen minutes into the twenty-five minute drive when Jazmine Sullivan's *Bust the Windows* pumped through the speakers. We both burst into a roar of laughter. It was the perfect ice breaker.

We arrived at the restaurant minutes later. Once inside, we took two seats at the bar. I shouldn't have been drinking that early, but I needed something to calm me down after learning of A.J.'s betrayal. I didn't even have to look at the drink menu before quickly ordering a glass of Paloma. I noticed him staring at me.

"What?" I snapped my neck. "Did you think this was my first time coming here?" I questioned.

Marko just smiled and ordered himself a glass of Fontaine Bleu. "So, is Nikki short for something?" he asked after our drinks arrived.

"Yes, it does. I'm Niquole. Niquole Wright," I replied. "And I actually prefer if you call me Niquole. I don't know you well enough for you to use my nick name."

He damn near choked on his drink when I told him my name. "Niquole Wright?" Marko asked as if he was meeting his favorite star. "I knew you looked familiar."

"Yes. The one and only," I faked a smile.

"Now, it all makes sense as to why you were giving the place a beat down." I laughed at his choice of words. "Ms. Kingquole Records in the flesh," he continued ecstatically. When he saw that I wasn't enthused, he calmed down. "I'm sorry about that. It's just that you are a force to be reckoned with. I've been following your story."

"Was," I corrected before sipping my drink.

Marko grinned weakly. "You still are."

I could tell that something else was on his mind, so I decided to help him out. "Go ahead. Ask me."

"Huh?" he asked dumbfounded.

"I know you want to know if I shot that guy." His facial expression read yes. "And the answer is…No. No I didn't," I lied because in my eyes, I didn't do it. I was forced.

Marko shifted his weight on the stool, then called the waiter over. He ordered me another drink when he saw that I'd already finished off the first one.

"I'm sorry for your troubles, Niquole. I know you got a

lot going on, but it's truly an honor meeting you. You had some great artists on your label, so I respect you as a black woman handling her business." I could tell that he meant every word which made me feel a little better. "I don't know about you, but I'm hungry as hell," he said, rubbing his stomach. He skimmed through the menu.

"So, you are trying to get me drunk?" I asked him when my drink arrived.

"Naw, I'm just enjoying your company and I want to keep you satisfied while you're with me." He winked. For some reason, his words made me smile. His young ass definitely had game.

After a few more drinks and a much needed meal, he drove me back to my car. Surprisingly, I actually enjoyed his company and a part of me wasn't ready for us to part ways.

"I think this belongs to you," he chuckled after handing me the tire iron through my window. I was a little embarrassed as I stared across the street at the damage I'd caused. "I'd like to see you again."

"I don't think that's a good idea," I replied. Playing hard to get sometimes was a good thing.

"Well, if you change your mind, here's my card."

I accepted it. After saying his goodbye, Marko walked back to his Range. I stared at his fine ass in my rearview mirror until he drove off. I flipped his card over, which read: *Marko "The Verse."*

I assumed he was a rapper or spoken word artist with a title like that. I had to find out more about what he did for A.J.'s label. If I wanted to get A.J. back, Marko might've been my way to do that. I smiled sinisterly. My relationship with A.J. was chaotic, but I knew that his feelings for me ran deep. I knew that seeing me with Marko would make his blood boil. He was always jealous, and hated seeing me with other dudes. This was going to be fun.

Carla Pennington

Chapter 3

This bitch on this phone is really working my nerves, I thought as I fumbled through my purse for a stick of gum.

"Look, ma'am, I told you that your card was declined for the fourth time. I'm not a magician. I can't make it work," I huffed hoping she would hear the aggravation in my voice after having me on the phone for over twenty minutes. "Look, you can't get the damn car if your card isn't working. Why can't you understand that? You can scream and holler at me all you want, but it still won't change anything."

At that moment, the woman immediately began screaming even louder and demanding to speak to a supervisor. Who would've thought that I'd be working as a rental car reservation agent at a call center? To add insult to injury, I had to go through a temp agency to get the piece of shit job. I didn't think I was going to get it with all the legal crap I had going on, but the agency that I went through didn't do background checks. They just needed to fill positions and get paid. I'd been working for almost four weeks, and couldn't believe I'd lasted this long. I wasn't used to rules and working a set schedule along with making nine dollars a damn hour. I was used to coming and going as I pleased as well as a paycheck that would make every bitch in the call center jealous. Something had to give. I'd applied for the bullshit job just to earn some money until my deal with A.J. went through. I'd planned on quitting once A.J. hired me to help him run the label, but obviously that shit wasn't gonna happen now.

As the woman continued to scream in my ear, I instantly tuned her ass out and thought about A.J.'s ass once again. After parting ways with Marko the day before, I went back to A.J.'s hotel only to find that he'd checked out. Even my hundreds of calls to him went ignored. I couldn't help but wonder if Marko had tipped him off about my rampage. Either way, he was gonna have to face me one day, but until then, someone else was about to feel my rage.

I wasn't trying to hear this bitch's voice any longer, so I politely ended the call. I didn't have to take that type of abuse. I needed a break. Tossing the headset off of my head, I watched as it landed on the keyboard before pushing my chair away from the desk. However, before I could even stand up, I saw my thick, supervisor charging toward me like a professional football player. His white ass was red as a tomato. I knew that my call had been recorded, but I didn't care. They didn't pay me enough to take the shit from the crazy ass people who called in. I'd been written up before because of my unprofessional attitude, and I'm sure this time was no exception.

"Niquole, I need to see you in my office…now," he spoke after adjusting the glasses on his fat ass face.

"For what?" I frowned. A few heads turned. "What in the hell are y'all looking at?" I snapped at the jealous bitches.

"So, you wanna talk out here…in front of everyone?" he questioned.

I looked around noticing that everyone was already staring at me, so I thought, *fuck it. Might as well well give 'em a show.* "Sure, why not," I said.

"Niquole, you've had a number of complaints ever since you were hired, and I've given you several opportunities to get yourself together but that last call has forced my hand. I'm sorry, but I've got to let you go."

"Let me go?" I laughed after hopping out of the chair. "Thanks. You just did *me* a favor." I grabbed my purse and started walking toward the door. I stopped when I heard a few of the females snickering. I turned to the blond, skinny, cheerleader type bitch and pointed at her.

Her snickering quickly stopped.

I turned back to the supervisor who was following me and smiled like I had a secret to tell. "I guess if I was sucking your dick like this illiterate bitch right here, I'd still have a job, huh?" He gave me a look of disbelief. "I've seen the two of you a few times in the parking lot and from what I've seen, it doesn't take long to make you cum." A few people giggled as I turned back to the Jessica Simpson looking girl. "You need to be sucking the owner's dick and not the supervisor's because he can't get you shit but an approved day off." Embarrassed, she jumped up like she was about to charge me until one of the other females held her back.

"You fake bitch! You walk around here all high and mighty like you're on top of the world, but everybody knows about you!" the skinny broad yelled. A few oohs and ahhs filled the room.

This bitch evidently didn't know who she was fucking with. "Look, you cheap trailer park whore," I said, staring her up and down like she disgusted me. "At least I fuck for more than just an extra thirty minute extended lunch break. You see the bags I carry and the clothes I wear." She swallowed that attitude real quick as she glanced at my attire like she hadn't done so already. "Until your Salvation Army ass can get on my level, don't come at me like that." As more giggles paraded the room, I could tell she was speechless and embarrassed.

"Get out of here Niquole!" the supervisor yelled.

"Isn't one of the rules for the call center not to raise your voice?" I laughed before walking away with my head held high. All eyes were on me. That's how I liked it. "They must not know who the hell I am," I barked while deep down inside, I was crumbling because I really needed the job.

Once outside, I hopped in my car and headed home; another place that I dreaded being. I pouted as I neared the neighborhood fifteen minutes later. I frowned when I turned onto the street and coasted through the area as if I was still showing off my 2010 Lexus to the nobodies. Although my 1993 Lexus ES was paid for, I had to end up selling my 2010 so that I could have money in my pockets. The only thing I had left were my custom made Kingquole Records rugs. But despite the year of the car, I knew people were still jealous of me. It wasn't like I was in a Hyundai or a fucking Smart Car.

A Lexus is a Lexus, no matter what it looks like, I convinced myself.

I frowned at the neighbors who were playing loud music in their raggedy ass Cutlasses, Impalas and Monte Carlos. There were even a few people sitting on their porches drinking beer, laughing and talking loudly while the untamed kids ran amuck. I even thought I heard a few of their bad asses curse. Although it was December, people were out like it was a cool day in spring. I caught a glimpse of two females stepping out of a Honda Civic with their knock off Louis Vuitton purses. I could spot a knock off a mile away as I tapped my Louis Vuitton Neverfull bag that was sitting on the passenger seat. Unlike theirs, my shit was authentic. I'd gotten rid of my car among several other things, but couldn't seem to part with my handbag collection.

All of a sudden, an orange light lit up on the dashboard of my car. I ignored it as I'd been doing for the past few weeks. But when the light was suddenly followed by a clanking noise under the hood, I finally slowed down. Even though I'd heard the same noise several times this month, I wasn't about to take it to a shop since I didn't have any extra money. I would see all the Auto Zone commercials, but chose to ignore them. I was too cute to be caught in such a place. As long as the car still rolled, I was fine.

I glanced out the corner of my eye and saw a guy walking toward me. His jeans were hanging off his ass and his corn rows were in desperate need of a touch up. "Hey, sexy. What's up?" he spoke through gapped teeth.

"Not you," I replied then sped up while silently praying that my car would make it to the house. *Damn, I hate this ghetto ass neighborhood*, I thought.

When I pulled into the driveway, I blew out a long, hard sigh. This house was a major step down for me. I missed my forty-eight hundred square foot home with a passion and wondered why I didn't pay it off when I had the chance to. Now, just like my Lexus and label, it was gone…foreclosed on actually. With my label going under, Germaine's bitch ass taking a large portion of my money, and the rest going to lawyers, investigators and anything else, I could no longer afford the mortgage. From what I was told, foreclosures were supposed to at least take a year, but my bank must've said, 'fuck that.' They started the foreclosure process after only two months of non payment. Maybe they'd heard about my situation along with everybody else. I laughed at the realization that I was now living with the person who I hated the most in the world…my mother. It had been exactly five weeks since I arrived, and I absolutely hated everything about it.

I stepped out of the car, took a deep breath and walked inside. It took my mother a while to even give me a key, but I guess she got tired of me knocking on the door waking her up all times of the night.

I halted my steps after closing the door. "Not again," I puffed after hearing her moan from her bedroom. That bitch fucked more than I did.

I just shook my head and walked to my room. Stopping at the doorway, I stared at the tiny room for a few moments and laughed. I was now sleeping in a twin size bed and watching a thirteen-inch battery operated TV that was used during power outages, and all of my designer clothes, shoes and purses were stuffed inside the small closet. They were even piled up on one side of the room and stuffed under the bed. My mom suggested that I sell some of the stuff, but quickly recanted her suggestion when she saw the look on my face. This was now my life and I hated it.

I fell onto the bed and closed my eyes. I wanted this all to be a dream. Hell, I'd take a nightmare if I could wake up from it and have all of this shit behind me. When I opened my eyes, twenty minutes later I was still in the same place...my hell on earth.

Letting out another high sigh, I walked inside the kitchen to get a glass of water. My mother was too cheap to buy bottled water, which was another thing that pissed me off. Walking past the living room, I frowned as I watched my mother and some stocky, shirtless man giggle and neck each other like two horny teenagers on the couch. I couldn't stand it. I hated when she moved her touchy feely sessions outside of her bedroom. When they saw me, they finally stopped.

"Who is this one?" I asked my mother with a slight snarl.

"Excuse me?" she asked insulted. "You need to watch yourself Nikki."

"I feel like I'm in high school all over again." Her eyes widened in disbelief because she knew where I was about to go with my speech. "You're the reason why I'm the way I am. You and all these different men are..." Before I could finish, she jumped up and headed directly toward my face.

My mother looked good for her age because she always kept her weight down. I'd never known her to wear over a size eight. But that bitch thought she was Tyra Banks or somebody with those hazel contacts.

"Maxine, baby, I'm going back in the room," her friend addressed her after grabbing a bag of chips off the counter. He left after smiling at me.

"Aren't you supposed to have a boyfriend? People in relationships aren't supposed to cheat on each other," I joked.

"This is *my* house, damn it!" she reminded. "If you don't like what I do in here, you can get the fuck out." That bitch knew she had me backed into a corner because I had no where to go. I watched her grab a cheap bottle of Chardonnay from the refrigerator, then she walked up to me once again. "If you ever

24

embarrass me like that in front of my company again, I'll put your ass out." She started walking off, but stopped as if she forgot something. "By the way, your share of the bills are due."

"I...I...I lost my job today, Mama," I stammered like a scolded child.

"Oh, so I'm mama now?" she laughed. "What does losing your job have to do with me? That's not my problem. The bills are still due and I need your half by Friday. It's funny how you had to end up coming back home. Welcome to the *real* world, Nikki." She walked off.

Completely furious, I retreated back to my bedroom and plopped down on the kiddie bed. "This isn't my fucking home! I don't need you! I don't fucking need you!" I screamed before throwing the pillow at the door.

I hadn't been in the house ten minutes and already I needed to leave. Racking my brain of who to call, I retrieved Marko's card from my purse and quickly dialed his number. After getting his voicemail, I hung up. The past six months of my life raced through my head like a runaway train. How in the hell could I be on top of the world one minute, then under it the next? In addition to all of that, my relationship with my mother was still just as fucked up as it was before. My unfortunate circumstances definitely hadn't brought us closer together. I wondered if things would've been different between us if she'd just told me the truth about my father in the beginning. Okay, Jalisa was his daughter...big deal. We could've still been the happy family that we once were before she decided to give him the boot.

Speaking of Jalisa, I wondered what she was doing with my boys and my husband and if they loved her like they loved me. I still couldn't believe that nasty ass bitch knew we were sisters when we had the threesome with a teacher back in high school. The thought of her knowing this and not bothering to inform me turned my damn stomach. I thought I had issues, but that bitch's issues were far more serious than mine.

As I continued to evaluate my fucked up family, my

phone rang. I was hoping it was Marko preparing to take me away like Calgon, but it wasn't. It was one of my defense attorneys. I didn't want to answer the phone for fear it would be more bad news, but I answered.

"Hello?"

"Ms. Wright, I have some news for you. Kingston is awake."

I dropped the phone.

Chapter 4

After hearing that Kingston had awakened after six months of being in a coma and against my lawyers' advice, I immediately rushed to Lyndon Baines Johnson Hospital. If anyone knew that I'd been sneaking to see him ever since he'd been in the hospital, I'd probably be locked up. I had to be in the know about Kingston's health because it was the deciding factor if I went to jail or not. So, until someone actually recognized me, I would continue to be Kingston's sister whenever I visited.

Once I arrived, I sat in the parking lot for nearly an hour contemplating what I was going to say when I saw him. All I could think about was me being the main reason why he was in his current state. I still couldn't believe that the man I thought I was in love with was now paralyzed. But looking at it differently shit could've been worse. Instead of the bullet hitting his spine, it could've hit his heart or some other major organ causing him to die on the spot.

When Kingston fell in the coma during surgery to remove the bullet, I was happy that he was still alive. If he would've died, my ass would surely be in jail for murder and my not guilty plea wouldn't have meant a damn thing. My lawyers were worth every penny that I paid them though. They kept getting my trial dates pushed back, which was where the bulk of my money went…keeping me out of jail. They even helped me avoid house arrest. We all hoped for the day when Kingston would come through with the truth. Maybe today would be it. I still couldn't believe that Germaine placed the gun in my hand and made me shoot Kingston. Then again, after all the shit I'd put him through, none of his actions should've shocked me.

Thinking back to that horrible day again, when the police walked inside my house and saw me kneeling over Kingston's body, my clothes bloodied and the gun at my feet, I could tell that they instantly jumped to the conclusion that I'd shot him. I kept crying out to Kingston so he could tell them that I didn't do it, but he was unconscious. He couldn't defend me. He couldn't help me and the cops didn't believe me. I remember being carted off to Harris County Jail for questioning like it was yesterday.

I nearly lost my mind when I walked inside. I didn't belong amongst the prostitutes, drug dealers, rapists, real murder suspects, arsonists etc. I was a nervous wreck because I knew my fingerprints were in the system from a petty theft charge when I was nineteen and they were on the gun; a gun that my dumb ass hadn't bothered to get rid of. Of all the dumb moves in my life, that was clearly one of them.

Those detectives were brutal and out for blood, but I kept my cool until one of them finally came into the interrogation room to inform me that my fingerprints had been discovered on the murder weapon. When they read me my rights, I blacked out.

With the detectives not knowing if Kingston would live or not, they first charged me with murder. After being processed, I was stripped down and handed a pair of scrubs. I couldn't believe that I would have another mug shot floating in the system. More embarrassing than that, my one phone call was to my mother who didn't seem shocked that I was there. I had to turn over power of attorney to her so that she could post the one million dollar bail after I was arraigned. Even more shockingly, she let me sit in jail for a damn near two weeks before posting my bail. I was scared shitless sitting behind those bars with those hard looking ass women who looked like they wanted to eat me alive…literally.

One of them even tried to cross me by tripping me in the hall. I was fresh meat, but I had to let them all know that I wasn't the one. I hopped to my feet and got gutter on her ass. She didn't know what hit her. She tried to charge me, but I hemmed her against the wall and choked her with my forearm. She fought for air, but I wasn't about to let her go especially when her face turned into Jalisa's, then Germaine's. I pressed harder thinking about everything they'd done to me. As soon as it looked like the inmate was about to pass out, several other inmates restrained me before the guards caught whim to what was going on. I guess my beauty fooled her. When I made it back to my cell, I threw up because I was scared out of my mind. The next day, I was released. I thanked my lucky stars because sleeping with my eyes open wasn't an option. Germaine and Jalisa were definitely going to pay for putting me through that ordeal.

After my trip down memory lane, I finally got up the nerve to walk inside the hospital. But I stood in the lobby for a few minutes, afraid to face him. I didn't know if he would receive or reject me, but I had to take my chances. Knowing that my fate lay in Kingston's hands, it was worth sneaking in to see him.

I started toward the elevator and caught a glimpse of a ten dollar get well soon teddy bear and balloon combo in the gift shop's window. I scrambled inside my purse and located eleven dollars. I should've stuck the money back inside my purse. I was slightly embarrassed at giving him such a cheap gift especially since the ones I had given him before were expensive and tasteful. Well, today would be the day that I would find out if the old adage was true; *it's the thought that counts.*

My heart beat a million miles per minute after stepping off the elevator when it reached Kingston's floor. As I walked toward his room, my stomach began bubbling.

"Not now," I mumbled to my stomach.

I didn't need the bubble guts. Knowing this moment was do or die, an upset stomach would've made shit ten times worst. I took a deep breath, then pushed his door open. As if I wasn't already nervous, I swallowed hard when I saw the two detectives who questioned me after I was arrested standing by Kingston's bed side. I wanted to run out, but my feet were cemented to the floor. Plus, I knew that would make me look even more suspicious. I felt light headed as I stood in the doorway and eyed the two men.

"Ms. Wright, what are you doing here? You're not supposed to have any contact with the victim," the Hispanic detective spoke defiantly. He slowly walked toward me with a stern look on his face. "I can haul your ass back to jail for this. You do know that, right?"

Before I could respond, the doctor walked past me and into the room.

"This patient needs to rest," the tall, red headed doctor addressed the detectives as if they had been there for a while. I took that as my opportunity to get ghost, but as I was about to flee, I saw Kingston slowly open his eyes. They fixated on me.

"N…Niquole," he painfully called out to me. I stared back at him with hopes that he could hear and see the plea in my eyes. I squeezed my tears back when he spoke my name. His body looked so frail.

"I need this room clear so that my patient can rest," the doctor spoke again as he checked Kingston's vitals.

I gave Kingston one final facial plea, then rushed out of the room before I was cuffed. I hopped on the elevator with the quickness so that I wouldn't have to share the ride down with the detectives. As soon as the door opened on the first floor, I discarded the teddy bear and balloon on the way out, and hurried to my car. Hopping inside, I turned the key, but the piece of shit car wouldn't start.

"Come on, damn it!" I screamed as I turned the key a few more times while thinking that this could not be my life.

I had to be living a nightmare. On the fifth attempt, the engine finally turned over. Before I could pull off, I burst into a wail of tears. All I could think about was Kingston telling the detectives that I did shoot him after I left. But it wasn't my fault. I needed him to tell them that.

As I was about to pull off, my phone rang. I quickly answered it when I saw the name. "H…Hello?"

"Niquole, it's Wayland. I've found your husband."

My ears had to be deceiving me. It felt like my throat and nostrils closed. I couldn't have heard him right.

"What?" I asked when I was finally able to breathe.

"I found him. I found Germaine."

※ ※ ※

Twenty minutes later, I pulled into the parking lot of the Waffle House on Westheimer Road to meet the Private Investigator, Wayland Downs. I figured his fat ass wanted to meet there because he was hungry as usual. As soon as I walked inside, I saw him chomping down on a steak, two chicken breasts and some hashbrowns in the back corner of the restaurant. Shaking my head, I walked over and took the seat across from him.

"Where is he?" I wasted no time.

"Would you like something to eat?" Wayland asked after slicing through the potatoes with his fork.

I tooted my nose up as I watched his three-hundred and sixty pound slouchy ass stuff his mouth. His clothes were even slouchy and smelled like he'd just pulled them from the attic. He was in desperate need of a shave and a haircut that he tried to hide under a ball cap.

"Not hungry. Where is he? Where are my boys?" I glanced at the manila envelope on the table next to his plate and figured it contained the info I needed. I reached for it, but he quickly snatched it back.

"Business out of the way first." I frowned knowing what was about to come next. He wiped his mouth and licked his tongue out at me. I almost threw up. When I started running out of money, sexual favors came into play. The good thing about it was that all he wanted me to do was sit on his face and let him eat me out. "I get off work tonight around ten."

"What kind of dirty things are running through that head of yours, Wayland?" I tried to sound seductive, but it was hard because it felt like I was talking to a damn walrus.

"You wanna know where your husband and kids are don't you?" he asked while waving the envelope in my face.

"You know I do, Wayland. Why are you teasing me? You know I want the information." I reached onto his plate and dabbed steak sauce on my finger then sucked it off. Again, I was trying to be sexy.

I could've sworn his ass had bust a nut since he suddenly started trembling.

"You study long, you study wrong," he said trying to speed up my decision. "You either let me taste that juicy pussy or give me five grand. The choice is yours."

"I got you, boo. I'll see you tonight." I winked while easing the envelope from his hand. *Stupid ass*, I thought.

"Your husband has been a pretty busy man. It wasn't easy finding him," he stated.

I pulled the contents from the envelope. I glanced through the photos and fumed as I saw Jalisa with my damn family. There were photos of her holding Johnathan and Nathan, playing with them at the park and going in and out of restaurants. There were even a few with her and Germaine holding hands as if they were a couple.

"He's changed his name, too," Wayland interrupted.

"Changed his name? What about my boys?" I replied shockingly thinking that Germaine must've really wanted to vanish.

"Your boys' names are the same, but Germaine has been using the last name Edwards. He used it to rent a house and when he registered Johnathan for karate class. But he still uses Evans when it comes to his credit cards and insurance. I don't understand his system, but at least he's been located."

"Where are they?" I asked getting a little choked up as I continued flipping through the photos.

"Your family is in New Orleans."

"Are you fucking kidding me?" I laughed. "What kind of dumb ass would try and disappear back to the place where we grew up and are well known?"

"Evidently, he knew something you didn't since you couldn't find him."

I glared at Wayland's fat, black ass for his snide remark. "That's what I paid you in pussy for," I shot back. He stuffed his mouth with another big chunk of steak. He knew not to say anything else. "What else do you have in here besides these photos?" I asked while continuing to flip through the contents.

"The home address should be in there."

Happy with the information I'd just received, I stood up. "Don't forget tonight," he reminded before I walked off. "Make sure it's wet for me and spray some of that peach shit that I like down there."

I walked out knowing good and damn well that was the last time I was going to see him. As soon as I reached my car, I saw the two detectives that were at the hospital drive by.

"These bastards are really out to get me," I mumbled.

I assumed they'd probably followed me from the hospital. My body tensed as I wondered if Kingston told them anything. I wondered if they were gonna hop out and arrest me. An overwhelming amount of nervousness took over my body once again. I didn't seem to calm down until they continued to drive past. Feeling a sense of relief, I finally headed toward my car. But before I could make it, I felt a hand on my shoulder. I turned around.

"I don't trust you," Wayland spoke.

"Look, I've got things to take care of. I'll see you tonight."

"Like I said, I don't trust you. Let's get this over with now. It doesn't make any sense for me to kick out fifty bucks for a room when we can just do this here."

"Are you serious?" I asked.

"My SUV is over there." I glanced in the direction he was pointing, then stared back at him realizing that he wasn't joking.

"I'm not letting you munch on me in a damn truck! It's bad enough that you take me to that shit hole Motel 6!" I blasted.

"Well, there's a little piece of information that I left out about Germaine and Jalisa."

"What is it?" I asked desperate to know.

"I gotta taste that pussy first."

"But I'm on my period," I lied.

"No, you're not," he laughed. "You know you're dying to find out what else I have on them so you may as well get this over with. I'll be at the SUV letting the seats down."

His wobbly ass walked away as if he knew I was coming for sure. Again, I was backed into a corner. I needed to know. I took a deep breath and walked to the tinted Suburban. I laughed internally when I saw the back doors open and his fat ass laying inside waiting for me.

"What the fuck am I doing?" I mumbled before climbing inside. His ass didn't even bother to help me.

"What'cha smelling like down there today?" Wayland asked as he unbuttoned my jeans. "Somethin' tasty I hope," he said before lowering his head toward my crouch. "Mmm-mmm...sweet jasmine." I couldn't help but wonder how he knew the names of all the body sprays and lotions I wore. Eager to get this over with, I removed my boots then my pants. "Slow down, baby. Let me enjoy this," he said after placing his hand on top of mine.

"Look, I told you, I got things to do. I need…"

"What you need to do is shut up and let me enjoy this," he interrupted.

Suddenly, things started feeling eerie especially when I saw him unzip his pants. "No way! This is not what I signed up for," I panicked trying to get back into my jeans. Before I could do so, I was pinned on my back with him on top of me. "Wayland, this wasn't the fucking deal!" I yelled while trying to push him off of me.

"Am I that hideous? So, I'm good enough to eat your pussy but not good enough to fuck it?"

"You made this fucking deal! Not me!"

"So, basically, you're telling me that if I had included sex in the deal, then you wouldn't fuck me?" I turned away from him because I didn't want him to see the *yes* in my eyes. "Niquole, I've never had a woman like you," he sulked.

I hated myself for beginning to feel sorry for him, but of all the three PIs I had working for me, he was the only one who produced results. I was seconds from giving in and fucking his fat ass until he said, "I'll just settle for whatever I can get from you." He maneuvered his face between my legs. Before he began his meal, I blew out a soft sigh of relief because I couldn't imagine myself fucking his nasty ass. I rolled my pussy all over his face for a good ten minutes then gushed all over it.

After I came, he laid on the side of me. "Can you jack me off?" he asked while stroking his puberty looking dick. I swallowed hard before closing my hand around it.

"Ooooooh, come on, Niquole! Stroke it, baby! Stroke it!" I fought back the urge to vomit when I saw his fat ass nearly slobbering. Exactly one minute later, he came. I held back my laughter. I located a piece of tissue in my purse to wipe his babies off my hands then got dressed.

"Now, what's the other info you have for me?" I didn't have time to play games.

"Oh, I lied. I just felt like you were gonna stiff me since you got all your info," he chuckled evilly.

No, his fat ass didn't think he played me, I thought. "Well, I was about to feel sorry for your fat ass and fuck you, but you opted for eating pussy instead. So, thanks for the nut." I smiled and jumped out of the SUV leaving him feeling like shit.

Chapter 5

The next evening around five, I hopped in my car to pick up some Thai take out that I had ordered. I needed to get my mind off the fact that I now knew where Germaine and my boys were. All this time, they were just a few hours away from me. But still, I had a huge problem. I couldn't get to them. My car definitely wouldn't make the drive. The bus was far from an option, and I couldn't even rent a car because all my credit cards were maxed out. However, the biggest reason of them all was that I couldn't leave the state due to my case.

I had tortured myself all night with these thoughts as well as what I would do when I finally arrived. I had no clue. If I saw my boys, would I grab them and run? Would I gauge Jalisa's eyes out for her back stabbing and conniving ways? And what about Germaine? What the hell would I do to him? Better yet, what would I say to him? With so many thoughts, I needed to clear my mind.

Before I could back out of the driveway, my mother's so-called boyfriend, Cliff pulled up behind me. "Now, I know this asshole sees my reverse lights?" I blew my horn for him to move. Moments later, he finally backed out and parked on the street. That was where that ugly ass Scion belonged...on the street. I backed out as well. As I was about to pull off, he flagged me down. "What in the hell does he want?" I mumbled before rolling my window down.

"I think you need to change your oil," Cliff said, then stepped up to the door. "I hear your engine knocking. You don't want it to lock up on you, then you're gonna have to get a new engine or a new car."

His words went in one ear and out the other. I didn't even bother to look up at him when he was speaking because I was too busy fumbling in my purse for my ringing phone. It was Marko. I started not to answer because he'd gone an entire day without returning my call, but because I found him interesting I changed my mind.

"Hello?"

"Hey, beautiful."

"Hey," I spoke dryly.

"Sorry I didn't get a chance to call you back." He didn't give me time to interject before he kept on talking. "A.J. called a last minute meeting and I couldn't miss it. I want to make it up to you though. Have dinner with me?"

I started to say no, but quickly realized that I could save the ten bucks I was about to cough up for the Thai food. Marko would've been better company anyway. I was getting sick and tired of watching my mother and one of her many men kissing every time I walked out of my crappy room. They were always in the living room hogging the forty-six inch flat screen. To make matters worse, my mother never even offered me any of the mouth watering food she cooked for her dates. She only offered me the leftovers and that's just what they were…leftovers. My stomach still growled afterwards. I guess she figured something was better than nothing. I saw it as petty and fucked up. I blew out a long, hard sigh as I thought about how my life had flipped upside down.

"Niquole, are you there?"

For a brief moment, I forgot about Marko being on the other end. "Yes, I'm here?"

"Dinner?"

"Sure." I needed to be in a nice restaurant again.

"Cool. I'll pick you up around seven?"

"No," I quickly answered not wanting him to know where I lived or the fact that I was now living with my mother. "I can meet you somewhere."

"How about the Galleria Mall?"

"Okay."

We hung up after coming to an agreement about what part of the mall we would meet at.

"I can change your oil for you, Niquole," Cliff offered.

"Now, when you saw me on the damn phone, why didn't you just leave?" I scowled.

"I just don't want you to get stranded somewhere," he said then backed up.

"I'm not your concern," I replied before pulling back into the yard.

I had almost two hours to get myself together for my date with Marko. I was happy that he'd called because I wasn't looking forward to coming back home. I kept my eyes on Cliff as I turned off the engine and stepped out the car.

"So, do you want me to change your oil?" he asked. "I can…"

"Cliff, I've got things to do," I interrupted before walking toward the house. Besides, if he didn't watch out, I'd have his ass changing more than just my oil.

❖ ❖ ❖

As soon as I neared our meeting place around six forty-five, I spotted Marko leaning against a jet black BMW 640i. My pussy thumped at the sight of the seventy-three thousand dollar beauty and wondered if the car belonged to him. Marko was engrossed in what seemed to be a heated conversation. He didn't see me as I whipped into a parking space a few cars down. When I stepped out of my car and walked toward him, he finally turned toward me. You would've thought I was Halle Berry by the look on his face.

"Yo', I gotta go," he addressed the caller when I reached him. "I'll take care of it." He ended the call.

"Is everything okay?"

"Nothing I can't handle. You look good," he said, undressing me with his eyes.

"Thank you," I replied with a smile.

I wanted to return the comment, but his baggy jeans, Gucci tennis shoes and black sweatshirt didn't match my attire. I rocked my short, black Marc Jacobs dress, fish net stockings, thigh high boots and a Vivienne Westwood coat. It felt like I was with Germaine all over again. Germaine's fucked up clothes never complemented my style. But instead of complaining, I sucked it up and allowed Marko to assist me into the car. The newness made my nostrils flare with excitement. My body fit perfectly inside the butter soft leather seat like it was made just for me. I closed my eyes and basked in the moment as I reminisced about my precious Lexus that I no longer had.

"Let me know if you need me to adjust the heat in your seat. It's cold out tonight," Marko said bringing me back to reality.

"Oh, it's fine," I assured. "So, where's your Range Rover?" I had to know. I figured he must've borrowed the BMW to impress me.

"It's at my pop's crib. I let him drive it earlier today."

"So, does the BMW belong to your dad?" I crossed my fingers hoping it didn't.

"No, both whips are mine," he answered before turning up the volume on the Miguel CD. "*No bite marks, no scratches and no hickeys. If you can get with that mami come get with me,*" Marko sang along. He sounded good. Part of me hoped we'd be doing what he was singing later on. "You're gonna enjoy what I have planned for us." He grinned before exiting the parking lot.

I got even more comfortable in the seat knowing that the BMW belonged to him. I sat back and enjoyed the twenty minute ride. During the drive, we chatted a bit more than we did on our first date. This time, I enjoyed the conversation. When we arrived at the destination, I just knew it had to be a joke.

"What are we doing here?" I asked trying not to sound insulted.

"We're about to have some fun," he said before jumping out of the car and hurrying to my side to help me out.

I hesitated for a few seconds before giving him my hand. All I could think about while walking to the entrance to Dave & Buster's was me pulling A.J. out of the place several months ago for sex. I wasn't dressed for this bullshit and even if I were this wasn't a place I wanted to be. I wanted to be sitting in a nice, dim, five star restaurant with a bottle of champagne. This was a huge step down from Gravitas.

"I can't wait to play that basketball game," he boasted. "Oh, and that motorcycle game, too."

As Marko bounced up and down like a kid on a sugar rush, I rolled my eyes. I wanted to yank my hand from his. I was way too grown and sexy for this shit. I continued ignoring him as he talked about all the other games he wanted to play when we finally walked inside. I watched as people came and went with smiles on their faces like they'd just had a good time or knew they were about to. Well, I was going to be the bitch of the bunch because I didn't want to be there. I quickly wondered if getting involved with his young ass was a huge mistake. I mean we were nine years apart.

"Oh snap!"

I jumped at his loud outburst. "What?" I asked slightly concerned.

"My lucky b-ball machine is available," he announced happily before gently pulling me to the machine. He sounded just like an excited twelve year old.

Oh hell no! This shit is not gonna work, I thought.

After quickly getting one of those Dave and Buster's Power Cards, then inserting it into the machine, I watched as Marko tossed the balls into the basket one after the other. At that moment, I wished I'd driven my own car because I would've definitely left his ass right there. This Lebron James wannabe shit wasn't for me.

By the time his ass started his third game, I huffed, puffed and shifted my weight to let him know that I wasn't having a good time. After each shot he made, he would glance at me. I didn't want to embarrass him in front of everyone, but I was on the verge of going off. That game went on for nearly ten minutes until Marko realized that I truly was about to snap.

"Let's get a table," he suggested.

"Yeah let's do that," I concurred with much attitude in my voice.

By the time we found an empty booth and claimed it before anyone else did, my arms were folded across my chest like a spoiled brat.

"Is everything okay?" he asked. Before I could respond, a waitress came over to our table.

"What are we having tonight?" she asked with a huge smile on her face. I rolled my eyes at her, too. She took notice and turned to Marko.

"Umm, can you bring me a pitcher of Bud Light?" he asked. "What are you having, Niquole?" Still, I ignored him. "Just bring the beer," he addressed the waitress. She trotted off. "What's the problem, Niquole?"

"Are you serious?" I laughed. "We're in a fucking adult arcade, Marko!"

"It's not a…" When he saw the glare in my eyes, he stopped mid sentence.

"Do you see what I have on?"

"Yes. You look nice."

"Marko, I figured we were doing something *grown up* tonight." The waitress returned with the pitcher of beer and two mugs. "Oh, you can take this back," I said, pushing one of the mugs back to her. She gave Marko an '*I feel sorry for you look.*'

"Well, can I get you anything else? Some wings for starters?" she suggested.

"Umm, can you come back in about ten minutes?"

Marko chimed in. I could tell that he was feeling a little uneasy, which was good. I wanted him to feel just like I felt.

"Sure," she replied before retrieving the mug then walking off.

"Grown up, huh?" he reiterated to me. "I can show you grown up."

Whatever, I thought but wondered how the hell he planned on doing that because when I got pissed…I was pissed. Reflecting back on my beer drinking days, I filled his mug with Bud Light then downed it. I needed to get my mind off of this fucked up date. Seconds later, he filled the mug back up, then eased it out of my hands. He emptied it within seconds.

"Wanna have a drinking contest?"

"Hell naw, Marko!" I answered bluntly to let him know that he'd insulted me.

"Niquole, I'm gonna get a positive reaction out of you before the night is over."

"Good luck," I said, rolling my eyes at him. *Maybe if we talk finances that'll make me feel better*, I thought. "So, when we met you said that you worked for A.J. What exactly do you do?"

"I'm a rap artist on his label." At that moment, Marko started bobbing his head like he could hear some imaginary music.

I knew it. "So, why did you say you work for him like you were the janitor or something?" I chuckled.

"Well, I didn't wanna come off as me riding my own dick by saying I was an artist. That shit is so corny to me."

"So, tell me about your music. How many CD's have you put out? Are you in the studio now?" I didn't want to say that I'd never heard of him before. That might've been insulting.

For some reason it seemed as if the conversation was a bit uncomfortable for him. Marko cleared his throat. "Well, I did put out one CD, but it didn't do as well as me and the label wanted. So now, I'm back in the studio working with different producers. I also have several mix tapes out. I like doing mix tapes more anyway. Labels want too fucking much out of their artists. It's too much pressure."

I shook my head. "Well, you know I understand. I still have relationships with different producers if you ever need some help."

"Bet. I might take you up on that offer."

Just as I was about to ask more questions, suddenly Marko eased from his side of the table and slithered next to me.

"What in the hell are you doing?" I asked, sliding away from him.

My question went unanswered as he inched closer to me. I was cornered in the booth, but didn't give a damn when he placed his hand on my thigh. I should've pushed it away, but once he started massaging it, that thought went with the wind. His fingers toyed around in the holes of my fishnet stockings as if they were trying to rip them off.

Slowly, he clasped the bottom of my jacket, then opened it to gain access to the inside of my thigh. At that moment, we were the only two in Dave & Buster's. No one else exsisted. I stared into his eyes and gave him the '*go for it*' look as I opened my legs for him to do what he and I both wanted. He stretched a few holes in my fishnets. His journey to my spot was taking too long so I reached under the table and ripped a few holes myself. He smiled when I did so. His lips were so close to mine that I could tell the temperature of his breath as he breathed. My chest rose and fell. My breaths were shallow. I wanted his ass…bad.

Marko continued massaging my thigh before finally leaning into my ear and whispering, "I told you I'd get a reaction out of you."

To my surprise, he glided back to the other side of the booth with a victorious smile on his face.

What the fuck? Did I just rip a perfectly good pair of fishnets for nothing? When I spotted our waitress, I flagged her down. Marko basked in his victory while drinking from his mug.

"You ready to order?" the waitress asked.

I stared Marko directly into his eyes before placing my order. "Yeah. Let me get a Wet Pussy and a Slippery Dick."

Marko instantly spat his beer out onto the floor. I guess my fake drink choices had shocked him, but I'd said that shit on purpose. I needed him to know what the hell could've been going down if he wasn't into playing games...literally.

The waitress giggled. "We don't have those, but how about a Sex on the Beach?"

"That'll work," I replied as she walked away to fill my order. "Seems that's the only way I'll be getting any is through a drink," I muttered while angrily retying my coat.

Chapter 6

It was a little after twelve when I staggered inside the house after parting from Marko. As much as I didn't want to admit it, I ended up having a good time. I knew that was due to me being drunk. I eventually caved in when he asked me to have a drinking contest again. Marko was shocked when I beat him at ski ball and air hockey and even more shocked when I almost beat him shooting hoops. He kept trying to psyche me out by bragging on his basketball skills. He even went as far as to tell me that if he hadn't been diagnosed with arthritis in the hand, he'd probably be in the NBA. I couldn't tell if he was lying or not. He put on a nice game face, but he was the typical man. He let a pretty face fool him. I gave him a run for his money.

I hoped our night would end up at his place or a hotel. All of the kissing and fondling like two horny teenagers had me ripe and ready, but he had other things to tend to. That damn A.J. called in between one of our lip locking sessions. I was mad as hell when Marko pulled away to answer the phone. I wondered if he and A.J. were fucking because no man in his right mind would pass up some pussy. Not for another dude anyway.

When Marko told me he had to go handle some business for A.J., I looked at him like he'd lost his damn mind. Even though he kept apologizing and saying that he would make it up to me, all of his apologies fell on deaf ears. And when he asked for a rain check, I was seconds from slapping his lil' boy ass. How dare he offend me in such a way; like I was a young chicken head who would've happily accepted his offer? If he were Kingston, I would've been fucked right there on the Fast & Furious car racing game. I stomped out of Dave & Busters with cum oozing down the inside of my thighs.

To me, Marko didn't seem like the thug rapper that I thought he was. If anything, he seemed more like A.J.'s damn flunkie. I needed to know how valuable Marko was to A.J. because I knew he would come in handy when I decided to pay A.J. back for his lies.

As I walked out of the bathroom, I heard keys jiggling in the front door. I glanced at the time on my cell phone. "She doesn't usually come back from the casino this early," I mumbled thinking about my mother's casino nights. "Oh, it's you," I spoke dryly when I saw Cliff walking in seconds later.

He reeked of cigarette smoke and alcohol, but didn't seem drunk. He was dressed in a cheap three-piece suit and a pair of worn down Gators. But in spite of his country style, he was still a handsome man. From what I saw the other night in the kitchen, his body was well toned. He just needed to upgrade his attire. The flashy rings he wore on his fingers was also a turn off. I wasn't too keen on his full beard either especially since he had a bald head. If he'd been a big man, he would've looked like an old ass Rick Ross.

"I didn't expect to see you here." His voice was full of sarcasm.

"Why not? I live here, don't I? What are you doing with a key anyway?" As many dudes as my mother had coming in and out of here, I was surprised she'd given him access to her house. *Maybe she finally decided to settle down.*

Cliff gave me a questionable look as if I should already know the answer. "Good night, Niquole."

"Been to that hole in the wall again haven't you?"

"What are you talking about?"

"I overheard you and my mom talking about that old

folks club on…"

"What's it to you if I have or haven't?" he interrupted.

"A little jumpy, huh? I was just wondering why your woman isn't with you. You needed some new pussy already? I can understand if you do. All of my mother's other men tend to get tired of her after a while then they eventually turn to me."

He seemed surprised by my response. "Stay in your lane, lil' girl."

"Lil' girl?" I laughed. "I was just saying that I know how those old women in those clubs can get. Drunk and horny and eventually…boring. Is that why your clothes are sort of out of place?" I smirked devilishly.

Cliff hesitated for a few seconds which led me to believe that I was getting to him. "Again, good night," he answered, then disappeared into my mother's room.

A minute or two later, I heard the shower. I walked back to my room snickering at my antics because I knew what was coming next. I had two birds to kill with one stone. Not only was I horny and needed to take care of the monsoon between my legs, but I also needed to get my mother back for embarrassing me in front of one of her men the other day.

When I heard the water in my mother's shower desist, I walked into her room and stood in the doorway with some sexy lingerie and nothing underneath. Cliff was drying off and didn't notice me. I giggled silently as he sang B.B. King's, *The Thrill is Gone*. That was sure proof that he'd been to the hole in the wall.

"We have to stop meeting like this," I spoke thinking back to our first encounter in the kitchen when he was shirtless.

"What in the hell are you doing in here?" Cliff quickly wrapped the towel around his waist.

"Too late for that. I've already seen what you're packing."

"You need to get out of here. Your mama done told me you're trouble."

Feeling a little more hatred and anger toward my mother,

I walked up to him and whispered in his ear, "She's right so let me show you just how much trouble I can be. Believe me, I'm the type of trouble that you want to be around." I rubbed my hands all over his upper body and twirled his chest hairs with my fingers. I could feel his chest rising and falling at a fast pace. "Do I scare you, Cliff?"

"No," he answered quickly.

"Don't you want to get into a little trouble with me?" Sticking out my tongue, I slowly made my way toward his nipples before licking them both in a circular motion.

"Y...Y...Y...You need to s...s...stop," he stuttered.

"Doesn't sound like you want me to," I said before licking my way up to his neck. "Let me show you what young pussy feels like." I seductively gripped his dick and rubbed it on my neatly shaven pussy hairs. He threw me for a loop when he harshly grabbed my arms and squeezed them, but I was a big girl and he didn't scare me. "Come on, Cliff. You know you want this." With a hungry look in his eyes, instead of tossing me out the door, he tossed me on the bed. "Mama said I've been a bad girl, Cliff. Teach me a lesson." I slowly opened my legs to reveal my garden that I needed him to tend to. "I was about to give all this good pussy to my dildo, but I think I made the better choice by coming in this room."

Cliff shook his head. "We shouldn't be doing this."

"We're not doing anything yet. Come on. Feel guilty later."

"We shouldn't be doing this in your mama's bed. That's what I meant."

"If you want this pussy, this is the only place you're gonna get it." I slid two of my fingers inside of my wetness.

"You don't have to do that. Let me help you," he offered before plummeting in with his tongue. If he had dentures, I hoped they were polygripped in tight because he was munching like I was Thanksgiving dinner.

"Ooooooooh, Cliff! Clifffff!" I found myself running from him until I couldn't go any further. I had clearly underestimated this old dude. I expected this to be a wham bam thank you ma'am and then split, but leaving was far from my mind now.

"This young pussy can't take this experienced tongue, huh?" Cliff mumbled then continued.

My mother's pillow was now in my mouth to keep me from screaming this man's name any louder than I already had. She really knew how to pick 'em. Just as I was about show him how grateful I was for his oral, he stopped.

"W…What are you doing?"

"Now that I know how young pussy tastes, I wanna see how it feels." He retrieved a condom from the nightstand and within seconds, it felt like my cherry was being popped for the first time all over again. It also felt like he was doing push-ups inside of me with his long, deep strokes. "I don't hear you talking now," he spoke smugly.

He was right. I had nothing to say. I was too busy trying to keep myself from cumming because I didn't want him to stop. I couldn't let this man see that he had me by the tits. I needed to regain control…quick! I maneuvered him onto his back with his dick still inside of me.

"Mmmmmm…you are much better than your mama," Cliff moaned as I rolled my hips. Little did he know, I was about to cash in on his words. I pulled him up to me so that we could be face to face. He then dug his nails into my back when my walls became a pair of suction cups on his shaft. "You're not playing fair, but I like it," he continued.

"I know, but if you want to keep playing this game, you gotta do something for me," I said between soft pecks to his lips. I squeezed my walls to make sure he was paying attention.

He squeezed one of my breasts when I offered it to him. It became his personal ball of caramel. "And what's that, baby?"

"Take care of my share of the bills to keep my mother off my back."

"I…I don't know about that, Niquole."

I squeezed my walls a little tighter and bounced a little

faster. I took his hand and placed three of his fingers inside my nest. "You sure you wanna give up this pussy?" He yanked my head back with his other hand, and latched his lips onto my neck. "You gotta pay to play, Cliff!" He quickly gripped my shoulders and pushed me onto my back with his tool still inside of me. "You can get this anytime you want, Cliff. All you gotta do is say, yes," I sang in my closest Floetry voice.

"Anytime I want?" he grunted while flipping me onto my back.

"Anytime, Cliff! Anytime!" I gripped his ass cheeks to push him deeper inside. "Just say you will! You know you want to!" I panted. I was near lift off.

"Yes! Yes!" he agreed as we both came. Moments later, he collapsed on top of me. "For future references, there's no difference between you and your mama," he breathed in my ear. "Pussy is pussy. It all feels the same."

"Get the fuck off of me," I said then shoved him. He giggled as he climbed off of me. How dare he say some shit like that to me? All my mother's other men had always told me that my pussy was better than hers. Cliff had a lot of nerve by telling me that there wasn't a difference.

"I need you to get up, baby girl so I can wash these sheets before your mama comes home." He obviously wasn't phased by my reaction.

"Don't you think she'll get a little suspicious when she smells fresh sheets asshole? Better yet, since you say our pussies are the same, why don't you just leave the sheets on the bed," I stated sarcastically. He needed to know that I was still pissed at his comment.

"They may feel the same, but they don't smell the same," he shot back.

"What in the fuck do you mean by that?" I asked furiously because I knew my pussy didn't stink. He ignored me and tugged at the sheets.

I allowed him to collect the sheets to take them to the laundry room. As I thought back to my recent deviousness, I heard a vibration coming from the night stand. I glanced over and saw that it was my mother's phone. "Her stupid ass left her phone trying to rush to the casino," I huffed.

As it continued to ring, my curiosity of who was calling her got the best of me, so I grabbed the phone. I wondered if it was another one of her men. I smiled devilishly as I wondered what would happen if I allowed Cliff to answer the phone. Better yet, what if I set up a rendezvous to meet the stranger. Either way, my mother was going to find out how embarrassing me wasn't a good idea. My curiosity peaked when I saw the number flash across the screen.

"Who could be calling her from New Orleans?" I whispered to myself. I knew the area code by heart. Now, my curiosity was in overdrive. I hopped off the bed and hurried to my bedroom before the caller hung up. "H…Hello?' I answered. I could hear the caller breathing. "Hello?"

Still, no response. If they had the wrong number, they would've hung up by now. My heart began to race when it dawned on me who the caller could be. I took a risk and called out his name. "Germaine? Germaine, is that you?" I could still hear the breathing. "Germaine?" I was getting a little antsy. I wanted to know who was on the other end. I had a strong feeling that it was him. "Germaine, if this is you, say something. You know you want to since you haven't disconnected the call yet." My eagerness to know turned into anger as I thought of my mother possibly knowing his whereabouts all along and not revealing them to me.

"Daddy? Daddy?" My body went limp and tears quickly spilled from my eyes when I heard John John in the background. Hearing my son's voice, my heart began to beat like skilled hands on African drums.

"Germaine, let me talk to Johnathan!" I cried. "Germaine, please let me talk to John John!"

I wondered how long he and my mother had been conversing. The thought angered me. I felt betrayed that she would keep this shit a secret. Now, I really didn't feel bad about fucking Cliff. If she wanted to be sneaky, devious and foul…so could I.

Within seconds, he disconnected the call. I spent the next ten minutes calling the number back, but of course he never picked up. There was no voicemail set up on the phone so I couldn't even leave a message. On my last attempt, I pretended the voicemail had been activated and spoke into the phone, "I'll see you soon, husband of mine."

Chapter 7

"What's all the noise going on in here, Nikki?" my mother asked after barging in my room.

"You need to start knocking," I scowled at her while trying to shove more of my clothes in the already cramped closet. "I do pay half the bills in here so you can at least give me that much respect."

She laughed as if I'd just told a fucking joke. "Honey, this is and will always be *my* house so I can do as I please."

"How many more times are you gonna keep reminding me about that?" I muttered. She needed to get the fuck out of my damn face for being so deceitful. I didn't know how much longer I was going to hold back from choking the life out of her. All this time, she knew where my boys were and kept it from me. That was fucked up in my book.

"I really don't feel like arguing with you. When I got in last night, I found this money on top of some bills in the kitchen. I won't even ask how you came up with it in such short notice," she said, counting the six hundred dollars in my face.

"Ask your man," I mumbled softly with a smirk.

My mother gave me a questionable look as she recounted the money. "What did you say?"

"I said I pay my dues. Now, will you please leave so I can finish organizing this jail cell?" I didn't want to be near her knowing that she'd been talking to Germaine. I didn't have money to go anywhere, and I refused to call Marko after he'd put A.J. before me, so straightening my room was the only thing I could do to alleviate my stress.

"I don't think you had this many amenities when you were locked up. You didn't have clothes or a closet to put them in," she shot back.

"Mama, will you just go!" I yelled trying to hold my composure. "I can't stand the sight of you right now! Get out!"

She gave me a look as if I'd hurt her feelings, but there was something else behind those eyes. I remembered the look all too well when I was younger especially when she had to tell me my father was gone. She must've wanted me to go off on her because she didn't budge. And since the bitch obviously wanted to feel my wrath, I decided not to hold my tongue any longer.

"Why didn't you tell me that you've been talking to Germaine? He has my damn kids…your grandkids." She needed to know that I was aware of what she'd been hiding from me. I couldn't wait to hear her explanation as her hands fell to her sides in disbelief. "I don't care how much you hate me. You still should've told me. He has my boys."

I had to calm down a bit because my voice started cracking. I refused to show her any tears. Her mouth opened, but the words seemed to be stuck in her throat. The look on her face was priceless.

"Nikki, what do you want me to say? I'm sorry for keeping that secret from you, but there was no need for you to know. What could you do anyway? You're stuck here with a potential criminal charge hanging over your head. Plus, everyone seemed happy without you." I must've been in a twilight zone because her words were not apologetic or sympathetic. "Nikki, it was best that you didn't know because all you would do is cause trouble."

"Trouble? Trouble? After all the shit Germaine put me through, you still wanna protect his sorry ass?"

"You caused all of this, Nikki and you know it."

"Mama, all the shit I'm going through is because of Germaine and Jalisa. All they had to do was leave me the fuck alone, but the biggest hypocrite of them all is you. You've never once had my back." I laughed thinking about Germaine's involvement in all of *my* so called drama. "Like I told you before, Germaine is not as innocent as you think and neither is that bitch Jalisa. You've always defended him…always! He's no damn angel, and you constantly take up for him! I'm your daughter! You're supposed to have my back! " I yelled even louder after jumping in her face. I was seconds away from spilling the beans about my sexual encounter with Cliff. I wanted her to hurt like I did, but decided to keep my secret a little longer.

"What? You're joking, right? Let's get all this out in the open right now. You turned your back on me. You betrayed me when all I've ever done was try to help and save you."

"Help me? Save me? Get real."

"Nikki, there's so much that you don't know. There's so much…"

"Just leave me alone. You've always been full of shit. What makes you think I would believe anything that you have to say now?"

"You know what, I give up, but let me tell you this one last thing before I go. You have one more time to raise up at me. If you do it again, your ass is out of here," she spat.

"At some point you need to stop faking. You need my money more than I do, so stop threatening to kick me out." My phone rang as she was on her way out the door. "Damn, I miss my house," I said, before retrieving my phone from the bed. "Good timing," I said when I saw Marko's number on the screen. "Hello?" I answered dryly. Although I wanted him to get me out of the house, I still had to seem pissed about him ditching me.

"Hey, Niquole. It's me, Marko."

"I know," I replied nonchalantly.

"I really enjoyed you last night."

Just imagine what else you could have enjoyed if you hadn't run off. "Oh really," I said unenthused.

"Is everything okay?"

It was time for *Niquole* to kick in. "I have a family emergency out of town that I need to handle, but my car…"

"Hey, I don't mean to cut you off, but I gotta catch this call coming in from A.J.," he interrupted.

"Are you fucking serious?"

"I'm sorry, Niquole. We have a lot going on with his label." Knowing that the label was no longer mine infuriated me. "I gotta take this call, baby but I wanna see you later. Meet me at the YMCA on Pease Street around six."

"You have a lot of fucking nerve, Marko. I knew I shouldn't have gotten involved with your young ass. You're not gonna keep putting me off." When I didn't get a response, I looked at the phone and laughed. He must've clicked over to A.J. right after he told me to meet him. "Bastard."

It didn't take a rocket scientist to figure out if I was going to the YMCA or not. It wasn't like I had anything better to do. Ever since my mother returned from the casino, she was all over Cliff, so his dick wasn't unavailable. But the shocker was hearing them in the room having sex at least three times since she came back. For an older man, he sure had a lot of fucking energy.

❖ ❖ ❖

I pulled up at the Y at exactly 5:45 p.m. I knew I was overdressed for the gym in my stilettos, oversized embellished tunic and some leggings, but Marko needed to know that I wasn't that type of chick. If and when he paid attention to my wardrobe then maybe it would click in his head that he needed to up his dating game with me. Dave & Busters and the YMCA were not going to cut it. Even though I didn't have money like I used to, I was a Louboutin chick…not a Jordan one.

I parked my car next to his BMW and stepped out. When

I saw a few people walking in my direction, I hurried to the driver's side of the BMW and pretended I had just gotten out of it. I looked the part with my candy apple red Birkin bag dangling from my wrist. I smiled at the group when they walked by. A couple of them stared at me and the car. I know they were wondering what someone like me was doing at the YMCA. They weren't the only ones. Marko just didn't know how good he had it.

As soon as I walked inside, I heard balls bouncing, shoes pounding and plenty of trash talking. I peeped inside the gym where the noises were coming from, and instantly spotted Marko on the court. Moments later, he noticed me and grinned. I was seconds away from turning around and leaving, but he was looking so damn good. It definitely didn't help that he was shirtless. My eyes fixated on the tattoo on his back that read: **Est. 1988**. I assumed that was the year he was born, which instantly made me feel like a damn cougar.

"Hey." Marko startled me when he sat down in front of me. I was still trying to figure out when I'd sat down. I assumed cloud nine guided me there. "I'm happy you came," he said after catching his breath, then taking a swig from his Gatorade. "Are you going somewhere after this? You look nice."

Your place would be great, I thought as I sized him up and watched the sweat drizzle down his face. "No, I don't have any plans. Not yet anyway."

"Come on, Marko!" one of the players called out to him.

"You're holding up the fucking game, nigga!" another yelled out.

"I think you better go," I said to him.

"They can wait. Besides, I like what's going on right here."

He winked. I beamed.

"Marko, come on!"

"Let me go whip these fools real quick," he said. "Don't go anywhere. I got a surprise for you." He kissed my lips then bounced back onto the court. It had been a while since my heart warmed. This boy definitely had my attention.

For the next hour, Marko took breaks to come and chat with me during the game, which pissed the players off every time. I assumed he was trying to make up for putting me off for A.J. If that was the case, it was slightly working. I was happy when the game finally ended because I was eager to know more about his surprise. I think a few of the players were happy it ended as well since Marko kept holding up the game for me.

"So, what'cha got planned?" he asked as we walked out to the parking lot.

"I told you nothing."

"You're not dressed for nothing." I watched him wipe the sweat from his face with his t-shirt as he stared at me waiting for a reply.

Was this lil' mofo trying to check me? If so, he was in for a rude awakening. "This is the way I dress, Marko," I replied slightly insulted and a little disturbed. "I'm not sure what you're used to, but I'm a *woman* not a girl."

"I'm just saying, Nikki…"

"Who gave you permission to call me Nikki?" I snapped.

"My bad, Niquole. I was just saying that no one dresses like that at a gym."

I took a deep breath, "Marko, you may wanna stop while you're ahead. You invited me to the gym…remember. It wasn't my idea to come here. Just like it wasn't my idea to go to Dave & Busters." He pulled me to him to hug me, but I pushed his wet, musty ass up off of me. "My clothes can't sustain your sweat," I said, rolling my eyes.

"You'll change your mind in a sec," he replied once we made it to his car.

I had to contain myself from jumping up and down in excitement since I didn't know what I was excited about. He popped the trunk of his car and pulled out a Nike duffle bag. I was a little curious when he pulled out a key and handed it to me.

"What's this?" I asked.

"Your surprise. I heard everything you said to me on the phone, Niquole."

"I don't understand."

"I can't imagine what you're going through with your issues. I figure your family emergency has something to do with your kids."

I was shocked. "How do you figure that?"

"I may be young, but I ain't stupid, Niquole. I watch the news, so I know what's going on. I also listen to all the rumors even though I'm not exactly sure what's true and what isn't."

"So, what's the key for?"

He pointed to a Toyota Camry parked next to my car.

"I know it's not what you're accustomed to, but it's yours for two weeks."

"You rented me a car? Why?" I asked stunned.

"Because I like you and I wanna help you."

"What do you want from me, Marko?" I quickly went into defensive mode thinking of all the shit that I went through with Kingston.

"I just want to help you, Niquole. That's it. I don't have any ulterior motives if that's what you're wondering. Just because there's bad blood between you and A.J. doesn't mean there has to be any between me and you."

If only you knew how much blood A.J. and I actually shared.

"But I can't leave the state, Marko."

"From the stories I've heard about you, I'm sure you're not gonna let that stop you from getting what you want."

I could only imagine the shit that A.J. had possibly told him. Seconds later, Marko handed me an envelope. I opened it up. My eyes widened when I saw the stack of one hundred dollar bills. I was stunned yet again. "Marko, I…"

"You can thank and repay me later," he winked then tapped me on my ass. "When I see something, well, someone I want, I let 'em know. I don't hold back my feelings. If I got it, you got it. If you need it, I got it. Have a safe trip." He kissed me, then hopped in his car and drove off leaving a trail of the Youngbloodz's song, *Damn* in the air.

"You just may come in handy after all, Marko but I hope you don't turn out to be another Kingston."

Chapter 8

It didn't make sense for me to prolong my trip to New Orleans any longer. Marko was right about one thing, nothing was going to stop me from getting to my kids. I couldn't wait to see Germaine and Jalisa's faces when I showed up. I was prepared to put my foot on both of their necks for all the chaos they'd brought into my life. I may have caused a lot of it, but hell, they took the shit way too far. When Germaine stole my hard earned money, he took it to the next level and so did Jalisa when her ass confessed to wanting Germaine all these years. So what, I tried to hook her up with him first, but it turned out that he wanted me instead. She should've left that shit alone. Now this bitch was in New Orleans living my life with my damn kids. There was no way they were getting away with any of this shit.

I ended up leaving my car at the Y. I could've easily driven it back to my mother's house then asked Cliff to drive me back to the Camry, but I knew that would've stirred something up. As much as I would've loved to have his dick inside of me, I had to get on my mission. Besides, my mother would've raised a suspicious eyebrow about the rental and I didn't have time for that interrogation. I was so happy to be rid of that raggedy ass Lexus. That shit could stay parked for the entire two weeks as far as I was concerned. Even if the shit got towed, I wouldn't care.

After typing Germaine's address in the GPS on my I-phone, I hit the road. I wondered how my boys would react when they saw me. The thought of the reunion nearly brought tears to my eyes, but I had to bat them back so I could focus. Of all the places Germaine and Jalisa could've fled to, I wondered why they chose our hometown. I would've left the damn country, but simple minds do simple shit. As many people in New Orleans who knew me and Germaine were married, I'm surprised someone hadn't seen them together by now and called me. But now that I think about it, I was labeled a bitch there also. That started back in high school when I was the cause of a teacher being fired and losing his family. Oh well. His ass should've given me what I wanted. That was the beginning of Niquole, the bitch and it festered from there.

As I drove down I-10, so many thoughts of revenge rushed through my head. I wondered if all of them could have been done at the same time. If Germaine opened the door after I knocked, what would I do to him? If Jalisa opened it, what would I do to her? Then again, it didn't matter who opened the door. Both of them were getting punched in the damn face, but Jalisa was going to get the worst of it. The thought of her fucking Germaine, although I didn't want him, and playing mommy to my sons pissed me off. There was no way she was getting out of this unscathed.

Two hours into the drive, my phone rang and interrupted my murderous thoughts. "Who in the hell is this calling me?" I questioned after seeing the unknown number pop up on the screen. "Hello?" There was no response. "Hell-the-fuck-o?" I said irritably.

"Ni…Niquole," the caller spoke in a raspy voice.

I immediately knew who the raspy voice belonged to. My foot had a mind of its own when it slowly lifted off the gas. Even after all he'd put me through, he still had a slight hold over me.

"Kingston?" I breathed.

A loud horn brought me back to my senses. My speed

had decreased form seventy-five to forty-miles per hour on the interstate. I wondered how Kingston had gotten my new phone number. It had to be changed when all the drama began. My phone rang off the hook from morning 'til night with reporters, prank calls and even a few harmless threats.

"Niquole, you...still there?" he moaned.

Hearing his voice made me pull onto the shoulder. It sounded like he was in a lot of pain. I wondered if he was angry that I didn't shoot Germaine or Jalisa instead.

"I need to see you," he stated in a low tone.

Those exact words struck a nerve. Whenever he would say them to me in the past, I would instantly hop in a car or on a plane to get to him, but things had changed. I still couldn't figure out why I was so head over heels for him even after he beat and raped me. Yet and still, I would always blame Germaine for that. Then again, if Germaine and his friend, Hummer, hadn't raped Kingston's sister, then Kingston would've never entered my life.

"Why do you need to see me, Kingston?"

"Not over the...phone. Come see me. You know where I am." In typical Kingston fashion, after giving his orders, he hung up.

"Fuck! Why did you have to call me now?"

I was torn between continuing with my original destination and turning around to find out why Kingston needed to see me. What could he possibly have wanted to talk to me about? If he was going to help me, he could've told me that over the phone. I sat on the side of the road trying to rationalize which was more important; seeing my boys or finding out what Kingston was up to. Maybe the detectives had gotten him to turn on me. He wouldn't do that or would he? The more I thought about it, whatever the case it would be dealt with when I got back.

"You're gonna have to wait, Kingston," I said, pulling back into traffic and continuing towards New Orleans.

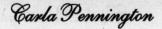

✦ ✦ ✦

Five hours later, I parked down the street from *my* two-story house on Forest Oaks Drive. Yes, it was *my* house because *my* money was paying for it every month. The suburban neighborhood called English Turn was nice. I could even tell that the houses cost a pretty penny, but I still didn't understand why Germaine was renting. Did he not want that commitment with Jalisa yet? Looking at the house that was surrounded by a golf course and a lake, my insides burned as I compared Germaine's life to mine. While he was living the life in a beautiful two-story home, I was imprisoned inside a cramped ass room that really did feel like a prison cell sometimes. There was no way this shit would continue to fly with me.

Looking around, I carefully surveyed the area. Luckily, no one was outside which was a good thing. I sat in the car for nearly thirty minutes contemplating my next move, but Germaine and Jalisa made it easy for me when they suddenly walked out of the house. Sitting up to get a better view, I watched as the two of them laughed about something and walked toward a maroon Jaguar XJ.

"A new car, too? I got a lot of shit to repossess," I said maliciously. There was also a silver Mercedes GL truck sitting outside as well.

I wondered what the fuck was so funny. I also wondered why my boys weren't with them. It was almost twelve a.m.

When Jalisa locked her hand inside of his, I fumed. "Bitch, you're gonna pay," I said, watching their every move.

Jalisa's locks were long and bouncy like she'd just come from the salon. She was wearing a cute, cropped leather jacket with some tall boots that I quickly envied, and she was still tall and gorgeous. I wanted to rip Jalisa's red lips off of her face as she smiled at Germaine when he walked her around to the passenger's side.

He, however, wasn't the Germaine I remembered. Although still handsome with a strong resemblance to Michael Ealy, his ears were now pierced, and he'd grown a sexy goatee. That man wasn't my husband. Jalisa had done him some good. Bitch.

Seconds later, they drove off. It was at that moment when I realized I had to get inside the house while they were gone. Jumping out of the car, I hurried toward the house while ducking and watching my surroundings at the same time. After reaching the backyard, I stopped running to quickly look at my sons' nice wooden swing set that I immediately envisioned them playing on. Even the patio was set up nicely with a stainless steel four burner grill that Germaine always wanted and an outdoor fire pit. Furious, after looking at what my fucking money paid for, I pushed the grill over that should've been covered up anyway. Germaine still didn't know how to take care of shit.

Shaking my head, I walked up to the back door and jiggled the knob hoping one of those dumb asses would've left it unlocked. No such luck. Thinking of my next plan, I picked up a brick from the pathway and walked to one of the windows. I felt like a sloppy burglar when I threw the brick and only caused the bottom half of the window to shatter. I stopped and waited for an alarm to sound but soon realized that the only thing I heard was a dog barking in the distance.

I didn't remember seeing any alarm signs out front and even if I had, they wouldn't have stopped me from getting inside, I thought while reaching inside to unlock the latch. After brushing the broken glass from the ledge, I lifted the pane.

"Shit!" I bellowed when I realized it was too high for me to climb inside.

The heels that I had on didn't help either. I hurried to one of the patio chairs, then dragged it to the window. After getting it in the perfect position, I stepped onto the seat cushion, before finally making my way into the house. The room I'd broken into was an office which I wasn't too interested in. There were way better things to snoop around in at the moment, so I kept it moving.

Not thinking about when Germaine and Jalisa would possibly return, I walked through the house like a spy. I took note of everything as I wandered around. Inspecting every single inch, I figured Jalisa must've hired an interior decorator because the furniture along with the rest of the decor was gorgeous. There were two green chaise lounges that I wanted to take with me along with a fish tank built in the wall that were filled with Little Nemo type fish. I was sure the boys loved that. Germaine and Jalisa seemed to be living large off of my shit.

"This bitch is just trying to outshine my damn house. Jealous ass. She always wanted to be like me," I said.

When I reached the living room, I paused when I saw all the *family* photos of them at Universal Studios, Six Flags and Disney World. They were scattered about on tables, the walls and the fireplace mantle. "I see they've been having a blast these past few months."

I angrily knocked the photos on the floor. Jalisa even had the audacity to have some of her modeling pictures scattered about the room like she was the woman of the house.

"You bitch!" I screamed. I broke one of the frames, pulled out the photo, then ripped it into tiny little pieces. "My money bought all this shit!" I glanced around the room. "There's no way in hell y'all are gonna continue enjoying this on my fucking dime!"

At that moment, I began to ransack the place. I snatched down pictures, broke several vases, knocked down lamps and flipped over tables. When I was satisfied with my tirade, I headed upstairs.

It was more than evident that the first door I opened upstairs belonged to Nathan. "You finally got the boys in separate rooms, huh, Germaine?" I said, walking over to Nathan's crib.

I smiled when I saw one of his pacifiers. Since we were always misplacing them in the past I knew Germaine had a few more around the house so I swiped it just to have a part of him with me when I left. I spent a few more minutes admiring the room before proceeding to the next.

I opened the door to Johnathan's room. His walls were plastered with posters of the WWE wrestlers, John Cena and The Rock. His bed and floor were filled with paraphernalia from them as well. The room was totally different from Nathan's who obviously had a Bob the Builder theme. I got a little choked up after realizing Germaine had been right all along. The boys did need their own rooms to express their differences. I noticed a drawing pad on the nightstand next to Johnathan's bed. I skimmed through it and gasped when I came across a drawing titled, *Daddy, Jeliza, Nate and Me.*

I wondered why I wasn't part of his drawing. It hurt my heart knowing that my son was forgetting about me already. The only thing humorous about the picture was that he'd spelled Jalisa's name wrong. I angrily folded the paper up and stuffed it in the back pocket of my pants, then hurried out of his room to continue my investigation.

I tried to hide my anger with laughter after opening the door to the master bedroom and seeing the California king sized bed. It wasn't like I'd never seen one before. I was just hating because of the twin bed I had to sleep in every night at my mother's house.

I stared at the bed for a moment and fumed at the thoughts of Germaine and Jalisa rolling around in it like I didn't exist anymore. I contemplated about masturbating in it. It would've been funny if the two of them had walked in while I was doing it, too. I erased the thought once my eyes locked onto the closet. Just like me, Jalisa loved clothes. I knew just how to fuck with her. I clicked on the light inside the walk-in closet. Surprisingly it could've been its own damn bedroom. It was just that huge. This bitch had clothes and shoes galore.

I yanked and pulled at every piece of clothing I could reach, then proceeded to rip each item. The jeans seemed to give me a hard time, so I could only step on those. I felt like Angela Basset in *Waiting to Exhale.* All I needed was some lighter fluid along with a cigarette. When I came across this bad ass Dior dress, I folded it up and stuffed it inside my leggings instead of destroying that piece. I was no damn fool. It definitely looked like my size, so I took the shit. Glancing at Germaine's small side of the closet, I quickly realized there was no need to do any damage to his sorry ass wardrobe, but I yanked a few items down just for show.

Once that was done, I moseyed over to the master bathroom as if I had time to spare. I spotted bottles of Veet and Nair hair remover in the shower. Jalisa's shampoo and conditioner were in there as well.

"You are making this too easy, bitch," I laughed devilishly after grabbing all the bottles. I poured all the shampoo and conditioner out into the sink, then replaced the contents with the Veet and Nair. "I know how much you love your hair, dear sister, but it's time for a new do."

When that was done, I cleaned everything up then sat the bottles back in their original places. Next, I grabbed a bottle of Clorox bleach that was on the side of the toilet and headed back to the closet. On my way, I spotted Germaine's athlete's foot powder. I grabbed that, too. I rushed in the closet and grabbed the clothes that I couldn't rip, then slung them onto the bed. With major get back on my mind, I doused the bed and all the clothes with lavender scented bleach. When the bottle was halfway empty, I walked back into the closet and emptied the rest of the liquid onto her shoes. Afterwards, I reentered the bedroom and searched the drawers for Jalisa's underwear. When I found them, I sprinkled the foot powder in the crotches of her panties.

"Let's see how well you fuck Germaine with an itching pussy, trick." I laughed sinisterly.

After that was done, I began to ransack the room just like I'd done downstairs. However, my rampage quickly came to an abrupt halt when I heard a car pull up. Running to the window, I quickly peeped outside and realized that the Jaguar had returned.

"Shit!"

I rushed to put the foot powder back into the bathroom because I didn't want that evidence around. The bleach didn't matter because there was no hiding all the stains and the odor. I then hurried downstairs. But before I could reach the office where I broke in, I heard Germaine and Jalisa cackling at the front door. I wasn't gonna make it, so I dipped inside the hall closet, and prayed they didn't open it or couldn't see me through the slits in the door.

"Oh my, God!" Jalisa gasped.

"Yeah, you're gonna need him, bitch," I mumbled under my breath wishing I could see her face. "Wait until you see up-stairs."

"What the hell?" Germaine joined in.

"Somebody broke in!" Jalisa yelled.

"I'll call the cops," he said taking charge.

Seconds later, I could hear someone running up the stairs, which I'm sure was Jalisa because I could hear Germaine on the phone calling the cops. She was about to get an eyeful.

"Will you hurry the fuck up and take your ass upstairs, too Germaine," I spoke softly while silently tapping my foot. I needed to get the hell out of that house before the shit hit the fan.

I nearly gave away my position when Germaine stood in front of the door. I held my breath and backed up. His cologne smelt so fucking good. It had been a while since I was turned on by him.

Then, like clockwork, she interrupted. "Germaine!" Jalisa screamed.

As soon as he rushed upstairs, I flew out of the closet and raced toward the office. Nearly home free, I suddenly stopped. My legs became putty when I saw my boys in the den. Nathan was now walking, and Johnathan was sitting Indian style on the floor playing his Nintendo PSP. I couldn't believe how much they'd grown. I wanted them to turn around and see me and say *Mama*. My eyes filled with tears that I let fall freely. I missed my babies so much. I wanted to hug them. I wanted to kiss their cheeks and tell them how much I loved them.

I was inches away from snatching them up and taking them with me, but I stopped myself. It hurt like hell to do so, but I didn't need a kidnapping charge added to my rap sheet.

"Turn around, John John. Turn around," I whispered through cries hoping he would hear me.

I wanted him to see me. I wanted him to run into my arms and if he had, there was no way I was leaving them behind. I'd face the consequences later. Then it happened, Nathan saw me. My heart stopped, but his brother's game was of more interest to him. Instead of walking toward me, he slithered into Johnathan's lap and watched him play the game. Their brotherly bond made me smile. My body shook with anger because I knew I had to leave them again. With tears pouring down my face, I continued toward the office. However, before I climbed out the window, I grabbed a huge stack of mail from the desk.

"I'm gonna see what you bastards are up to and then I'm coming back for my sons."

Chapter 9

      Coming out of my heels so that I could get to the car a little faster I ran like hell toward the rental while looking back every few seconds to see if someone was on my tail. Once inside, I cranked up the car then fled as fast as I could realizing that I was just in time. No sooner than I made it out of the subdivision, a police cruiser raced past me with flashing blue lights. Driving for at least twenty-five minutes, once I felt safe, I pulled over and cried. Seeing my two sons and not being able to make my presence known to them, ripped my heart in two. Knowing that I had to leave them behind with the two people who'd ruined my life had me infuriated. My sons needed to be with me; their mother. I had to get them back regardless of what it took. It seemed like my tears wouldn't stop falling, but eventually I managed to regroup when I glanced at the mail in the passenger seat. Wiping the tears from my eyes, I snatched a few envelopes. The first one that I decided to open was an RSVP to Nathan's first birthday party at Chuck E. Cheese in a week.

      I shook my head at the thought of how much I'd missed out on in just few months. I knew his birthday was coming up. I just tried to keep it in the back of my mind for fear that I wouldn't get a chance to see him just like I'd missed Johnathan's birthday three months ago. I wondered if my mother had sent him a gift since she'd known their whereabouts all this time. Once I got back on my feet, I was going to be done with that cruddy bitch. That was one secret she never should've kept from me. She'd done enough damage in my life already, but keeping my boys away from me, was the worst. When I got them back, she would never see me or them again.

"Nathan, mama will see you at your party," I said to the photo on the invitation. "No one or nothing will keep me away this time."

As I continued through the mail, two more RSVPs to the party slightly angered me because I wondered who the hell these people were. That anger quickly disappeared when I felt what seemed to be a card in one of the envelopes addressed to Germaine Evans.

Just like Wayland, I also didn't understand why Germaine only changed his name in certain cases. When I opened the envelope, a grin instantly spread across my face. It was an Amex card.

"This is a great way to start my payback," I said wickedly.

With me knowing Germaine's social security number by heart along with his new address, and even his mother's maiden name if they asked, it was gonna be easy to activate the card. "You stole from me asshole. Now, I'm stealing from you," I spoke as if Germaine was sitting beside me. "Niquole is back!" I headed toward the French Quarter singing Drake's *Money to Blow*.

Despite the fact that I needed to get back to Houston before those detectives found out I was gone, I drove to the French Quarter. I needed a place to crash, since I was a dead tired from the drive and all the chaos that I'd unleashed in the house. I was happy for the money Marko had given me especially when I spotted the Loews Hotel. In a desperate need for some lavishness in my life, it's where I was going to lay my head for the night. When I pulled up, I valet parked the Camry, even though I was slightly embarrassed for treating the car like it was luxury, but then again I was Niquole Wright. Regardless of how broke I was, my attitude made me look like money. The new Niquole had jumped back onto the scene.

When I retrieved my room key, I went into the gift shop to purchase a tooth brush, toothpaste and a cheesy souvenir t-shirt to sleep in since I'd left without packing an overnight bag. After that was done, I headed toward the elevator but stopped midway there.

I was spooked by a man who resembled my father at the front desk. It had been almost fifteen years since I last saw my dad, but this man had the same build like I remembered. The skin complexion was the same and even though the man kept his head low, I even think I saw a mole near his right cheek, which was another feature my father had.

After the man checked in, and in a desperate attempt to see if my assumptions were accurate I followed him inside the elevator. He got off on the fourth floor and so did I. I reminded myself to never get a job as a detective or a spy because I truly sucked at it. I think he even knew I was following him, but didn't say anything. Thinking this man could possibly be my dad, thoughts of my childhood rushed into my thoughts like a flood. I remembered being envied by every kid on the block. Everyone wanted to be me especially around Christmas and my birthday. The kids would always be at my house to see what I got because I had stuff that it took their parents a few years to get. Those were the good ole days until my mother fucked it up.

"You wanna join me in my room?" the stranger spoke. I was so wrapped up in my thoughts that I didn't realize that I'd followed him straight to his room.

"What?" I asked with a slight attitude after realizing he wasn't my father.

"I got a king size bed in here. Ya' wanna help me mess it up?" He smiled showing his stair step teeth. They were that fucked up.

"Go to hell," I snarled and hurried back to the elevator. When I arrived at my room on the eighth floor, I immediately took a shower, then changed into the t-shirt. I washed my underwear in the sink so they would be dry for the next day. Although I was tired, I decided to go through the rest of Germaine's mail. After seeing two envelopes from Ikon Models addressed to Jalisa I smirked, especially after opening one envelope and seeing confirmations from two modeling gigs that she'd accepted. That bitch really had it going on, but not for long. I was going to ruin her reputation. Project *Destroy Jalisa* was well underway. If that wasn't enough to make me happy, when I opened the second envelope and a fifteen thousand dollar check fell out, I instantly gasped. I stared at the check for several minutes trying to figure out how I could cash that shit myself. Since she'd helped Germaine spend my fucking money, it was only right if I took it. Then again, I didn't need any check fraud drama added to the mix, so I decided to do the next best thing.

"Bitch, you won't see this fifteen grand," I said, tearing the check into several pieces. Satisfied with my day and completely worn out, I finally put everything away, then went to sleep.

❖ ❖ ❖

My cell phone woke me up around 10:00 a.m. the next morning. I was already irritated since it felt like I still needed some rest, but even more so when I looked at the unknown number. Wondering if it was Kingston again, I answered. "Hello."

"Where are you?"

"Cliff?" I asked after sitting up.

"Are you with someone?"

Was he for real? "This is not how this shit works, boo."

"You said anytime I want it and I'd like to have it now. Your mama is…"

"Wait a minute, Cliff. I know what we agreed to, but you're not gonna be demanding me whenever you feel like it. You didn't pay enough to get it like that. Don't get sloppy with this," I said sort of wishing I would've just dealt with the dildo that night instead of him.

"I'm sorry. It's just that it was so good. So much better than your mama's."

"So, now you're finally admitting it, huh?" I said sarcastically. "I thought all pussy was the same."

"Look, stop wasting time. She's gone to the casino and…"

"Cliff, I'm out of town."

"What? When are you coming back?"

"Later today," I answered not wishing it were true since I wanted to stay a few more days. I wanted to see my boys again, but knew that wouldn't be wise. I needed to get back to Houston for several reasons, more importantly I needed to handle things with Kingston.

"I'll be here."

"I know you will." I hung up.

Two hours after the call, I was on the road again. I wanted to stop by Germaine's house again, but decided not to torture myself. I'd see them soon enough at Nathan's party.

❄ ❄ ❄

I pulled into my mother's driveway only to be stopped by an unknown car. I should've blown the horn for them to move out of my spot, but I didn't want to start anything so soon. I couldn't help but wonder if my mother had replaced Cliff so soon with a new guy. That would've been hilarious and sad for me at the same time. His Scion in the driveway confirmed that he hadn't been kicked to the curb yet, but I still didn't know who the strange car belonged to. After parking on the curb, I headed inside the house. I couldn't have been no more than a few feet away from the door before my bags hit the floor and my mouth fell open. I couldn't believe when I saw my sister Adrienne and Cierra sitting in the living room with my mother and Cliff. I was pissed at Cliff for not telling me about this surprise visit. For his sake, I hoped he didn't know anything about it. The room felt eerie and awkward. Adrienne and I stared at each other waiting to see who would break the silence first. It sure as hell wasn't going to be me because I didn't have anything to say to her. We didn't get along when we were younger and damn sure didn't get along now.

Besides, what would I say to her? The last time we saw each other, Cierra was two and now she was knocking on eight. I tried my best not to look at Cierra, but my curiosity took over. I took a quick glance at her. Yes, she was definitely A.J.'s daughter. Thank God she didn't look anything like me. I proceeded to my room, since this was one family reunion I didn't want to be part of.

"Nikki, I need to talk to you and mom," Adrienne spoke. She sounded serious.

I took a deep breath. "Can I get myself together for a second?" I asked sarcastically as I continued toward my room. "What can that bougie bitch possibly want with me anyway? What in the hell are they doing here?" I questioned while putting down my purse. After giving myself a pep talk, I headed back to the living room. "What's going on?" I asked, sitting as far away from Cierra as I possibly could.

"I've got a job offer overseas that I can't pass up. A hundred grand a year," Adrienne said.

And, I thought to myself. I wondered why the hell she needed me in this conversation.

Oddly, after all these years, Adrienne still looked the same…boring. She didn't look anything like me or our mother. She must've received her looks from her father's side. Hell, she may not have been my mother's child for all I knew. She had her hair pulled back in a tight ponytail without any makeup on her face. That was probably the reason she couldn't have kids because no man wanted to fuck her plain looking ass.

"I'm going to be here for a few days then after that I'll need help with Cierra," Adrienne continued.

I glanced at Cierra and wondered what kind of help Adrienne could need. Cierra didn't look sick and all of her visible body parts seemed to be operating. I didn't want to stare, but I couldn't help but notice how pretty she was. She seemed tall for her age and slim with a head full of thick, black hair that was pulled back with a green and silver head band to match her clothes. Adrienne had taken good care of her.

"I don't understand why I'm here," I said since Adrienne wasn't making any sense. I caught Cliff sexing me up when my eyes passed him to get to Adrienne.

"Nikki, after I leave, I need you to take care of Cierra until I can come back and get her," Adrienne stated.

All eyes in the room locked onto me when I laughed. Forgetting that Cierra was all down my throat, I replied, "And what the hell do you expect me to do with her?"

My words shocked them all and I wondered what they possibly expected me to say. I didn't know this kid and she didn't know me. I may have given birth to her, but she was Adrienne's daughter…not mine. I turned to Cierra who was now sniffling. I saw so much of A.J. in her and I hated him so therefore, I hated her.

Cierra jumped up from the sofa and screamed, "I don't wanna be here anyway!" She ran out the front door after her outburst.

"Who in the hell does that lil' sassy ass heifer think she's talking to?" I asked. "Is that the way you raised her?"

My words obviously infuriated Adrienne. She blew a head gasket. "You know what, Nikki? You're still a selfish bitch! You're never going to change!"

I shook my head. "I knew it wasn't going to be long before we started arguing. You barge in here with a child that I don't even know and expect me to take care of her while you're overseas! How in the hell did you expect this conversation to go, Adrienne?"

"I didn't expect you to hurt Cierra's feelings," Adrienne fired back.

"Well, she's your fucking daughter! Go comfort her!" I

yelled. "Besides, it's crazy people out here in this world. You better go outside and make sure she's okay. I thought you were supposed to be a good mother, Adrienne."

"Niquole, stop it! Stop it right now!" my mother finally jumped in. "Cierra is your blood. You may not have raised her, but you're still her mother!"

I knew my mother was pissed when she called me Niquole.

"Whoa," Cliff responded to the news he evidently knew nothing about. My mother was good at keeping secrets, so it didn't shock me that he didn't know. "I don't think I need to be here for all this. I'll check on Cierra before I leave. See you ladies later," he said directing his words at me before leaving out the front door.

"Niquole, even if you don't see Cierra as your daughter, she's still your blood; your sister's daughter," my mother added.

"Mama, there's no reasoning with Nikki and you know it so don't waste your breath trying to talk some sense into her. She doesn't value family. She's out for herself. No one matters but her."

Adrienne's words pissed me off and she was about to know that. "I don't need this shit! I have way too much going on in my life to sit here and listen to you belittle me. You talk about me not valuing family. You're damn right I don't value this damn family because it's filled with lies! You're damn right I'm out for myself! Who else is gonna look out for me? Y'all sitting up here jumping on me about not wanting to take care of Cierra when I don't even have my damn sons! Did either of you factor them into this equation? Let's not forget if I go to jail. Who's gonna take care of Cierra and my boys then Adrienne? Now, digest all that shit while y'all sitting here with them stupid ass looks on your faces!" I barked before walking out of the room.

Chapter 10

"You're damn right I'm selfish," I mumbled to myself as I stomped to my rental car. "Who in the hell do they think they're talking to like that. I…"

I paused when I saw Cierra leaning against the driver's side door. Taking a deep breath, I pressed on even though I didn't want to deal with her little ass. I hoped she would get the hint that I was about to leave.

"Why don't you like me?" she asked when I unlocked the car door.

I turned to Cierra just in time to see her wiping tears that I'd obviously caused. I knew kids were more sensitive than adults, but I didn't know what to say to her. Not only did we lack a mother/daughter bond, we didn't even share an auntie/niece bond. Adrienne was to blame for that. I hadn't seen Cierra in years, so it was her *mother's* fault why we didn't have a relationship. I guess I could've put forth more effort to get to know her by at least calling, but, in my eyes it wouldn't have changed anything. I still would've been distant. I didn't want anyone to find out about Cierra because secrets had a funny way of coming out. So, I guess you could say I was the real one to blame for my relationship with Cierra or lack of.

"You better go back inside lil' girl. It's cold out here."

"Mama said you were mean," she responded.

I chuckled as I wondered what else Adrienne had put into her head about me. And my sister wanted me to keep this heifer? "Well, it seems to me that you and your mother are the ones with the problem. Now, move out of my way," I replied, then gently pushed her to the side.

Eyeing the stunned look on her face, I gave Cierra a '*get over it*' look, slid in my car then drove off. I couldn't help but laugh when I looked in the rearview mirror and saw her stick her tongue out at me.

"Yeah, you're my daughter with your lil' grown ass," I said.

I drove around for nearly an hour. Adrienne showing up unannounced with that fishy ass story about going overseas to make money didn't sit well with me. Hell, I should've been asking what I needed to do to sign up with her. I needed money like a drought needed rain. I wondered why she needed the money anyway. She had a cushy job as a paralegal at some big time law firm and received a hefty child support check from A.J. every month. Before my money problems, I sent her money as well. A.J.'s five grand a month should've been more than enough to take care of her and Cierra. If her story was a lie, it would eventually come to light.

Stopping at a red light, I happened to look out of the driver's side window and surprisingly saw Marko's BMW parked outside. It wasn't hard to spot since he'd pulled a corny ass move and put *VERSE* on his license plate. Couldn't have been too many people riding around Houston with that shit.

Seconds later, he walked out of the store wearing a pair of sweat pants and a pull over sweat shirt. I assumed he'd just come off the basketball court. "Come on light," I fussed, wanting to catch Marko.

When the light finally turned green, he'd just pulled out of the parking lot, which worked in my favor because instead of flagging him down, I decided to follow him. I wouldn't necessarily call myself a stalker, but more so curious as to where he was headed.

Fifteen minutes later, he pulled into The Plaza @ River Oaks Apartment complex. It was an okay spot but not anywhere I would live especially if I was driving a BMW and a Range.

"I wonder if he's about to see another chick." I had to catch myself because I was sounding slightly jealous. But there was only one way to find out.

I parked and watched Marko walk to the apartment. When I saw him slide the key in the door, I felt a little bit more at ease. I looked myself over in the mirror and played with my hair. After doing a quick breath test, I sprayed on a little smell good that I kept in my purse, then made my way up the stairs.

"What the hell are you doing, Niquole?" I chastised myself thinking that I may have been making a huge mistake.

But it was too late to turn back now. I needed a distraction from my dysfunctional life. If it meant walking into a fight, so be it. I knocked on the door. When Marko opened it a few seconds later, he choked on the smoke from the blunt he was inhaling.

Oh, so that's why his lips are so dark, I thought.

"What are you doing here? How did you find me?" Marko asked after getting himself together.

"Don't think I'm insane when I say this, but I followed you from the liquor store." Even though he didn't call me crazy, the look on his face said that he thought I needed to be evaluated. "Trust me…I didn't know you were at the store. I just happened to see you coming out while I was at the light, so I took a chance."

"Oh," was all he said.

"Am I interrupting something?" I asked while looking past him. I didn't know how I was going to react if I saw another female. We weren't an item yet, but I didn't fuck with shady people.

"Naw…naw. You're good."

"Are you sure because you look like you're doing something sneaky?"

"I'm just blown away that you're here."

I stepped up to him and nibbled on his earlobe. "Well, if you let me inside, I can blow something else."

Displaying a slight grin, it only took seconds for Marko to pull me inside. When he did, my assumptions about the apartment belonging to a woman were wrong. It was definitely his apartment. There wasn't an inch of a woman's touch anywhere. I tooted my nose at the shabby black leather furniture, dusty coffee table and three Dallas Cowboys jerseys on the wall. He wasn't living the way I thought he would be. Guess he took more pride in his cars.

"So, you followed me here, huh? Why?" he asked while taking two shot glasses from his cabinet then filling them with Patron.

When he handed me one of the glasses, I downed it quickly then relieved him of the blunt. After taking a long pull, I pressed my lips against his and blew the smoke inside his mouth followed by a long, hungry kiss.

"You left me hanging the other night. You owe me," I said, placing my hand inside his sweat pants. I gasped when my hand wouldn't close around his package. Marko was packing something lethal.

"I apologize. It won't happen again," Marko said as he tried to remove my hand. But I wasn't having that shit this time.

"I'm about to make sure of that." When I eased to my knees, he quickly backed away like I had some type of disease. *What the fuck?*

"Now, is not a good time, baby."

Was he serious? Did he not just see me drop to my knees to give him head?

I frowned. "Why not? Are you expecting someone else?"

"No, it's just that…"

"Then there's no fucking problem," I replied then scooted to him.

This time, he didn't move. I slowly whipped out his thick weapon then swallowed it whole. It was wet and salty. Either he'd definitely been playing ball or he'd just finished fucking

someone else. The second thought pissed me off a little especially if I was slurping on another bitch's pussy juices, but I had
to finish what I started.

Finally starting to relax, Marko leaned back on the wall
and let me have my way. I enjoyed blowing him. My blow jobs
were a man's heaven so I knew it wasn't going to be long before
he got into the groove of things. I placed my hands against the
wall and went to town. I stared up at him and saw that he was
biting the inside of his bottom lip.

"Damn, baby. Where they do this at?" Marko moaned. I
had to suck on him a little faster to keep from laughing.
"Niquole, I'm about to bring it, baby!"

Already, I thought. Young dudes were supposed to last
longer. I clasped my hands around his girth to let him know that
I wanted to drink his serum. He slapped his hands on the side of
my head and pulled my hair from the root. That shit hurt like
hell, but I didn't let it stop me. As soon as I worked the muscles
in my mouth a little more, he released a thick load of his juices
in my mouth.

Feeling like I gave him a taste of his own medicine, I
stood up in preparation to leave especially since he came so
damn fast. I wasn't about to waste any more my time with his
ass.

"I'm out," I said, turning around to walk away.

"It doesn't work like that, Niquole," Marko replied after
stopping me at the door. He backed me into the cheap, computer
desk

"How does it work?" I asked knowing that the blowjob
would make him want more.

"You're about to find out."

As he slowly removed my heels, his eyes were filled
with hunger. The look he gave me made him totally irresistible.
He lifted me on top of the desk and slowly pulled my leggings
and underwear down. He then scrambled through the CDs and
papers on the desk and located a condom.

"So, is this where all the action goes down?" I asked sarcastically.

"No, this is where it all begins."

Marko jerked me to the edge of the desk after rolling on the condom, then eagerly pulled my thong to the side and licked me wet. He tongue fucked me for a few minutes before giving me the real deal. I jumped upon entry and grabbed the side of the desk. His dick felt so good, but I refused to show any emotion.

"I don't know why you keep acting like you're hard and shit but like I told you last time, I'm gonna get a reaction out of you," Marko breathed in my ear. He cupped my arms with his and deep drilled me.

"Oh shit, Marko!" I couldn't deny him victory any longer. While still inside of my nest, he carried me over to the wall and banged my back out. I locked my legs around him. He definitely had me fooled. He was no two minute brother.

"That's right! Show me how much you want this!" he said cockily.

He had reason to be cocky and his cock was the reason. Moments later, he set me down, then slapped my hands against the wall like I was about to be searched. He then placed his hand on the small of my back and bent me over a little.

"Damn, Marko!" I howled when he entered me again. My durability and his strength made the standing/kneeling position awesome. He pressed my face into the wall and started gnawing at my back. "Oh Marko!"

"Talk to me, baby! Talk to me!"

When I didn't respond, he bent me over the sofa then punished me. It wasn't that I didn't want to respond. I was just muted by his skills. Neither Germaine, A.J. nor Kingston could measure up to Marko. Their sex was great, but they had nothing on this young buck. I should've been robbing the cradle a long time ago. Without warning, I came. I turned my head to the side at his sex max and noticed the condom on the floor. He'd taken it off, and collapsed on my back to catch his breath.

"Whenever you're ready, I can show you the rest of my

crib where the action continues," Marko whispered in my ear then stood up.

He walked to the back of the apartment like he was the king. Shit, as good as his dick felt, that was a title that he could carry. However, I couldn't get the condom out of my head. Not thinking about cleaning myself up, I got dressed. Seeing his deceit on the floor, I needed to get out of there.

"Are you leaving?" Marko questioned when he returned completely naked. "I thought we could take a shower together. After shooting hoops and you showing up, I sure could use one. Hop in with me," I stared at the condom and so did he. "I'm sorry, Niquole. I just got caught up in the moment."

I tried my best not to look at his toned body. "I need to leave, Marko."

"I'm sorry. I'm clean if that's what you're thinking."

I gave him an awkward look. "Are you sterile, too?" I asked defensively.

"Well, I don't have any kids if that's what you're asking."

I needed to get away from his inexperienced ass because he was about to make me blow up on him. "I've gotta go. Even though what you did was fucked up, I have so much other shit on my mind, I can't even deal with that condom issue right now."

"Don't leave. Please, stay. I promise you that it won't happen again," he spoke sincerely. His words and apologetic look were believable. "You can talk to me about your problems. Is it about your kids?"

I stared at him and wondered if he truly gave a damn or was just using his game to get me to stay. It was time to test him. "Marko, I want my boys and I need some help to do that."

He stared at me for several seconds. "So, what are you saying?" he questioned then walked over to the kitchen to pour two more shots of Patron.

"I'm saying I want my boys back and I'm prepared to do anything to make that happen."

"Why are you telling me this?"

Does he need me to draw him a damn diagram, I thought. "Because I want you to help me."

He stared at me again before swallowing both shots. "Help you how?"

"I don't know just yet, but I need to know if you're on board."

"Well, that depends. You need to give me more details."

"I don't quite have the details now, but I will in due time."

"So, what about your sons father?" he questioned.

I looked at him. "What about him?"

"Is he still in the picture? Like are you all still involved with each other?"

"Are you serious? Absolutely not."

"But you are still married right?"

"Yes, Marko I am. Why?"

He shrugged his shoulders. "Just curious, that's all. So, is anyone gonna get hurt whenever you give me the details?"

I still couldn't believe sometimes that this dude was a rapper. He seemed so fucking soft sometimes. Then again, maybe he was one of those conscious rappers like Common or Lupe Fiasco. Right now, I needed a street nigga on my team.

"No one is going to get hurt," I tried to convince. "But let me ask you a question. If what I needed help with involved my husband, would you be down?" I hoped his ass could read between the lines this time.

I could tell that he was contemplating the idea, but I needed him to confirm that he would help.

"I guess. I would have to think about it," Marko answered. "Is that cool?"

His response was good enough for now. *Maybe once I give him more pussy, that answer will turn into a yes*, I thought. "Cool," I said then started stripping. "Now, what was that about a shower?"

Chapter 11

I woke up the next morning to a loud horn blowing outside. When I opened my eyes, I found myself lying on Marko's chest with his arm wrapped around me. With my hand resting on his chest I could feel his heartbeat. It made me feel warm inside. It was a feeling that I couldn't recall ever happening with anyone, not even Germaine or Kingston. It must've been infatuation that I was feeling because there was no way this twenty-three-year-old could mean anything more to me than that. I slipped out of his arm and stared at him for a minute or two. He looked so peaceful and innocent and it made me wonder if I should bring my madness into his life. But then again, he chose me and not the other way around, so he would have to deal with his decisions.

After tiptoeing to the restroom, I grabbed one of the thin, scraggly wash cloths from the linen closet to wash my face. I then picked up the cheap tube of toothpaste from the sink and used my finger to brush my teeth. I giggled while thinking back to the few times Marko woke me in the early hours for sex. Whenever I thought I was about to venture off to la la land, he would poke me. I guess he had something to prove. He proved that he could go all night. The soreness between my legs would be a reminder for the next few days. In addition to it being a reminder, it also jarred memories of my times with Kingston whom I needed to see. Thinking back to his phone call, I realized I needed to get to the hospital. I took a quick shower hoping not to wake Marko even though a tornado could've come through and he still wouldn't have budged. He was that knocked out from the Patron, pussy and the weed. I dressed back into the clothes from the night before, stuffed my two day old panties in my purse then left.

I drove to the hospital freaking out about the unknown reason Kingston wanted to talk to me. I hoped he was going to tell me that he would let the authorities know shooting him wasn't my fault. Although I knew I was taking another chance on showing my face at the hospital again, I was willing to suffer the consequences to learn if Kingston was going to help set me free. Hell, I'd take a lesser charge and probation at this point. Anything but doing time.

Minutes later, I arrived at the hospital, with my body shivering with fear. I took a deep breath before making my way inside. My hands trembled as I stepped off the elevator onto the fifth floor. I squeezed them tight hoping the trembling would stop. I was a nervous wreck. I stood in front of Kingston's room for a few seconds before slowly pushing it open. Fuck! The two hound dog detectives were standing on both sides of Kingston's bed once again.

Damn, these assholes are really out to get me, I thought while trying to hide the petrified look on my face. Kingston had just come out of his coma and they're already trying to press him for answers. Hell, I couldn't blame them. I needed his help, too.

"So, you're just itching to go to jail, huh?" the short, black detective with the fucked up hairline asked.

"If you truly wanted to arrest me, you would've done so when you saw me here the last time," I snapped knowing they could still arrest me if they wanted to. "Besides, Kingston called me," I stressed, then rolled my eyes at him before landing them on Kingston whom I hoped would say something in my defense.

I needed to know why he called me and I assumed I

wouldn't find out until the detectives left. Then another thought hopped in my mind as I glanced back and forth from him to the detectives. What if he called all of us together so that he could make me take the fall for everything; shooting him and Hummer's death? It would've been brilliant on his behalf since I was the one who caused all the mess. When he shot Hummer, I should've gotten rid of the blood splattered jacket when he ordered me to. I not only brought loads of drama into my life, I also brought tons into his. I came out of my stupor when I heard him try to speak. I inched closer to him and pulled my cell phone from my purse. I wanted everything he had to say on camera. I didn't trust those detectives. They wanted to lock somebody up after all this time, but it wasn't gonna be me.

Kingston stared at the Hispanic detective then spoke, "She didn't…" he paused and moaned in pain. He tried to move which caused him to moan even louder.

I hated seeing Kingston in pain like this, but still couldn't hide my excitement from what he'd just said. "Did you hear him?" I spoke frantically. "He said I didn't do it!"

"Ms. Wright, he didn't say what it was that you didn't do," the Hispanic detective burst my bubble.

I forced my way between the detective and Kingston. Like a mad woman, I grabbed Kingston by the shoulders and shook him hysterically. "Tell them I didn't shoot you! Tell them, Kingston! You destroyed my fucking life! You owe me, Kingston! You owe me! Tell them! Tell them!"

The detective grabbed me and pulled me away from Kingston who was now moaning even more. At the moment, I couldn't sympathize with him.

"Ms. Wright, you need to control yourself," the black detective scolded.

"Fuck you! This is my damn life that's in jeopardy!"

"Cuff her," the black detective advised his partner.

Just as the Hispanic detective stepped over and attempted to place my hands behind my back, I heard the words that I'd been longing to hear for months.

"Niquole…didn't shoot me," Kingston announced.

The detective released me immediately. Disappointment formed on both of their faces. "Are you sure about that, Mr. Braxton? Do you want to wait until…"

"Asshole, you heard him!" I blasted the Hispanic detective. "Why in the hell are you badgering him? He said I didn't do it!"

"Ms. Wright…"

"Don't Ms. Wright me! You're trying to make him change his statement! He said I didn't do it!" I repeated. Turning my phone on video mode, I walked up to Kingston. "Please repeat what you just said."

Kingston closed his eyes for a moment, then opened them back up. "Niquole…didn't shoot me."

"Do you know who did shoot you, Mr. Braxton?" the black detective inquired.

Kingston looked like he wanted to say something, but finally shook his head no.

While the detectives continued pressing Kingston for information, I sent the video to my lawyer's email to let him know what was going on. After that task was done, I noticed Kingston staring at me. He'd never stared at me in that way before. I felt like he wanted me to forgive him for all that he'd done to me. The look was an apologetic one. I knew I shouldn't have, but I walked over to him.

My heart melted when he whispered, "I'm sorry."

I held back tears. Never in my wildest dreams would I have imagined Kingston apologizing to anyone. I leaned over to kiss him, but instead of heading toward his lips, surprisingly I ended up on his forehead. I shocked myself with that move.

"Thank you, Kingston. I'm sorry, too."

As I was about to walk away, he gently grabbed my hand. His touch almost made me melt and fall back into his life again, but Kingston was nothing but trouble. He didn't give a damn about me and I no longer gave a damn about him. I got what I wanted and needed from him. The prize that my eyes were locked on now were my boys.

"Don't…leave," he said.

I slowly pulled my hand away and shook my head at him to let him know that we were done. If I ever saw him again, it would be too soon.

Chapter 12

After leaving the hospital, I felt like celebrating so I did something I hadn't done in years. I went to the casino with some of the money I had left over from Marko. I spent two hours on the Black Jack table and an hour on the dollar slot machines. I walked out with two grand that I blew on a few pair of shoes along with a few more sweaters and some jeans from the mall. I was on a natural high. Nothing could take me off that cloud I was floating on. It got even better when I pulled up into my mother's driveway and neither her car nor Adrienne's was there. The Scion was there though. If Cliff wanted sex, he was gonna have to take a raincheck because I was in no mood or predicament to screw him. Plus, after fucking Marko I don't know if Cliff could ever get some again.

"Where were you?" he asked as soon as I walked inside the house as if he'd been waiting for me.

He'd actually startled me by standing on the side of the door like a fucking rapist ready to leap.

"None of your damn business." I frowned at him.

"It is my business when you live here."

"Last I checked, Cliff, I was grown and you were my mother's man, not mine," I barked.

"If we're gonna make this work…"

I quickly interrupted him. "Make what work, Cliff?

You're tripping." His actions made me think that I'd made a huge mistake.

"Just be available when I need you especially since I'm paying for it."

Did this son-of-a-bitch just call me a whore on the sly? "Paying for it?" I asked slightly insulted. "Need I fucking remind you that you gave me money only one time. If you think you're gonna get it like you want it, you need to keep the money rolling."

He walked up to me and removed my jacket. "It's worth every penny," he breathed on my neck.

If that's how he saw me then I was about to play the part to the fullest. I pushed him against the wall. He was about to pay me in another way. I stroked his jolly stick until it hardened. "Y…Your mama and your sister should be back in a few hours. They went…"

"I don't care where they went," I interrupted. "All I'm worried about now is having you inside of me." He hungrily groped my breasts. "Not here. Go wait for me in my mother's bed. I've got a surprise for you."

I took one quick lick of his lips then skipped to my room to find that some of my things had been snooped through. I figured Adrienne's jealous ass was the culprit, but I'd deal with her later.

Taking off my clothes, I grabbed some lingerie along with a red thong from my drawer and slipped both items on. "Ahhhhh," I moaned in pain at the soreness between my legs. Marko had really done a number on me. To add to my sexy look, I zipped up a pair of Jimmy Choo thigh high boots, then sprayed on Dolce perfume. With my boobs perked up nice and high, I stepped into my mother's room.

"Damn!" Cliff gawked. He was lying in bed butt naked with his pipe in his hand. I sleazily crawled up to him. I blew on the tip of his baby maker, then allowed a portion of my saliva to drop onto it. "Stop teasing me," he begged.

"I need you to do something for me, Cliff."

"Anything to make you put your mouth where it belongs."

"I need you to act like my husband and activate his credit card," I said just before landing.

After calling American Express on my way back from New Orleans, they wouldn't allow me to activate the card since I wasn't Germaine. Thinking they needed to hear a man's voice, I decided to go to Plan B.

"What? Ooooooooh," he bellowed when his dick hit the back of my throat. A minute later, I pulled out. "W…Why you stop?"

I reached toward the foot of the bed and grabbed my purse that I'd brought into the room with me. I pulled my cell phone and Germaine's credit card from it. "Your name is Germaine Evans. Your birthday is May…" I started coaching before being rudely interrupted.

"What the hell, Niquole? Come on now. Your mama is gonna be back soon. We don't have time for that."

"Listen to me, Cliff. I need this card activated and you're the only one who can do it."

"Look, I told you I would pay your bills."

"I know that, baby," I said before climbing on top of him and teasing the tip of his dick with my wetness. He grabbed my thighs and tried to push me down, but I hopped off. "Are you gonna call for me?"

"Whatever you want, Niquole," he huffed impatiently. "Whatever you want me to do."

After coaching Cliff with more of Germaine's information, fifteen minutes later, not only was the card activated, but I'd been added as an authorized user. I had my own personal card expedited to come to my P.O. Box along with the statements so that Germaine would be clueless for a while. As soon as I'd done enough damage, he could have his shit back.

"That's done now, come on." Cliff latched onto the inside of my thigh with his wet lips, but I gently pushed him away. He gave me a puzzled look when I got up out of the bed.

"The bills aren't due yet, Cliff. You'll get this when they are."

"Stop playing, Niquole. I know you're not gonna leave me here with my dick hard."

"Watch me."

"You fucking slut!" I heard Cliff yell as I walked to my room, then secured a chair behind the door in case he was just that pissed to come in and rape me.

I couldn't help but laugh at what I'd just done. I glanced at my phone on the bed and saw that I'd missed three calls from Marko. I didn't want to seem too excited by the number of times he'd called, but I was. He was probably calling to tell me how good of a time he had with me. The feeling was definitely mutual. I picked up the phone and called him back. I was fighting the urge to, but I couldn't help myself.

"Why didn't you wake me before you left?" he asked after picking up.

"You were sleeping like a baby. I didn't want to bother you."

"It's all good. I needed the sleep anyway. A.J. has been running me ragged about this damn party and shit."

"What party?" I asked curiously.

"The grand opening party that I'm about to invite you to at THRONE this Saturday night. I want you to roll with me."

So, A.J. named the new label THRONE, I thought. I hated to admit, but the shit didn't have a bad ring to it.

"Roll with you?" I asked.

"Yeah as my date."

"Marko, let me ask you something."

"Shoot."

Before I could get my question out, Cliff started banging on the door. "Open the damn door, Niquole! What the hell is wrong with you leaving me with this fucking hard on?" He banged some more. "Niquole, I know you hear me!"

"What's all that noise, baby?" Marko asked.

I needed to distract Marko. "Do you really think I would

98

want to step foot in that place since I no longer own it? That jackass, A.J., promised to keep it as Kingquole Records and changed the damn name! What the hell do I look like going to that fucking party?" I ranted.

"Nicole!" Cliff yelled again. I couldn't wait to curse his ass out.

"Baby, I know it might be difficult for you, but I want you with me. Don't let that nigga get to you. Fuck, A.J." Those words made my pussy smile. "So, are you gonna roll with me?" Marko asked again.

"What has A.J. told you about me?" It was time for that question to come out.

"All I know is that he bought your label. Is there any-thing else I should know about?"

If only you knew. "There's nothing else," I lied.

"So, are you gonna roll?"

Feeling a little devious, I answered, "Yes," I was so glad Cliff's banging finally stopped.

"Cool. I'll pick you up at…"

"No, I'll meet you there."

"I don't think I can take too much more of me not being able to pick you up. Are you hiding something?"

Yeah, my life. "Let's just keep it like this for now. Okay?"

"If you say so, baby. Have I earned the privilege to call you Nikki yet?"

After last night, you can call me anything you want. "I guess so."

"So, Nikki, what's the chance of me seeing you again tonight? I can get another sack and another bottle of Patron." Hearing my mother and Adrienne's voices suddenly threw me off. I needed to get off the phone to put on some clothes.

"Marko let me call you back." I hung up and jumped in my clothes. Seconds later, someone tried to open the door.

I kicked the chair from the door then swung it open.

"Nikki, what are you doing in there? Why couldn't I get in here?" my mother drilled.

"Maybe if you stop leaving your man in here alone with me, I wouldn't have to barricade it," I replied to get a rise out of her.

"What is that supposed to mean?" she asked while giving me a death stare.

"It means that I don't feel safe being alone in a house with a man that I don't know." I had to cough to keep from laughing.

"Just make sure you stay out of his way," she threatened.

Too late. "Make sure he stays out of mine. By the way, if he's going to be here all the time, we need to be splitting these bills three ways."

"Look, you don't call the shots around here. He does what I need him to do."

"That ain't all he does," I mumbled.

"What?"

"Nothing."

"Speaking of money, it looks to me that you've come across some extra cash. You're driving a new car. You've got new clothes and shoes. What is that all about?"

"The only thing you need to worry about is my half of the bills. Anything else is none of your business." I wasn't in the state of mind to engage in any type of conversation or argument with her. I was still pissed at her knowing where Germaine was and not telling me. She must've picked up on that vibe.

"Nikki, if this has anything to do with Germaine…"

"It has everything to do with him!" I growled.

"Look, I'm sorry."

"Your apologies are meaningless so save 'em. I have my own game plan in place now anyway."

She gave me a sorrowful look, shook her head, then walked out like her feelings had been hurt. It must've shown on her face because Adrienne walked in my room to put her nose where it didn't belong a few minutes later.

"Adrienne, save your breath and get the hell out of my room. Oh, and I know you've been snooping through my shit, too."

"I wouldn't be caught in those whorish clothes that you wear and I'm not going anywhere until you hear me out."

"I can't wait until I get out of here!" I screamed while throwing my hands up in defeat and plopping down on the bed. Marko's invitation to the party was looking even better.

"I don't appreciate how you treat mama."

"Does it look like I care about what you do or don't appreciate? Besides, Adrienne mind your own business."

"She is my business. Do you know that she calls me and cries about how you've treated her all these years?"

"Guilt trip."

"Nikki, you're so damn selfish. If only you knew everything that our mother has done to protect us and especially you." I wanted to question Adrienne about her statement, but my anger wouldn't allow me to. "You're gonna have to change your ways for Cierra."

"Look, I told you that I'm not responsible for her. My goal is getting my boys back. Did *our* mother tell you that she knew where they were all this time and didn't tell me?"

"That's irrelevant right now. Cierra is here."

It took everything in me to stop from ripping out my sister's esophagus for calling my situation with my sons irrelevant. "I'm gonna say this one more fucking time. I'm not responsible for *your* child. I'm sure they have schools and shit overseas. Her snobby ass needs to be with her snobby ass mother."

I stood up when Adrienne started walking toward me with vengeance in her eyes. I allowed her to step in my face and get some things off her chest, but she knew not to touch me. She knew from our younger years when we lived together that I was a dirty fighter. The scar on the side of her neck was proof when I burned her with a pair of curlers.

"I wish our mother had let your father stay in the house because you deserved however he was going to treat you."

Her words had my mind boggled. What in the hell was she talking about? What was she talking about in regards to my father? I needed to know. "Can you elaborate on what you're talking about?"

"I'm not saying another word and I hope you find out the truth one day, then maybe you'll stop treating our mother like the ground you walk on."

As Adrienne turned around and proceeded to walk out. I held up my middle 'fuck you' finger. She could go to hell with her advice and so-called words of wisdom.

Chapter 13

I was excited and nervous at the same time about the grand opening of THRONE. I couldn't wait to see A.J.'s face when he saw me and Marko together. I couldn't get out of the shower fast enough to get dressed for the event.

"What in the hell are you doing in here?" I snapped at Cierra when I walked into my room and saw her in the mirror modeling a pair of my platform pumps. I quickly yanked her little ass right out of them.

"So, you're the one whose been going through my stuff, huh?"

She nodded but showed no fear. When I glanced at my dresser and saw a few bottles of perfume and lipstick tubes opened, I looked back at Cierra noticing her nude colored lips. It smelled as though she'd bathed in the perfume. At that moment, I also noticed that my purse was open. I rushed to it to see if my last two hundred dollars was still there. It was.

"I don't steal. My mama taught me right from wrong," Cierra defended the visual accusation.

"Your mother must not have taught you too much since you're touching other people's belongings without their permission." She rolled her eyes and neck at me. "If you roll your eyes at me one more time, I promise you that'll be your last time. Now, get your grown ass out of my room. Now!"

She stomped out like the spoiled child she obviously was.

I sat on the bed to lotion my legs and caught a glimpse of Johnathan's drawing in my purse. I pulled it out and fumed at the stick figure of Jalisa all over again. Even in a kid's drawing, she looked flawless. I wasn't jealous of her. She just didn't belong in that picture or their lives. I poked my newly manicured finger though her face until there was a big hole replacing it.

"This is not your life, bitch. These are not your kids." I rummaged through my purse for an ink pen. When I found one, I drew a stick figure of me on the paper and titled it *Mommy*. "Now, this is better," I smiled cunningly before folding the picture and placing it inside the night stand drawer.

An hour later after getting dressed, I walked out of the room. I frowned at the fact that my mother wouldn't allow a lock on my door like I was a thirteen year old girl trying to hide a boy. I couldn't get out of her fucking house fast enough. I walked towards the living room.

"Nikki, where are you going?" my mother asked when I grabbed the door knob. When she whispered something in Cierra's ear, Cierra got up to leave, but stared at me eerily like that little girl in that movie *Orphan* before disappearing in the back. She could try to cross me if she wanted to.

"Can't you see that I'm on my way out?" I snapped.

"Your mama asked you a question. Where are you going?" Cliff added.

That asshole had truly overstepped his boundaries with me as well as my mother, who didn't say shit to put him in his place. I wasn't about to let it go because I knew what he was doing. He was trying to make sure that I didn't give this nookie away, but he was going about it the wrong damn way.

"First of all, Cliff, I don't know who you think you're talking to. I'm not a fucking child, so I would appreciate if both of y'all stop acting like TSA and stay the fuck out of my business."

And with that...I walked out.

✺ ✺ ✺

When I arrived at my old label, my anger shot through the roof. It was like Kingquole Records never existed. Not only had A.J. replaced the windows that I burst out, but the building had been repainted gold and black. He'd even gutted out one side and added on a few extra square feet. Looking at all the exterior renovations, I knew he'd paid some serious cash to have everything done in such an extremely short period of time. To add insult to my injuries, the THRONE marquise was of him sitting on a throne wearing a crown.

"Fucker," I seethed.

Cars were lined up and down the street and it was only 10:00 p.m. The rear parking lot was just as packed. Luckily there was a spot in the back right beside Marko's BMW. There was a reserved signed posted up, but I figured it must've been for me so I moved it and parked. I stepped out of the car and took a deep breath because I was unaware as to what I was about to walk into.

When I walked up to the door, I didn't anticipate being stopped. "Are you on the list?" the Fat Joe look-a-like asked.

"You're kidding me, right?" I was insulted. "Do you not know who I am?"

"Name please?" he asked with authority.

I glared at the big bear then gave him my name. "Niquole Wright." He didn't even bother to look on the list. He stepped out of the way to allow me inside.

"Asshole."

"Right back at you bitch," he countered. His actions led me to believe that he knew who I was from the jump. From that point on, I definitely knew the night would be interesting.

As soon as I walked through the door, heads turned and mouths dropped. By their reactions, you would've thought that Michael Jackson had risen from the dead. Those that were eating and drinking froze with food and cups almost reaching their lips. The chatter soon began. I loved every minute of it.

"That's Niquole Wright," I heard someone say.

You're damn right it's me. Did they really think I wasn't going to make a grand entrance to my own damn label? The name and owner may have changed, but Kingquole Records was still alive and in effect…in my heart.

As I walked through the lion's den, I noticed that A.J. had extended one of the studios. It looked good, but I was pissed that he'd made all the unnecessary changes and upgrades. My label was just fine the way I'd left it. I continued my walk through with eyes still glued on me. I was about to head to my old office, but Marko's appearance stopped me. When he saw me, he gave me a sexy, side grin. Those eyes that were glued to me popped out of their sockets when Marko walked up and kissed me. I liked the way he operated. The chatter increased two-fold followed by a few camera flashes. It felt so good to be me.

"I was just about to call and see if you changed your mind," Marko said as he slipped his fingers between mine.

"I wasn't going to miss this for anything. Does A.J. know you invited me?"

"He will when he sees you." He winked, then led me down to the basement where the music was coming from.

My curiosity peaked higher. My insides boiled when I saw the party room. I would've never thought to do that to the basement. As far as I was concerned, it was a storage room, but A.J. saw something totally different and it worked. I followed Marko through the crowd, then suddenly, he stopped.

"Dance with me," he said.

"What?" I giggled.

He smoothly grabbed my hips and pulled me to him. The perfect song was playing for the onlookers; Raheem Devaughn's *I Don't Care*. Marko and I rolled and grinded all over each other like two teenagers at a prom. Once again, I stepped out of character for him. After the dance, we walked to the bar.

"Well, well, well, if it isn't Ms. Niquole Wright." I recognized the voice, but couldn't put a face with it at the moment until I turned around. It was a face that I hadn't seen in years and didn't need to see now.

"Tara Townes," I greeted.

"*Mrs.* Tara Townes," she corrected with a slight attitude. I don't know why she was so proud to be A.J.'s wife.

It wasn't hard for me to smile in her face with all the sneaking around that I'd done with her husband over the years. She hadn't changed a bit with her short hair cut that resembled Nia Long's back in the day. She had light brown eyes and a figure that would put any *America's Next Top Model* to shame. I had to give it to her…she was a knockout.

I didn't care for her and she didn't care for me. She was always upset that A.J. spent a lot of time with me back in the day when I was recording my album. I was a threat then and little did she know, a threat now.

"So, what brings *you* here?" she asked before sipping her champagne. "Aren't you out of the business?"

I saw the bitch cutting her eyes at me while she waited for a response. I knew she was being sarcastic since her husband now owned my label. Before I could respond, Marko handed me a glass of champagne.

"You ready to hit the floor again?" he chuckled, then leaned in to kiss me.

"Hi, Marko," Tara spoke.

"What's up, Tara?" he said nonchalantly as if she disturbed him.

"Are you with her, Marko?" Tara questioned.

"Yeah, I am. Why?" he answered.

I could sense a little animosity, but I brushed it off when he leaned down to kiss me again. The kiss couldn't have come at a more opportune time. The crowd began clapping when A.J. walked down the stairs. His eyes must've had radar because they landed directly on me and Marko not Tara. I knew she picked up on it.

A.J. walked toward us with a murderous look on his face. "What's up, man?" Marko greeted him when he walked past us. A.J. didn't respond. He kept walking.

"What's up, people?" A.J. spoke after grabbing the microphone. "I see everybody is getting comfortable, full off all the good food and drunk already. That's how I like it." Tara joined him and tried to hold his hand to show that she was a supportive wife, but he stepped away from her. I knew she was embarrassed, but still kept her cool. "I see we have a special guest in the house tonight," A.J. continued. I damn near shit my pants when he turned to me. "If it wasn't for this chick right here, THRONE wouldn't be here."

Tara threw stones at me with her eyes when A.J. raised his glass to me. To keep Marko from getting suspicious or notice the animosity, I grinned and raised my glass back to A.J.

"Ms. Niquole Wright in the house, everybody!" A.J. emptied his glass, then left with Tara riding his coat tail.

My anger toward A.J. festered at an alarming rate and he needed to know that. I knew it was going to be hard to get to him with Tara lingering around, but I had to. My opportunity came when Marko was called away by the DJ. I hurried up the stairs just in time to see Tara stomping down the hall nearly in tears. A.J. had obviously said something to upset her. I waited until she was out of eyesight before I headed to my former office. I didn't bother to knock.

"Tara, I told you…" A.J. paused when he saw that it was me. "You know my wife just left right, so don't try any freaky shit."

I quickly glanced around realizing that he'd changed everything. There was even a pool table in the corner now.

"Yeah, I saw her, and don't flatter yourself because I'm not interested in your dick anymore."

"I figured you'd be coming up here," A.J. said. "Oh, word of advice. Messing with the artists is beneath you. Actually that nigga doesn't even have a contract, so he's not an artist anymore."

"I assume you're referring to Marko," I replied wondering if he was jealous.

"Are there any other niggas here who I should be referring to? You know how *you* roll."

"What you did downstairs was fucked up, A.J. and I don't appreciate it."

"Maybe you need to tell somebody who gives a shit." He sucked on the Canadian Mist bottle that he was holding while raping me with his eyes.

"Get your mind out the gutter. I told you that I didn't come up here for that."

"Then what did you come up here for?" he asked slightly disappointed.

"Adrienne and Cierra are in town."

"And?"

"Adrienne has trumped up some story about going overseas for a job and she's leaving Cierra here."

"Okkkay…so what does that have to do with me?"

"I'm gonna need money to take care of Cierra if that happens."

"That shit is between you and your sister. I'm paying enough in child support already."

I knew that wasn't going to work, so I quickly played my other hand. "A.J., I want my label back."

He laughed. "Is that why you're fucking, Marko? Trust me, he can't help you get it back. First, you're asking me for money for Cierra and now you're asking me for something you can't afford to buy back? You've got a lot of nerve, Niquole."

"Who said anything about buying? You're gonna give it back to me."

He gave me a confused expression. "I have no idea what you're talking about."

"A.J., you need to listen to me carefully. If you don't want our little secret to come out then you'll give me what's mine."

"Tell the fucking world about Cierra! I'll just deny it

anyway!"

I chuckled. "Cierra has a brother. A full brother."

"Last I checked, she had two."

"You don't get it, do you?"

"No, enlighten me."

"Johnathan is her brother and… your son."

He froze for a few seconds to let my words marinate, then he went completely ballistic. "This is some bullshit, Niquole!" He threw the Canadian Mist bottle against the wall causing it to shatter. "This is some fucking bullshit! When I asked you if he was my fucking son years ago, you told me that he wasn't!"

"Well, I had to keep some things to myself, A.J. just in case I had to use them as a wildcard one day like I'm doing now," I spoke boldly.

"You fucking, bitch! Now, you're coming in here trying to blackmail me."

Before I even had a chance to defend myself, A.J. stepped closer and slapped me so hard that I flew across his desk. I tried to crawl to the door as fast as I could, but he caught me. He then kicked me in the stomach, causing me to instantly throw up. As if that wasn't enough, he picked me up by my neck and proceeded to choke me.

"This is some fucking bullshit!" I clawed at his hands until I scraped off some of his skin. "You bitch!" He threw me on the floor.

Once I caught my breath, I crawled to the wall and sat up against it. I couldn't move. Luckily for me, Marko walked in. I stood up and bolted toward the safety of his arms. Marko held a concerned look on his face as he wiped my bottom lip. That's when I realized that I was bleeding.

"What the hell is going on?" Marko questioned A.J. with much authority.

"Nigga, don't question me like this bitch is worth it! Let her ass go! Me and you need to fucking talk!"

"But…" Marko tried to say.

"Nigga if you want another deal, you'll do what the fuck I say," A.J. fired back.

I wasn't sticking around for an argument or a fight. I pushed Marko out of my way, then ran out the door just in time to miss the pool ball that flew past my head.

Chapter 14

A.J.'s tirade against me the night before had me baffled and it didn't help that Marko hadn't even called to check on me. I wondered what went on between him and A.J. after I left and went straight home. I wondered what was said. Not knowing was killing me.

"Will you stop touching my lip, Cliff?" I barked while riding him. I thought screwing him would make me forget about the drama, but it didn't. He reminded me of it everytime he touched my lip. "I just want to know what happened to you, Niquole."

"If you don't leave it alone, I'm getting up."

"You're staying right here," he grunted after pressing down on my thighs so that I couldn't move. The sex wasn't as good as before and I could only wonder why.

"Do you use Viagra?" I asked not giving a damn if he was insulted.

"What? No! I don't need that shit!"

"Yes, you do because something is definitely wrong."

"I can't concentrate with that damn phone of yours ringing off the hook! Can't you just turn it off?" he snapped after it rang for the hundredth time.

"Shut up, Cliff. You can't concentrate because you didn't take your damn blue pill," I said after glancing at the phone knowing that it was A.J.

Cliff didn't respond which made me realize that I was right. Seconds later, my phone beeped to let me know that I had another voice message. I'd never seen A.J. so upset before, but I couldn't blame him. Once again, I had meddled in his life and it was only a matter of time before he was paying child support for Johnathan.

Not hearing from Marko wasn't sitting well with me. In the little time that we'd spent together, I felt we had created some kind of connection. I hoped A.J. didn't tell him about our kids and caused Marko to get ghost. But then again I knew A.J. would want to keep our children as quiet as possible, so he probably hadn't said a word.

"Turn that phone off!" Cliff yelled when it rang again. This time, it was a different ringtone. It was the one that I'd set for my attorney. I immediately hopped off of Cliff's bare dick and snatched the phone. We'd forgotten to use a condom this time. "Fuck, Niquole!" he kicked and screamed. "I'm sick of this shit!"

"Hello?" I answered as I ran back to my room naked with juices dripping between my legs.

"Ms. Wright?" my attorney said..

"Yes, it's me."

"I have some news for you."

"I'm listening." I crossed my fingers hoping the words *you're free* would seep out of his mouth.

"Mr. Kingston Braxton is dead."

I nearly dropped the phone at the news. Kingston…dead? "How?" I asked. My heart rate instantly began to increase.

"Complications during an emergency surgery."

"Oh my God." Although I wanted to know more, knowing the state of my freedom was more important. "Where does that leave me?" I said, pacing the floor. "Did the detectives say anything?" I panicked.

"Ms. Wright, you're a free woman. With Mr. Braxton's confession to the detectives, the District Attorney has decided to drop all charges against you."

I could've broke down and cried. "Oh my, God! Are you serious?"

"I sure am. I'll call you if I need to discuss any further details. Congratulations."

"Thank you…thank you so much for everything," I said before hanging up the phone and jumping for joy. Then suddenly, I stopped when it hit me that Kingston was dead. My ex lover, the man who had turned my life upside down, the man who was the root of all this was gone. I thought my heart would crumble after hearing the news, but it didn't. That was a sure sign that I really didn't love him anymore.

"Now, that you're done with that call, can we finish what we started?" I turned and saw Cliff standing in the doorway.

"I don't have time, Cliff. I've got bigger and better things to do." I hurried to my closet and pulled out my suitcase.

"Oh no…not this time, baby doll." He grabbed me and threw me onto the bed.

"Cliff, stop! Stop!"

"You're gonna stop teasing me! If I'm paying for this pussy, I get it when I want it!" Before he could enter me, there was a knock at the front door. "Shit!" Cliff said.

He hurried off of me and rushed out of my room. I jumped up and threw on a pair of jeans and a T-shirt. This sneaking around shit wasn't gonna last much longer. I knew I would eventually have to cut Cliff off. Things were getting way too complicated. I hurried to the front door thankful for the interruption. When I opened it, I closed it right back when I saw two Jehovah's witnesses. They didn't bother to knock again after my rudeness. I turned around and saw Cliff peeping around the corner. He was fully clothed.

"I should've let them in for you!" I scowled at him.

"Niquole, I'm sorry," he apologized as he walked toward me.

"Don't come any closer!"

He stopped.

"Before this gets out of hand, let's squash this. The deal is off."

"If you don't want my mother to find out about the shit you just tried to pull, you will continue paying my bills."

"Look, I don't mind paying for ass, but you will keep your damn mouth shut. Besides, what makes you think your mama won't kick you out instead of me *if* she finds out?"

"Because I'm still here, asshole! If she wanted me out, I would've been gone a long time ago. No matter how much we fuss and fight, I'm still her daughter. I'm not replaceable, but you are." He rubbed the back of his neck. I figured that I must've struck a nerve. "As a matter-of-fact, won't you go ahead and break me off something now before your head bursts from thinking too hard. I'm getting ready to get in the shower. When I get out, I'll be expecting some cash in my hand."

Exactly twenty minutes later, I walked back into my room to find Cliff sitting on my bed. He stood up and handed me two fifty dollar bills and four twenties.

"That's all I have for now," he stated. "I'll bring you more later on."

"You must not have a place to stay," I began belittling him. "Or you must really like my mother. Any other man would've told me to kiss his ass then left."

"I'm not just any man. I like what I like and want what I want. If I gotta pay you to keep your mouth shut, then the original agreement still stands," he frowned after getting up in my face. "I'm still going to get something out of the deal though." He walked out of the room, then out the front door.

"This shit with Cliff is going too far," I mumbled after falling back on the bed. I grabbed my phone and went through all the missed calls from A.J. hoping that one or two of them may have been from Marko. None. "Fuck this." I hurried to my closet and immediately started pulling clothes from the hangers.

About ten minutes later, Cierra walked into my room. I caught a glimpse of her staring at me in the mirror. "Did you fall on your face?" the little brat asked as she watched me apply make-up on my bruised lip.

"What did I tell you about coming in my room without knocking?" I snapped.

I was stunned when she didn't leave. Instead Cierra walked in and took a seat on my bed. She definitely wasn't afraid of me, which was something I'm sure she'd gotten from my side of the family. I kept my eye on her in the mirror. It angered me to see how much of a spitting image she was to A.J.

"Did someone hit you in your face?" she continued her questions. Ignoring her, I continued applying my make-up, but knowing how A.J. had treated me and seeing his twin in my room bothered me. "My mama said..."

"I don't care what your mama said!" My bark frightened her. I grabbed Cierra by her arm and shoved her out of my room. "Next time...knock!" Before I closed the door, I saw tears streaming down her face. Moments later, my mother barged in the room.

"What did you do to that child? Cierra is in my bed bawling her eyes out!" she lashed out.

"I don't have time for this," I said, throwing clothes into my suitcase. Once it was zipped, I grabbed it along with my purse and walked past my mother like she wasn't even there.

"Where are you going? You need to stay here and help me with Cierra."

"Cierra has a mother. Where in the hell is she anyway? She's been MIA for the past two days. Doesn't Adrienne know she has a responsibility to her child?"

"Adrienne is gone, Nikki," my mother informed.

"So, she took the so-called job overseas for real?"

"No, she didn't."

"Then where in the hell is she?"

"Nikki, Adrienne is in Georgia. I knew she was dropping Cierra off to get things together for her and her new man."

I almost burst my gut laughing. "And you talk about me? Your precious Adrienne is no better than me or you." I shook my head. "She abandoned her child for a man. I never did that.

Even when I was dealing with Kingston, my boys were always part of my plan. You need to be ashamed at how you raised us. We learned all of this shit from you." I could tell that my words were getting to her, but she needed to hear the truth. She needed to feel like shit because all of this was her fault.

"Nikki, I was fifteen when I had Adrienne and twenty when I had you. I didn't have any help in raising both of you. I didn't know what I was doing. My mom died a year before I got pregnant with Adrienne. When my dad found out, he kicked me out saying that I was a disgrace to the family. You don't know how hard it was for me until I met your dad and…"

"And you got pregnant with me," I finished her pathetic statement. "So what? You're forty-nine now! In all of those years, you had time to raise us right, but you were too busy jumping from man to man. I wish my father would've taken me away from you just like Adrienne's father did."

"You wouldn't have wanted that, Nikki," my mother replied.

"How do you know? Was I ever given a damn option?"

"You turned your back on me, Nikki. You shut me out. You've never let me in."

"And I'm not letting you in now. It's too late to be my mother."

"It's never too late! You have to want it!"

"I don't want it! You had your chance!"

"Then be miserable all your life, Nikki. Your sister wants to be happy and she deserves a chance at it."

A feeling came over me that I'd never felt before. It felt like my heart crumbled. "What about me? What do I deserve? Am I that much of a bitch that I don't deserve to be happy?"

"You deserve to be happy, Nikki. You just choose not to be and in regards to Cierra, she can make you happy because she's *your* daughter. You gave birth to her. She's your first born. That should count for something. I know that I told you before that you should've aborted her and I apologize for that. Truthfully, I was willing to help you raise her, but you were headstrong on keeping her a secret."

Getting emotional, I fought back the tears. It was a mixture of hatred, anger and hurt. "Cierra is not my problem and she's definitely not my daughter. Since you and Adrienne concocted this unwanted family reunion, then the two of you should deal with her. I'm going to get my boys. They're the ones who matter most to me and they're the ones that make me happy."

I never looked back as I grabbed my things, stormed out the house and left.

The tears burned my eyes as I drove to the post office to see if the American Express card that I'd expedited was there. My mother's words burned a hole through my heart. Adrienne's happiness was always more important than mine and she proved it. "I'm supposed to just take care of a kid while that bitch goes off and lives in the lap of luxury? Fuck you and fuck her Mama!" I screamed as if my mother was in the passenger seat. "No one ever thinks about my happiness! When can I be happy? Tell me that!"

I swerved into the post office parking lot and walked inside. Tons of mail fell out of my box when I unlocked it. All that I didn't give a damn about remained on the floor. Luckily the card was there. That was all that mattered. After quickly activating it, I drove like a mad woman straight to the airport. When I arrived, I left the rental car in the long term parking lot just in case my time in New Orleans was extended. Part of me was afraid to give my name when I went inside to check available flights. I prayed that my name wasn't on some type of no fly list. For once, God heard me. When I was able to purchase a ticket, it was sure proof that I was a free woman. *Maybe things will start going my way again,* I thought.

❖ ❖ ❖

As soon as the plane landed in New Orleans, I rented a car and hightailed straight to Germaine's neighborhood. I was about to park down the street like I did before, but caught a glimpse of Jalisa climbing into the Jaguar. Just like I'd done with Marko, I decided to follow her. I made sure to stay a safe distance away in case she spotted me. I had one more day to hide before making my existence known at the party. Ten minutes later, Jalisa turned into the parking lot of a spa, which instantly pissed me off. Here I was struggling while this bitch was going to spas and shit. Not to mention, she had a new car, which was more than likely purchased with the money Germaine stole from me.

Parking a few cars down, I waited until that bitch walked inside before grabbing a tube of lipstick from my purse. Not really giving a shit who saw me, I walked to her car and dug my key into it as far as it would go and did a little bit of art all along the driver's side door and the trunk. I then used the lipstick and wrote: *C u soon, bitch* on the driver's side window. Feeling slightly vindicated, I left with a huge smile on my face.

Chapter 15

For about twenty minutes, I sat in the Chuck E. Cheese parking lot on General DeGaulle Drive and watched parents and their kids come and go. I wondered if the people who walked inside were attending Nathan's party. I was nervous yet excited about seeing my boys, but the faces that I really wanted to see were Germaine's and Jalisa's. As soon as that thought popped into my mind, I figured there was no reason to prolong the reunion any longer. I stepped out of the Chevy Malibu that I'd rented and grabbed the bags filled with Nathan's gifts from the trunk. Thanks to his father's credit card, Nathan would have more presents than he could ever imagine and they all would come from his mother.

"Go get your boys, Nikki." I gave myself a pep talk before walking inside.

"It's a great day at Chuck E. Cheese! Are you here for a party?" the overly ecstatic teenager greeted.

"Yes. Nathan Evans," I said looking around.

She checked her list, then pointed me in the direction where his party was taking place. I was near an anxiety attack as I walked through the crowd of boisterous kids and their parents chasing after them. I assumed Germaine wanted to give Nathan a different party than we'd always given Johnathan over the years. Johnathan always had theme parties in our backyard. I couldn't help but wonder what kind of party he had this year since I'd missed it. I would definitely have to make up for that. Actually this Chuck E.Cheese shit was an insult to my kids' lifestyle. They were better than this.

"Watch it!" I snapped at one of the kids who'd stepped on my Prada boots. I looked down to see if he'd scuffed them. Luckily he didn't or I would've been choking his ass out in some corner.

As I neared the table, I recognized a few of the people from my past. A lot of them were from Germaine's family. A few were from Jalisa's. There were actually two tables reserved for Nathan's party. The other table was filled with people that I didn't recognize and a few friends that I'd left behind when I moved to Houston. New or old, they were all about to get a real shock.

"Mommy!" Johnathan screamed with joy as soon as he spotted me. His eyes lit up like bright stars. But when he tried to run to me, that bitch Jalisa grabbed his arm to stop him. He gave her a misunderstood look.

As the chatter around the tables instantly stopped, everybody including Germaine and Jalisa stared at me like I was a circus freak.

"Did you think you were gonna have a fucking party for *my* son and I not show up?" I growled at Germaine.

I pushed the gifts that were on the table to the side and replaced them with mine. A few of the originals fell on the floor. The guests who knew me were speechless and those who were seeing me for the first time had curiosity all over their faces. I walked up to Germaine, who was holding Nathan. When I reached for him, Germaine pulled back.

"What are you doing here?" my soon to be ex-husband asked.

"Why the fuck do you think I'm here…for my son's party." I reached for Nathan again.

"He doesn't know you," Germaine said, backing away.

"And why is that? Oh! I know! You took him from me!"

Jalisa stood up as if she was about to say or do something, but Germaine stopped her. "Please let her go. I've been waiting six months for this ass whooping!" I pointed at her. "How in the hell do you think you're gonna replace me? I've told you over and over again…you will and can never be me! There's only one me, bitch!"

Jalisa heaved like she was itching to punch me. I wanted her to because I was going to turn Chuck E. Cheese the fuck out if she did. I had plans on scrubbing the floor with her ass. I turned back to Germaine. "Give me my son before I cause a scene." I reached for Nathan again. This time, Germaine didn't pull away.

"Why did you give him to her?" Jalisa questioned Germaine.

"Because he's my son and not yours," I answered for Germaine, then turned back to Nathan. I thought he would resist me because of the time we'd spent apart, but he didn't. My heart melted when he smiled at me as if he remembered. I saw Johnathan trying to pull away from Jalisa. "Jalisa, let my son go!" I could tell she didn't want to, but Germaine removed her arm as if to say 'please do what she says.'

Johnathan ran to me and hugged me tight. I batted my tears away when I saw him release a river of his own. Both of them were obviously happy to see me.

"How did you find us?" Germaine asked.

"Does it really matter? Besides, did you think I wasn't going to find you? It was only a matter if time," I responded.

"Why aren't you locked up?" Jalisa jumped in the conversation without permission.

"If you really must know, Kingston told the cops that I didn't shoot him." I instantly saw Jalisa and Germaine swallow lumps. "No need to worry though. Kingston is dead. I'm sure he didn't tell anyone about your involvement in his shooting. Well, then again I'm not too sure about that," I chuckled deviously. After my words, a few of the guests got up to leave. "All I know is that he cleared me." The two of them stared at each other as a few more guests left. I noticed Jalisa staring me up and down as if something about me looked familiar.

"Is that my damn Dior dress?" she questioned.

"I don't know. Is it?" I winked.

I handed Nathan back to Germaine and walked over to Jalisa before she could say anything else. "I never knew you wore wigs, Jalisa." I snatched the cheap-looking synthetic thing off her head and immediately burst into a roar of laughter. "I can't believe that shit actually worked!"

"I knew you had something to do with this! You fucked up my hair, you crazy bitch and all of my damn clothes! Then you come in here wearing my shit?" Jalisa roared.

"Technically, everything you speak of belongs to me since I'm sure my money paid for it and that goes for that Jag, too." I stared at Germaine when I spoke those words.

"You keyed my fucking car? I only flattened your tires and…" Jalisa paused.

A light bulb went off inside my head. "So, it was you who flattened the tires on my Lexus at Germaine's friend's wedding that night? Wow! You've really been after me, huh?" I laughed. "I guess payback is a bitch though."

I assumed my statement angered her because at that moment, Jalisa charged at me. Germaine snatched Johnathan and Nathan to safety just in time. There was no way this fight wasn't going to happen. It was long overdue. As soon as she made it in my space, I flipped her ass over one of the tables so hard and fast, she didn't have a chance to figure out what had just happened. Two of Jalisa's cousins that I remembered jumped up. But before they could get to me, they were stopped by two of the guys at the table. I was ready to take anyone on. Before I could get back to Jalisa to really put my fist down her throat, Germaine pulled me back while one of Jalisa's folks detained her.

"Here you go taking up for this bitch again!" I chewed him out. "I can't believe you let that bitch be a mother to my boys, Germaine!"

"Nikki, calm your ass down! Look at John John and Nathan! They're crying!" he yelled at me.

I turned towards Johnathan and Nathan. Their faces were wet with tears. Now, they looked frightened and I was partly to blame. Those were the faces that I didn't want to see. "You did this Germaine! You did this!" I snarled at him.

"The cops are on their way," the manager said after rushing over to us. His Caucasian face was red with anger. As soon as the words spilled from his mouth, two uniformed officers walked in.

Damn, that was quick, I thought trying to get myself together. I had something for Jalisa's ass. I yanked from Germaine's grasp and hurried to the officers first.

I pointed to Jalisa then screamed frantically, "She kidnapped my kids!"

Germaine and Jalisa were stunned as the officers walked over to them with me close beside. I waved for Johnathan and Nathan to come to me, but to my surprise, they didn't. They clung to Germaine's leg. I died on the inside because it felt like they'd turned my kids against me.

"Is what she saying true, sir?" one of the officers addressed Germaine. He had a bald head, and was quite handsome for an older white guy.

"No, she's lying," he answered cockily.

"You're lying!" I yelled. "These are *my* kids and he is *my* husband." That snide look disappeared from Germaine's face.

"Sir, is that true?" the officer asked.

Germaine turned to Jalisa. "Don't look at that bitch! She can't help you!" I fired back.

The taller officer turned to me. "Ma'am, please calm down."

"Yes. She's my wife and these are our kids," Germaine finally answered.

"Well, who is she, sir?" the taller officer asked of Jalisa.

"Yeah! Who is she?" I tossed in my two cents.

"Ma'am, I'm gonna need you to calm down," the tall officer warned.

"She's a friend of the family," Germaine responded.

Jalisa huffed at the title Germaine had given her.

"She's no friend of my damn family," I spoke.

"Well, actually, she's the boys' aunt," Germaine corrected which pissed me off even more.

"Sir, is there a restraining order against your wife that we need to know about?" the handsome officer inquired.

I frowned at his question. "No, there isn't," Germaine stated.

"Then why is she saying you kidnapped the kids?" the officer questioned.

"I…I don't know," Germaine stuttered. "She's the one with the legal issues. Ask her the damn questions." I couldn't believe that asshole had thrown me to the wolves.

"I think we need to take this downtown and get this cleared up," the tall officer suggested.

"No, we don't! These are my sons! This is my husband! She's trying to steal my life!" I freaked out because I didn't want to step foot in another precinct. I didn't have time to explain and have them contact the Houston police to find out if what Germaine was saying was true or not.

"Ma'am, you've already caused a disturbance. We can take you downtown for that alone. The only way for us to clear up this accusation is if we go downtown and check out your story," the handsome officer informed.

"There is no story! Those are my kids!" I yelled.

The tall officer walked over to the manager and asked him if he wanted to press any charges. The manager quickly told him that he didn't, but he wanted me out of the building. I watched Germaine comfort our boys when I should've been the one doing that. My heart sank even further as I watched Johnathan walk over to Jalisa. She picked him up and comforted him.

"Ma'am, the officer addressed me. "The manager is not pressing charges, but he wants all of you to leave the premises.

If you want to follow through with your complaint, it has to be done at the precinct."

"Don't do this, Nikki. You've already caused enough trouble. You know you're wrong for what you've done," Germaine said to me.

I glanced around Chuck E. Cheese and watched all the onlookers stare at me. The parents held their children close to them while mine clenched to another woman. I watched Jalisa walk over to the table where Nathan's gifts were. She covered her head with the wig and retrieved Nathan's gifts. Of course leaving the ones that I'd brought.

She walked back over to us then said to Germaine, "We need to leave." She was stern with her words.

"Don't walk out of here with my boys, Germaine. Don't do this to me," I damn near begged.

There was an inkling of hope in his eyes, but that was short lived. "You're never gonna change, Nikki or is it still Niquole? I can't have this nonsense around my sons anymore," he said just before walking out.

"Looks to me like my team is winning," Jalisa addressed me fiercely before walking out behind him.

I pierced my eyes as I watched them put the boys into the car. "Don't think this shit is over, bitch," I mumbled.

Chapter 16

I was furious when I left Chuck E. Cheese. Germaine had embarrassed me in front of everyone, especially Jalisa. He was about to pay for it dearly though starting with my accommodations. I paid for five nights at the JW Marriott on Canal Street. I wasn't leaving town that fast, so I could care less about the $289.00 a night price tag. I even got a suite. The tab was on Germaine, not me. If and when he ever received his Amex bill, he was going to see and feel my wrath. Germaine was real big on making sure that his credit was nearly superb, but I was about to fuck it up. After securing my room, I went on a well deserved shopping spree in Saks that totaled four grand, along with purchasing several dresses from BCBG and cute costume jewelry from Betsey Johnson.

Upon returning to the hotel a few hours later, I received a text from Cliff.

When are you coming home? Your mama ain't putting out because of your kid so you need to come fix this shit and me.

I laughed at the text and walked inside Shula's Lounge inside the hotel to grab a bite to eat. After finishing off my chilled half maine lobster, the waitress returned to inform me that my card had been declined.

"Run it again," I ordered. "It's an American Express." When she left, I reached inside my purse and grabbed fifty dollars in case the card still declined. Damn, I'd just gotten the card, and it was giving me problems already. When she returned, she informed me that the charges still weren't approved.

A little embarrassed, I handed her the fifty bucks and hurried out of the restaurant. As soon as I made it to my room, I called the card company. After making me verify some information along with some of Germaine's, the representative finally told me what I didn't want to hear.

"What do you mean I can't make any more charges? Why?" I lashed out at the woman after receiving the devastating news.

"Ms. Wright, it looks as if all charges have been suspended on this account."

"Why? I just activated the card today!"

"Yes, I do understand that, but there was quite a bit of activity on the account today, which the computer flagged as fraudulent."

"Fraudulent? No, I made those charges myself. I can tell you everywhere I went today, so tell your damn computer to take the suspension off my account."

"I'm sorry, Ms. Wright but once the computer flags the account, American Express will have to contact the main card holder to verify the charges as well. You're just a second authorized user."

Shit, the last thing I needed was for them to call Germaine so soon. I had to think of something quick. "Well, Mr. Evans has changed his phone number. Can I give you that?" I had planned to give them Cliff's.

"I'm sorry, Ma'am but you can't make personal changes to the account either," she sounded like a trained robot.

"Are you serious? So, basically I'm stuck out of town with no money! What in the hell am I supposed to do?"

"Ms. Wright, I do apologize but the only way for us to approve…"

"Shut the hell up bitch. You're no help," I said, hanging up the phone. "Shit! Shit! Shit!"

I stared at the bags of clothes and shoes on the floor and quickly erased the thought of returning them. It had been months since I was able to shop like that, so I was keeping all that shit. I only had eighty dollars left from the money Cliff had given me. I was seconds away from calling to tell him to wire me more when suddenly Marko popped in my head. It was time to put my game face on. I conjured up fake tears then called him.

"What's up?" he answered like he had a lot on his mind.

"Marko, someone robbed me and I don't have any money," I screamed, cried and sniffled.

"Where are you?" Finally I'd gotten a concerned reaction.

"I'm in New Orleans!" I cried even harder. "They stole my money, Marko! All the money you gave me is gone! I came out here to see my children and now I have to deal with this!" I poured it on even thicker with that last line.

"Damn, I can't believe some punk ass dude would rob a female. Wish I would've been there."

I snickered silently.

"I'll wire you a few hundred bucks through Western Union so you can get home."

"Marko, you've done so much for me already. I can't accept anything else from you. I just wanted to let you know what happened." Hopefully my plan was working.

"You're down there broke, Niquole! Do you think I'm gonna leave you out there like that?" he chastised.

"No," I whimpered trying to keep from giggling again.

"Go pick up the money in half an hour. I told you I got you. Call me when you get it," he said then hung up.

I wiped away the crocodile tears before heading out the door. *I'm so good at what I do.*

As I rode the elevator down, I started feeling a little guilty for using Marko. If I played my cards right, which I was already doing, I'm sure I would have him eating out of my hands. But then again, I thought the same thing about Kingston and look what happened. Kingston moved mountains for me, but it ended up being all for his benefit…not mine. The more I thought about it, until Marko showed his true colors, I'd ride the horse until it toppled over.

I collected my car from valet then drove to the nearest Western Union. I didn't expect the eight hundred dollars that Marko wired me, but I was grateful for it. I was about to drive to Germaine's house to stir up some more trouble, but my car pulled me in the direction near the Hollygrove community.

"I hope I'm going the right way," I said, turning from street to street after reaching my old neighborhood.

Some things seemed familiar while others didn't. It had been a while since I'd been there. The neighborhood looked horrible. I assumed a lot of vacancies and boarded homes were due to Hurricane Katrina, which didn't make a lot of sense when that shit happened six years ago. It was okay when I was living there, but it had gone way down hill since that time. The houses in the neighborhood weren't the best, but everyone made do with what they had. Our house, on the other hand, was the best on the block. Fuck living like the Joneses. We were the Joneses. My mother and father threw parties every weekend and we were loved and respected by all; my father was anyway.

I'm sure the neighborhood was still crime ridden, but back then everyone knew not to fuck with my father. I often heard rumors of him shooting people, but most times I would just shrug them off. But eventually I figured the rumors must've been true since no one ever bothered me.

"That's it," I said when I almost passed my old house. I slammed on brakes, then rolled my window down to get a better visual. Just like a lot of the other houses in the neighborhood, it was boarded up as well.

"Colie?" I jumped out of my trance when I heard my childhood name being called. "Colie, is that you?"

I was about to pull off, but that voice stopped me. How

could I ever forget that voice? They say you never forget your first and Milwaukee was definitely unforgettable. I remembered it like it was yesterday. He'd been flirting with me for the longest, but I wouldn't bite because I was fourteen and he was twenty-two. One night when my parents were having another one of their shin digs, he came over to attend. Only an hour into the party, everyone was either drunk or high as usual, but not Milwaukee. He snuck into my room and popped my cherry. I was resistant and scared at first, but that thump between my legs had a mind of its own. He yanked me out of my thoughts when he tapped on my window. He still looked the same and hadn't aged a bit.

"Hey Milwaukee," I greeted him.

"Girl, where you been hidin'? Last I heard you were about to get locked up?" I was about to pull off and roll over his feet for that remark, but then he said something to cause me to think otherwise. "I see ole Bishop in the hood all the time."

"You do?" I asked. The sound of my father's name made my heart skip a beat.

"Yeah, he was just here a couple of nights ago."

I glanced down the street and saw a few crackheads and drug dealers. I couldn't help but wonder if my father was now among the group.

"Hey Milwaukee?" I turned my head to see who was calling him. It was a crackhead. "Yo! Yo! You got that?"

"You got my money?" Milwaukee asked the guy with much aggression.

I glared at Milwaukee wondering if he sold my father drugs and that was the reason he was in the neighborhood. My nose flared with anger at the thought.

"Look, Milwaukee, man, let's do the same pay as the other night." Milwaukee tried to pull the crackhead away from the car so that I wouldn't hear what he was about to say, but he didn't pull him too far. "I'm sorry about nuttin' so fast the other night. I couldn't hold it for the way you were rollin' that ass on me."

"Oh my God. You roll like that now? You nasty loose booty ass!" I spewed at Milwaukee then sped off.

I glanced at the two of them in my rearview mirror. The crackhead's words had caused him to get a beat down. Damn…a lot of shit had changed since I'd been gone. The further I drove away, what Milwaukee said about my father stayed glued in my head. I couldn't believe that he could possibly be on drugs and knowing that Milwaukee was probably supplying it to him was killing me. I needed to find my father. I drove around the hood for a while searching for him, not realizing that I may not even recognize him after all these years.

"Get away from my car!" I growled at one of the crack-heads who ran to it when I slowed down.

"Hey! That's ole Colie right there!" someone from one of the small crowds hollered. I looked up and saw that it was one of my mother's old friends wearing a pair of those clear stripper shoes along with a dirty jean skirt with the matching jacket. I knew that bitch was cold. I also knew that she was more than likely on drugs, too.

"Hey Colie, where yo' mama been hiding?" I turned up my nose to her and pulled off. *Everybody around here is going down*, I thought.

I had to get out of the neighborhood. Too many memories and people that I'd suppressed were resurfacing. As soon as I was far enough to bury those memories and people again, my phone rang. That old hag had talked up my mother.

"Yeah?" I answered irritably.

"When are you coming home to get Cierra?"

"I'm not. I told you what I was doing. I'm trying to get my boys and now that I've heard that my father is around, I'm trying to find him, too."

She got quiet for a few seconds. "Why the hell are you looking for him?"

"Because I wanna see him. You sound scared that I'll find out something if I find him or something."

"You need to leave that alone, Nikki," my mother responded.

"You would want that since you're probably the reason he's on drugs."

I hung up not giving her time to deny or confirm. I turned the radio up because she ended up calling back a few more times. The more she called, the more infuriated I got. She wasn't helping my situation any. I was a ticking time bomb ready to explode.

"Will you please stop calling me?" I screamed at the phone.

There was too much going on in my head and I needed it all to go away. I was seconds from going back to the neighborhood to score a sack of weed from Milwaukee, but the liquor store that was in my view turned out to be a better choice. I would erase the demons with a bottle of Jose Cuervo Silver. I bought two just in case, then hurried back to the hotel to get my pity party started.

✿ ✿ ✿

"I got loooooooooooove all over me! Baby, you toooooouch every part of me," I slurred along with Monica on the radio.

If I was still singing, I would've given that heifer a run for her money. I danced around in my bra and panties in my hotel room spilling alcohol with every step. After dancing a little more, I took a long chug from bottle number one then dropped it on the floor. Seconds later, I fell to my knees and tumbled over.

"Why is this my life?" I asked no one. "Why me?"

I didn't even realize that I'd fallen asleep until I heard my cell phone ringing. Standing up to retrieve the phone off the bed, I glanced at the clock-radio on the nightstand. It was damn near two a.m. which meant I'd been knocked out for hours. The phone rang again.

"H…Hello?"

"What room are you in, Niquole?"

"Huh? Who is this?"

"It's Marko."

"Marko?"

"I'm downstairs. What room are you in?"

I was shocked. "What are…you doing here?"

"Is someone up there with you?" he asked.

"No."

"Then what damn room are you in?"

I glanced around the room like a newborn opening their eyes for the first time. "Hell, I don't know."

"Look on the phone, Niquole." I tripped over my shoes walking toward the night stand. After reading off the room number to him, he said, "I'm on my way up."

I was in no mood or shape to straighten up the room. A few minutes later, Marko knocked on the door. As soon as I opened it, he gave me a weird look.

"You sure you alone up here?" he asked, then hurried inside.

"No one is…here, Marko."

"Are you drunk?" he asked.

I giggled. "I was. I drank one bottle of Jose, even though I bought two. One for each one of my sons. But since I'm awake now, I guess I'll start on that second bottle."

Marko watched as I picked up the bottle, but quickly pulled it from my hands. "Give that back, Marko. Jose makes the pain go away." I don't know where the tears came from, but they seeped from my eyes at a fast pace. Marko swept a few of them away with the back of his hand.

"Niquole, I don't like seeing you like this. I'm here for you, baby. What do you need me to do to help you with your husband?"

As if that's exactly what I needed to hear, I instantly let out a barrage of tears.

Chapter 17

I woke up around eleven a.m. the next morning. Once again, I was lying on Marko's chest with his arm wrapped around me. He wasn't playing fair. This wasn't the direction I had planned on going with him. I didn't expect him to pop up out of the blue unannounced especially since I had things to tend to regarding my boys. I was happy he'd offered to help me with Germaine, but I didn't need him just yet. I had a lot more havoc to stir up.

I quietly slipped out of bed, showered and dressed. I grabbed the wad of mail I'd stolen from Germaine's house from the floor, then sifted through the envelopes for the information pertaining to Johnathan's karate awards ceremony. Shit, I had less than an hour to get there. When Marko shifted in the bed, I grabbed my purse and jetted out of the room before he woke up. Luckily, he was such a deep sleeper. Once I retrieved my car from valet, I typed in the address of the facility on my I-phone then headed to my son.

I arrived at the karate dojo fifteen minutes later. As I was about to walk in, I heard tons of loud clapping. I assumed one of the kids had received his or her award. I hoped it wasn't Johnathan because I wanted to witness his accomplishment. I walked into the room wearing my new bold blue, cowl neck sweater along with a pair of jeans and some five inch Dolce Vita studded pumps. I was clearly overdressed, but that was the idea. If that bitch Jalisa was there, I wanted her to know that I still had it.

Germaine, Jalisa and I spotted each other at the same time. Petrified looks quickly formed on their faces. By now, they had to know that I wasn't letting this shit go so easily. I took a seat within a few feet from where they were just to piss them off even more. My timing couldn't be any more perfect. Johnathan's name was called up next to receive his award. I jumped up.

"That's my son! Yaaaaaaay, Johnathan! That's my son!" I clapped as hard and as fast as I could. A few of the parents stared at me in disbelief. "What's the problem? I can't cheer for my damn kid?" I barked at them.

I turned back to Johnathan who was now receiving his trophy. I couldn't make out the look on his face. It was like he didn't know if he should be happy or sad to see me. My son was obviously confused and that hurt me.

"Way to go, John John!" I continued.

As soon as Johnathan took his trophy and sat back down, Germaine clutched my arm and pulled me out of the ceremony and into the hallway.

"How many times are you gonna embarrass your kids, Nikki?" he scowled at me. When I stepped up close and tried to hug him, he hesitantly pushed me away. "No! This shit has got to stop! You can't keep popping up like this! You're confusing our boys!"

"I'm happy you finally said it. Yes, they are *our* boys." Jalisa walked up just as I was saying that last line. Knowing Germaine didn't see her, I walked up to him again and rested my hands on his face. "I'm not doing anything any other mother wouldn't do," I spoke softly. "You can't blame me for how I'm going about things. You took my boys away from me. You left me out to dry and take a murder wrap that wasn't my fault, and you stole my money. Now, you tell me, if all of that happened to you, how would you react?"

Germaine rubbed his hand over his head. I could feel that he was inches from touching my lips with his. Jalisa must have felt it, too.

"Germaine, what are you doing?" she asked sounding a little jealous.

He quickly pushed me away.

"What do you mean what is he doing? He's with his wife, bitch," I answered, then gently snatched Nathan from her arms. "Hey, baby," I cooed at Nathan. Immediately, he started crying and tried to jump out of my arms. The Chuck E. Cheese fiasco must've still been floating around in his head. Germaine pulled Nathan from me.

"Nikki, you need to leave and stop causing all this damn drama. You broke into my house and now, you're showing up everywhere stirring up shit. When is it gonna end, Nikki?" he asked as he handed Nathan back to Jalisa.

"It'll end when I get my family back." My words stunned them. "Yes, I said it. I want my damn family back!"

"It's too late for that, Niquole. Your family doesn't want you," Jalisa ejected.

"The longer it takes for me to get my husband and boys back, the more I'm going to make your life a living hell. You should know the depths I'll go through to get what I want, dear sister. By the way, how's the cooch?"

She looked confused. "What?"

"I see you're trying to disguise the fact that you're twitching around. Itching? Need to scratch?"

"Bitch, what the hell did you do?" she asked.

"Let's just say that you may wanna wash all your underwear or just toss 'em out and buy new ones."

"You're a damn maniac!" Jalisa yelled.

"You, of all people, should know that, Jalisa. You're my fucking sister."

Jalisa furiously handed Nathan back to Germaine, then shot off her demands, "Get rid of this bitch, Germaine before I do something crazy."

"Like what?" I laughed. "Get your ass whooped again for trying to be me?" I leaned toward Germaine and tried to kiss him. He turned his head, causing my kiss to land on his cheek. I wanted Jalisa as pissed off as possible.

"Your day is coming, Niquole. Your day is coming," she threatened.

"Whenever you're ready, just let me know," I shot back.

"Germaine, I'll be inside waiting for you when you're done with this trash," Jalisa said, rolling her eyes at me. She walked back into the room.

"Why are you doing this, Nikki?" Germaine questioned.

"Why do you think?"

"You need to leave us alone."

"You don't want that, Germaine. You still love me. It's written all over your face," I said, breathing on his lips. I was caught off guard when Nathan started playing in my hair. "Can I hold our son, Germaine?" I didn't have to wait for an answer. Nathan rolled into my hands on his own.

"Nikki, I never wanted this. You did this with all of your lies and deceit."

"What about yours? Some of this is your fault, too, Germaine," I countered.

"If you're referring to that Kingston shit…"

"I'm beyond that, baby. I'm thinking more about our future."

"I can't do this again with you, Nikki. You need to leave all of us alone. We were doing fine until you showed up." I ignored him and laughed with Nathan. "Do you hear me, Nikki? You gotta leave us alone and if you don't, I'll have you locked up again."

"How do you plan on doing that, Germaine?" I asked still not giving him eye contact.

"I know you're in violation of crossing state lines."

"Did you not hear me the other day when I told you that I was a free woman? Kingston came through for me. You can't get your buddy, Tyrell, to trump up any outlandish charges this time. Oh, that's right! He can't anyway because he's locked up himself for evidence tampering. So, you see dear husband, I'm not going back to jail."

"There's a better way to go about this than what you're doing, Nikki and you know that."

"Germaine, don't play all innocent with me. Let's be honest with each other for a change."

"That'll be a first," he huffed.

"You're here playing house with my sister. You never had any plans of contacting me. Don't stand up there and lie to me."

"Nikki," Germaine paused as if he was choosing his words carefully. "I would've eventually contacted you when the time was right."

"And when would that have been? When I was behind bars?" I asked. "But you know what...I can forgive you for all the shit you've done," I lied.

Germaine was quiet for a few seconds. Maybe he did feel bad for what he did.

"I've gotta go. Give me back Nathan." That was the queue that he was trying to get away from the conversation.

I hugged Nathan extremely tight while staring at Germaine with conniving and seductive eyes. I knew the look was irresistible because he couldn't take his eyes off of me. I whispered in Nathan's ear loud enough for Germaine to hear.

"I'm gonna make your daddy love me again like he used to and when that happens...we'll be a family again."

141

Chapter 18

Later that night, Marko and I were on our way to dinner. I could tell that something was bothering him. When I came back from Johnathan's karate awards ceremony, that's when it began.

"Where'd you go?" he asked when I walked inside the room. He was just coming out of the shower. My mind wasn't focused on his words. Instead, they focused on his thick piece of meat that dangled in front of him. "Nikki?"

"I went for a drive," I lied. "I needed to clear my head."

"Did the drive work?" Marko asked like he didn't believe me.

"No, it didn't. That's why I'm back here." When I walked up to kiss him, he gave me a pathetic peck, then walked around me. "Wanna grab something to eat?" I offered after realizing that he had an attitude.

"Naw, I'm good. I need to run out for a few," Marko said as he dried off then got dressed. "I'll be back later and we can eat then."

I wondered where he had to go especially since I assumed he came to New Orleans to help me out. I didn't question him. I just let him leave.

"Marko, what's up?" I asked after coming back from my trip down memory lane.

"What do you mean what's up?"

"So, all I can get is the silent treatment?"

He took his eyes off the road and looked at me. "What's up with you and A.J.?"

I swallowed…hard. "What do you mean?" I knew the conversation would come up sooner or later. "What did he tell you?"

"All he said was to watch out for you and that you're not what you seem. What did he mean by that?"

"Marko, that's the nature of this business," I tried to laugh it off, but was slightly worried. For now I was glad that A.J. hadn't told him anything worse. "A.J. and I have been going at it for years. That's just us and I'm a little bitter having to sell my label to him. That's all."

"I feel like there's something neither of you are telling me."

"There's nothing, Marko. I promise."

"There was blood on your lip the night of the THRONE party. That's more than nothing. Did he hit you?"

"No, he didn't and I've had enough of that conversation. So, where'd you go earlier today?" I prayed that he would agree to change the subject.

"I had to take care of some shit for A.J."

"Are you fucking serious? Does he know you're here with me?"

"He doesn't know that I'm here with you, but he knows that I'm here."

"Why are you always taking care of something for him? I thought you were just an artist on his label. Are you his errand boy, too?"

"Don't insult me. I know what I'm doing."

I was so happy when my phone rang because I felt an argument coming on. However, I also wasn't too happy about the caller, so I sent her to voicemail. She called back, but I sent her to voicemail again. I saw Marko cutting his eyes at me. I know he was wondering why I wasn't answering my phone. Seconds later, my phone beeped letting me know that I had a message. I called the voicemail.

"Nikki, Germaine called and asked me for your new number. I gave it to him and Cierra is…"

I hung up when my mother mentioned Cierra's name. I also couldn't believe she had the audacity to give Germaine my number without permission. I couldn't wait to curse her ass out. Seconds later, I received a text.

Nikki, this is Germaine. You're right. We need to talk. Meet me at Pat O'Brien's on Bourbon in an hour.

This was my chance to get in Germaine's good graces. Now, all I had to do was get away from Marko. That argument I was trying to avoid was probably about to take place. I braced myself.

"Marko, I need to go back to the hotel to get my rental car."

"Why? What's wrong? Did you leave something?"

"No, something came up that I need to take care of."

"Does it have something to do with that phone call?"

I didn't feel like lying. "Yes."

"If it has anything to do with your kids or their father, I can take you, Nikki."

"Not this time, Marko. I need to do this on my own."

"Why? You asked for my help and I'm offering it to you."

He was visibly upset, but I could care less at the moment. Germaine was top priority at the moment. I needed my plans with him to work. "Look, lil' boy, take me back to the hotel. I don't have time for this shit. I need to go."

I thought I saw steam coming from his ears. "What the fuck did you just call me? After all I've done for you…that's how you see me? I drove all the way here from Houston to support whatever it is that you're trying to do. You do know you're in my fucking car, right? What if I just slammed on brakes right now and made your ass get out?"

"You wouldn't do that, so stop acting like a damn child."

Surprisingly, he wasn't bluffing. I probably should've had on my seatbelt when he slammed on brakes in the middle of the street. I was happy my hands were operational because they stopped my head from hitting the dashboard. Cars swerved around him. Horns blew. Headlights blinked. I freaked out.

"Marko, you're tripping!"

"No, you're tripping. You're hiding something."

"I'm not hiding anything from you! Now, pull off before we get hit!"

He made a dangerous u-turn in the middle of the street and headed back toward the French Quarter. Marko didn't say one word to me until we reached the hotel a few minutes later and he ordered for me to get out. I did so with much haste. But instead of him catering to my attitude, he sped off.

"You deserved that, Niquole," I told myself. I couldn't even be mad at him.

When I was about to get my car, it hit me that Pat Obrien's was actually in walking distance. I decided to walk to clear my head and to figure out what my next move with Germaine was going to be.

✼ ✼ ✼

Germaine showed up thirty minutes late. I was sipping on my second Long Island Iced Tea when he finally arrived. He looked a little nervous as he scoured the room for me. When I stood up and waved at him, he quickly walked over.

"You look nice," he complimented.

"I know," I responded sarcastically. I was irritated with his tardiness. "Where are the boys?"

"They're with Jalisa," he answered while waving for a waitress to come over. "I need two Heinekens and a Hennessy and Coke," he ordered when she arrived. "You want another Long Island?" he asked me. I shook my head no.

I wanted to ask why he'd left my sons with that trick, but decided against it. "I see you're still drinking."

"And smoking, too." He pulled out a pack of Newports. "I think I deserve this after all the shit you've put me through."

"Are you serious right now?"

He gave me a stern look. "Yeah, I am."

After the waitress returned with his drinks, I took a swig from one of the Heinekens, then handed it to him. He stared into my eyes. Before Germaine turned up the bottle, he said, "I wish I didn't love you the way that I do."

"Whoa! Where'd that come from?" I almost fell out my chair.

"Shhhhh. Don't talk. Don't ruin this for me."

"Don't ruin what?" I played dumb.

Without warning, he leaned across the table and kissed me. It felt like he'd been holding that in for a while. I wasn't going to deny him his moment. When I opened my eyes, I caught a glimpse of Jalisa standing a few feet away from us. I figured she must've followed Germaine. Well, she was about to get another eyeful. I stood up and walked to Germaine's side of the table. Still unaware of Jalisa's presence, he stood up. I wrapped my arms around his neck and we kissed again. As he squeezed me tight, I made sure this kiss had way more passion. I expected her to storm out, but she didn't. Instead, she stormed toward us.

"Why? Why Germaine?" she demanded answers. Germaine pulled away from me and gave Jalisa a startled look.

"Did you follow me?" he questioned her.

"Yes, I did! I heard you whispering on the phone with Maxine. I figured Niquole had something to do with your *cigarette run*. Why? Just tell me why?" She started crying.

I could tell that Germaine didn't want to hurt her, but she was naïve to believe that he could turn his feelings off for me so fast. "Jalisa, Niquole is my wife. She's my wife!"

"What about me? What about all the plans we've made? You told me once your divorce was finalized then you and I were getting married," Jalisa informed.

"I've never said that, Jalisa. You made all those plans not

me," Germaine replied. "Hold up…where are the boys?"

"They're with the neighbor," Jalisa responded in between sniffs.

"Bitch, you left my sons with some neighbor?" I snapped. Everyone in the restaurant looked in our direction. We'd caused yet another disturbance.

"Don't say shit to me right now, Niquole," Jalisa fired back.

Germaine tapped my hand. "Don't worry, they stay with the neighbors sometimes. They're perfectly safe there," he assured me before turning back to Jalisa. "Look, thank you for helping me out with the boys, but…"

"What? Helping you out? Was I just a fucking nanny for you? What about all the times we made love?" Jalisa belted.

I couldn't hold it any longer. I burst out laughing. "I'm sure he was thinking about me while y'all were doing it."

"I know what you've been doing behind my back, Niquole," she blasted at me. "I just received a phone call today about two of my modeling jobs that *I* supposedly cancelled. I know it was you. I can't believe you caused me to lose out on over two hundred thousand dollars in modeling contracts and ruining my reputation!"

Germaine slowly backed away from me. "Don't listen to her, Germaine. She's just as manipulative as I am. Look at what she's done," I said.

"Germaine, don't fall for her tricks! You know how she is," Jalisa chimed in.

Germaine stood and stared at us both like we were two looney tunes. I couldn't blame him though. We were like the head cheer leader and head majorette fighting over the quarter back of the football team. He didn't know who to listen to or who to believe, but Jalisa was about to win the battle.

"Germaine, ask her about Cierra."

I wanted to grab Jalisa by her throat and choke her lifeless.

"Cierra? Who is Cierra?" Germaine questioned.

"Tell him, Niquole. Tell him about your secret love child. Better yet, tell him who the father is," Jalisa continued with a victorious look on her face. She stepped up to me and whispered in my ear, "Bitch, I have tricks up my sleeves, too." When I gave her the look of death, she laughed. "In the end, I'll still get the man." She walked up to Germaine. "I'll be home when you're done with this tramp," she said before walking out.

Why the fuck did I confide in her about Cierra? I couldn't believe that she'd used that shit against me. I had to admit, it was a brilliant move on her part though. I actually wondered why she waited so long to use it.

"So, are you gonna tell me about this child that I know nothing about?" Germaine asked. He was ticked off.

"Germaine, it happened a year before I met you."

"What? And you felt the need to keep that shit from me? Is the kid dead or something?"

"No, my sister Adrienne has been raising her and now, she's back home with my mom."

"Are you serious, Nikki? You've kept your daughter a secret from me all these years. If this was something that happened before me, I don't understand why you wouldn't say anything unless it has something to do with the father. Who's the father, Nikki?"

"Look, it doesn't matter, Germaine. Let's just leave it alone and move forward."

"No, I don't think so. Who's the father, Nikki?" he asked sternly.

There was no way of getting out of it. "A.J."

"A.J. who?" His eyes bucked as if he was hoping I wouldn't say who I knew he was more than likely thinking of.

"A.J. Townes."

"The nigga I worked for? The nigga who hired me to help with your album? Please tell me you're fucking joking?" he laughed. I shook my head no. "Does he know about this kid?" I nodded my head yes. "Wow! Unbelievable!"

"Germaine, just hear me out."

"Don't touch me." He swatted my hands away. A few people in the restaurant tried to ignore what was going on, but it was hard for them to do. "I can't believe that I was about to fall for your shit again."

"That was before your time, Germaine."

"You're right. It was, but you kept it a secret. It only makes me wonder what other shit you're hiding." I stood in silence. I was afraid to open my mouth fearing that I could let more cats out of my bag. "Goodbye, Nikki."

I couldn't let him walk out. "Okay, I have another child…so what. That has nothing to do with what you and I are trying to build back up, Germaine. Don't let Jalisa get in your head like that."

"This is not her fault, Nikki! Tell me why you had to keep your child a secret? Tell me that!" I had to be quick on my feet. He was heated and I needed him to calm down.

"A.J. didn't want her. He thinks I gave her up for adoption. I couldn't turn her over to a complete stranger so my sister stepped in." I crossed my fingers hoping that he bought the lie

"That's still was no reason to lie to me about it."

"I know. I know. I'm sorry." He stopped me from trying to grab his hands.

"I've gotta get out of here, Nikki. Here, have a few more drinks on me," Germaine said before tossing down a hundred dollar bill. He grabbed one of the Heinekens from the table, then chugged down its contents. When he was done, he slammed the empty bottle down and walked out.

"Ooooooooooh Jalisa, you're gonna pay for this shit," I seethed.

Chapter 19

As I walked back to the hotel, I grabbed a Hurricane from another bar. I needed something to cool me down. I was trying to figure out ways to pay Jalisa back since there was no way in hell she was going to get away with what she'd done. She hit below the belt with that one. Of all the dirty shit she could've used against me, she used a deal breaker. I was so happy that I never confided in her about Johnathan because that would've probably landed me in my grave.

Suddenly, Marko popped in my head. I knew he was probably still pissed, but he'd have to get over that shit. I sipped the Hurricane like it was Koolaid. It was delicious. I hadn't had one in years so I savored every drop. It brought back memories of my time in New Orleans. Jalisa and I were inseparable when it came to Bourbon Street. Two young, dime pieces were a hot commodity. Although we were teenagers, we could get into any bar we wanted and have any man we wanted. As I reflected on those days, I knew just how to pay Jalisa back. It was time that I let Marko in on some of the action.

I acquired my car from the hotel valet and drove to my old neighborhood to score a sack of weed from Milwaukee. He didn't want to serve me at first because he was still embarrassed about the incident that I'd witnessed between him and the crack-head, but money talked. When I secured my package, I headed back to the hotel hoping the cannabis would be a peace maker between me and Marko. I didn't know what to expect when I walked into the room. Hell, I didn't even know if he'd decided to stay in New Orleans. But if he was still around, I just hoped he'd cooled off by now. I needed him to be for what I was about to get him into.

When I opened the door, I saw him sitting in the chair watching ESPN. I felt a little crappy when I saw the McDonald's bag on the table since we were supposed to have dinner. Hell, at least he got to eat. My stomach was still empty and growling for food.

I walked over to him. "I'm sorry." When Marko picked up the remote and flipped through the channels like I didn't matter, I spoke up a little louder. "Did you hear me?"

"Last I checked, *lil' boys* have fucked up attention spans," Marko said as he continued flipping through the channels.

I knew this was going to be a challenge. I kicked his knees open then dropped to mine before placing the sack of weed on his crotch area. He huffed like that wasn't going to resolve what transpired between us.

"You're a trip. You know that?"

"If that doesn't work, I know what will." I slowly unzipped his pants.

"What are you doing?" He placed his hand on top of mine to stop me. "I don't get you. I offer you my fucking help, you reject it and now, you're doing this."

"That's because I need your help now." I pushed his hand away and continued at my task.

"Oh you do? And what's that?"

"I'll tell you in about five minutes." He gripped the sides of the chair when I latched onto his meaty muscle.

"You know you're wrong for this shit, right?" I plunged even lower when he said that. "Fuck!" Marko lifted his ass when I tugged at his jeans. I wanted all of him in my mouth. I slurped and licked like his dick was a melting ice cream cone.

"Damn!" He started rising out of the chair. I wondered what he was trying to do. This was my show. He wasn't about to take over. I squeezed his thighs and made his ass sit back down. A few minutes later, I finished him off by swallowing his babies. "You know I got to have you after that, right?" he breathed heavily.

"In due time, baby. We need to talk." I stood up.

"Can we talk about it later? You got me feeling right. We can smoke this sack and drink the rest of that tequila and talk afterwards."

Marko stood up and pulled me to him. I smoothly pulled away then walked over to the table and opened the bottle of Jose Cuervo. I retrieved two paper coffee cups and filled halfway with the warm tequila. I handed one of them to Marko.

"What's up, Nikki? You look like you got a lot on your mind," Marko said.

"I need your help now." I wasted no time.

"I'm listening," he said before emptying his cup.

"Things have become a bit more complicated, Marko."

"How so?"

There was no easier way to say what I was about to say. "I need my husband out of the picture. You know like *really* out of the picture."

"Whoa…wait. When you said you needed help with him, I didn't know you were talking about that kind of help."

"Marko, there's a lot of money involved in this for me…I mean us. He stole my money and the only way I see me getting it back is to get rid of him."

"Hold up. Is this about money or your kids? You never said anything about money."

"Both, Marko."

"How much money are we talking about?" he asked, licking his lips.

"A lot. He took over nine hundred thousand of my money." I hoped like hell Germaine hadn't spent the entire nine hundred and fifty thousand. But just as a backup, I still had a million dollar life insurance policy on him that I still paid for.

At that moment, Marko grabbed the bottle of tequila and sat down in the chair. He then pulled a cigarillo from his pocket, cleaned it out and replaced the contents with the marijuana. He lit it up and took a long drag. His actions were confusing.

"Marko, did you hear me?"

"I heard you, baby."

"You can help share the money with me." I walked up to him and pulled out his python again. To my surprise, it was still pretty stiff. "Ours, baby," I reiterated.

"I guess we need a plan then, huh?"

"I've already got one." He stared at me inquisitively. "We've gotta get someone else out of the picture first."

"Who's that?"

"My sister Jalisa."

His eyes got bigger. "What does she have to do with this?"

"She's with him and my sons."

"Don't tell me that this is some type of vengeful shit for your sister taking your husband?" His words angered me and I squeezed his dick to let him know. "What the hell? That shit hurts!" he yelled out in pain, then pushed me away.

"Don't you ever say anything like that to me again!" I reprimanded. "No one takes anything or anyone from me without a fucking fight!" His eyes showed a slight concern.

"My bad, Niquole. Damn!" he said, rubbing his third leg to sooth the pain.

"Are you gonna help me or not? Because if you don't, I'm sure any amount of money will sound good to a broke nigga off the street." He gave his thickness one last rub before putting it back into captivity. He stood up and walked to me.

"I told you I got you. What do you want me to do?"

"I want you to seduce my sister."

Marko stepped back in disbelief. "What?"

"I want you to fuck her so we can get it on tape."

"Hold on. That shit don't sound right."

"It is right, Marko, so don't cop out on me. You said you would help."

"I know what I said, but how is fucking your sister gonna help? You can get any nigga to do that for free."

"But I want you to do it, Marko. I don't trust *any* other nigga." I could tell he was a little apprehensive about the idea, but he'd already climbed on board when he agreed to help me. There was no way he was backing out now. "This is the only way. I'll show the tape to my husband, then he'll kick her ass to the curb."

"And then what? You go back to him and be one big happy family?" He sounded a bit envious.

"No, baby. This is all a part of the plan. With her out of the way, we can get close to him to do what we need to do."

He paused for a moment. "Okay, if I agree to this, how do you plan on doing it?"

"I got that taken care of. When I ran into an old friend in my old neighborhood earlier…"

"An old friend? If he's an old friend, how do you know you can trust him?" Marko questioned.

"I got something on him, so he can definitely be trusted. He agreed to help for a small fee."

"A small fee of how much?"

"A thousand."

"Do you have that kinda dough right now?"

"No, but I was hoping that you did?"

"How you gonna just…"

"Look, you're either in or out! This is time sensitive. I've reserved a room at another hotel and…"

"And nothing! If my money is involved in this then I need to know everything. Besides the thousand dollars, what else and how much more?"

"All together…about three…maybe four grand. With the room, the make-up artist…"

"Rewind. What make-up artist? You're inviting too many people into this shit, Nikki."

"They're needed, Marko. My sister is a model. We're gonna have to pay her to come here, and we'll need supplies. This shit has to be done right."

Marko paced the room for a few seconds while drinking from the tequila bottle. He looked slightly worried.

"Again, what's the plan?"

"I'm gonna call her modeling agency tomorrow to set up a fake photo shoot and that's when it'll go down. She's so desperate for work right now that she'll take the job real quick. You'll be the photographer. I already have the ecstasy for her. Now, all we have to do is go get a nice camera and some other shit to make it look legit when she walks in."

Marko drank from the bottle again. I needed him to confirm that he was on board.

"You owe me big time for this," he finally said.

"How about I start paying off my debt now?" I pushed him on the bed.

Chapter 20

It didn't take much to get Jalisa to the hotel for the fake modeling shoot. After what she said I'd done to her reputation, she was probably willing to do any gig at the moment. Her agency was very ecstatic when I called pretending to be one of A.J.'s assistants from THRONE. My story was that we needed a model for A.J.'s new clothing line. I knew a lot about A.J.'s business ventures and having Marko there to back me up helped as well. I didn't think Jalisa would agree to it since she was near super model status, and the fact that it was such short notice, but she did. Exactly twenty-four hours after the call, Jalisa was in the hotel. Bright eyed and bushy tailed. Her stupid ass thought she was so big time that she didn't even bother to bring anyone from her camp. She came alone, which made things even better.

"Wow! This set up is nice," Jalisa beamed from ear to ear when she walked inside. I had to fight back my laughter and anger as I stood in the closet with the camera.

"Hi, Miss Jalisa, I'm Devvon Peterson," Marko lied as he extended his hand to her.

"Hi, Devvon, nice to meet you. You look kind of young to be a photographer."

"I'll take that as a compliment," he smiled at her. "We're gonna have you set up here," he said, leading her to the make-up table.

I still couldn't figure out how Milwaukee got that crack-head so cleaned up. She looked real professional sitting there waiting to make Jalisa look like a clown.

"Umm…G…Gina here will take good care of you, Jal-isa. Then you'll do wardrobe."

I almost lost it as he nearly botched the lady's name. *Get it together, Marko.*

"Here's a bottle of water for you," Marko offered while opening it. Little did Jalisa know, it was already open and filled with two ecstasy pills.

"Thanks. I appreciate it," Jalisa said. "Now, this is for a clothing line, right called THRONE."

"Yeah," Marko answered.

"Never heard of it, but I can't wait to see the clothes."

And I can't wait until you're exposed, I thought.

"Oh, I hope my hair is okay?" Jalisa asked tugging on the wig. "I just got it done, so that should actually save the client some money by not having to redo it for the shoot."

I guess that bitch was embarrassed. Good. I didn't feel sorry for her ass.

"Sure, that's cool," Marko returned.

As Jalisa took the bottle and sipped it a few times, Marko walked back over to the cameras and pretended that he knew what he was doing. Milwaukee was there pretending to be Marko's assistant. He wanted in on the action when I asked for his help. Marko damn near went ballistic when he found out how much the Nikon cameras were going to cost along with the back drop and a few lights.

"Are we ready?" Marko asked Jalisa when her make-up was done thirty minutes later. Luckily, Jalisa hadn't looked in the mirror because the shit looked terrible.

"W…W…What am I wearing?" Jalisa slurred when she stood up. The drugs had taken affect already.

"Your clothes are here on the bed. You can take them in the bathroom and change," Marko informed.

As Jalisa staggered to the bed, Marko caught her when she almost fell. "I think I…I…I'd look betterrrrrrrr in yours," she said, while tugging on Marko's shirt.

"Come on now, Miss Jalisa, we've got work to do," Marko responded as he sat her on the bed. For some reason it looked like his ass was starting to be sympathetic towards that bitch.

You better not back out on me, Marko, I thought.

I watched him swallow the lump in his throat then he turned to the closet as if he wanted me to jump out and tell him not to do it. But that wasn't happening. If push came to shove, I'd get Milwaukee to do it. All I needed was the bitch on tape.

"Marko, get it going before that bitch passes out," I said lightly.

Taking a deep breath, Marko finally stepped up to Jalisa and removed his shirt. He then leaned down and kissed her. Of course she didn't resist. She placed her hand on his cheeks and pulled him onto bed with her.

Whore, I thought. I got my camera in position and started taking several pictures. As Marko unbuttoned her shirt and pummeled her breast, I switched the camera to video mode.

I could tell that ecstasy was working because her ass was all into it. She grabbed Marko's hand and placed it between her legs. Watching Marko, kiss and finger her like he liked it ticked me off a little bit, but it made me horny at the same time. Even Milwaukee looked turned on when I glanced at him over in the corner. The only person not paying attention was the crackhead who was giving herself a fix.

"Oh Devvon!" I heard Jalisa call out.

I turned back to find Marko driving his dick inside of her. He seemed to be enjoying himself. I kept telling myself that he wasn't liking it and was just playing the part, but he was doing the shit a little too well. I crossed the thoughts out and turned back to Milwaukee, who now had his hands inside his pants. He had the right idea of self pleasure. Watching Marko and Jalisa also made me wet, which I needed to take care of.

While trying to keep the camera steady, I slowly lowered my pants, then began to finger myself to the brink of eruption. Within moments of my orgasm, Marko came as well. He climbed off Jalisa who was now passed out, and hurried to the restroom. It looked as though he wanted to vomit. I paused the camera and stepped out of the closet. I was about to check on him, but another idea popped in my head. Jalisa hadn't paid enough yet.

"That shit was hot, wasn't it Colie?" Milwaukee cheered when I walked over to him.

"I want you to fuck her."

"What?" he gulped.

"I didn't stutter."

"I...I can't do that, Colie."

"Why cause you're gay," I taunted.

"I ain't gay!" he said defensively.

"Then fuck her or give me my money back."

I knew he wasn't coming up off that money. After looking at me like he wanted to swing, Milwaukee climbed into bed with Jalisa and did as he was paid to do. I took a few more pictures, then turned the camera back on.

This is what you get for fucking my man.

❖ ❖ ❖

Later that night, Marko and I hit Bourbon Street to celebrate. He wasn't up for it, but I coerced him into doing so. He was getting on my nerves with that having a weak side shit. If he was gonna roll with me, he needed to get rid of his conscience.

As we walked down Bourbon Street with our Hurricanes, a few people recognized me and requested an autograph. It felt good to still be noticed in a positive way again. As we were about to enter a third bar, someone called out my name. Marko turned around, but I didn't. The recognition was sort of getting on my nerves since I was tipsy by that point.

"Colie Cole!" I halted when I heard *that* name.

I immediately dropped the Hurricane I was sipping on. Trembling, I turned around to the voice because only my father added that extra *Cole* to my nickname. It was him. I started breathing fast and heavy. I felt like I was having a panic attack. I slowly calmed down as I watched my father walk toward me. He was just like I'd remembered…suave. For a fifty-six year-old man, he was dashing with his salt and pepper hair and physique that thirty-year-old men would envy.

"Colie Cole, is that really you?" my father asked when he stopped in front of me.

A huge smile was on his face. He then flashed the two gold teeth that I remembered so well as I child. I couldn't believe he still had those things. A woman about my age was hanging on his arm. I could tell that she was trying to figure out who I was because I was sizing her up as well. When my father whispered something in her ear, the girl rolled her eyes at me then walked off.

"My Colie Cole!" my father cheered as he opened his arms to me. I fell into them with tears pouring from my eyes. I cried so hard it felt like I was about to pass out. "Calm down, baby," he tried to comfort me, but his words fell on deaf ears.

I held him tight and continued crying. Between my make-up, tears and snot, I knew his shirt would be fucked up, but I didn't care. I wanted him to know just how much I'd missed him. When I finally came up for air, he twirled me around like he used to do when I was a little girl.

"My Colie Cole, you're still beautiful as ever."

"Thanks, dad," I said smiling through the tears.

"How's Maxine doing? Where is she now-a-days?"

"Mom and I live in Houston."

"Oh yeah…that's right. I'm gonna have to pay y'all a visit sometimes."

My heart warmed at his offer. Marko cleared his throat to let me know that he was still there and wanted to be recognized. At the moment, he was irrelevant, but I gave him the satisfaction and introduced him anyway. I chatted with my father as we walked up Bourbon Street hand in hand for nearly twenty minutes until his young girlfriend interrupted us.

"Bishop, we've gotta go. We've got that thing to do," she said to him.

"Don't you see us talking, girl?" I snapped as I cut my eyes at her.

"My Colie Cole, I see you still got that fire in you," my father said as if he was proud of me. "Hey listen, I really do have to go. There's a party going on at my house that I need to get back to. I had to step out for a minute to take care of a small situation."

I wondered what that situation was.

"Actually, why don't you and your friend come to the party, Colie. We've got a lot of catching up to do."

I agreed. "Yeah, okay. That sounds like fun."

"So, are we driving my car, Nikki?" Marko asked.

"I don't think that's a good idea, Marko. I want to spend this time with my father by myself."

By his facial expression, I could tell once again that I'd stomped on Marko's heart.

"It's okay, Colie Cole. Let him come. The more the merrier." I wished my father had kept his words to himself. I didn't want Marko to go. I wanted to spend that time with him alone.

I nodded my head. "Yeah, sure."

After giving us his address, my father gave me another kiss before we parted ways.

Thirty minutes later, Marko and I pulled up to my dad's huge mansion. Cars were lined up and down the street, and the music was extremely loud. I couldn't believe this is how he lived. My first impression of his life was obviously wrong.

"There's no way my father is on drugs if this is really his house," I mumbled to myself.

I anxiously jumped out of Marko's car as soon as he parked. Not bothering to wait for his ass, I began climbing the brick steps leading up to the front door. Marko caught up with me before I walked inside and grabbed my hand. He eased his fingers between mine. I assumed he wanted the people to know that we were together. Marko had a lot to learn about me. I called all the shots…not him.

I didn't bother to knock on the door. The music was so loud, my knock or ring wouldn't have been heard anyway. When I opened the door, the visual took me back to the parties he and my mother used to host when I was younger. The old school music and the marijuana engulfed the room. All of a sudden, the volume on the music lowered.

"Everybody listen up!" It was my father. He had a champagne flute in one hand and a cigar in the other. "My baby girl is back!" he announced proudly as he pointed in my direction. Everyone turned to me. I recognized a few of the faces that automatically smiled at me. "My Colie Cole is back!" My father was still over the top.

After turning the music back up, I received tons of embraces and smiles. Somehow in the ruckus, my hand was no longer in Marko's. When I turned around to see where he was, I spotted him walking to the bar. That figured. He was probably still having issues about what he'd done earlier. *Weak ass*.

"Colie Cole, come on in and join the party, baby. Let me show you off," my father said.

After about an hour of reconnecting with my dad's friends and him bragging about me and my accomplishments, Marko finally found me. I was having such a good time that I forgot that he was even there.

"Nikki, are you ready to roll out?" he asked, grabbing my hips.

"No, Marko, I haven't seen my dad in years. I'm not ready to go."

"Well, I am. These old cats are getting on my nerves."

I didn't appreciate his attitude. "Then leave," I suggested harshly.

He stared at me in disbelief. "So, you're gonna choose them over me?" he asked jealously.

"Why in the world would you ask me some shit like that, Marko? You know right now you're showing your fucking immature age. Just go back to the hotel and wait for me, I need some more time with my father."

He didn't look too pleased with my suggestion, but I didn't give a damn. I didn't want him there from the start anyway. After giving him a quick peck on the lips, he left with a few beers in hand while I continued having fun with my father and his friends. Two hours in, I checked my cell phone. Marko had called me over ten times and left a dozen text messages, but instead of calling back, I turned the phone off. If he wanted to talk to me, he should've stayed.

As time passed, I was getting a little restless. The alcohol that I'd consumed didn't help. I tried to hide my yawns. I didn't want the older crowd to think that I couldn't hang, but I was tired from everything that had taken place over the past few days. I found my father at a card table playing Spades and told him that I needed to leave.

"Nonsense, Colie Cole," he said, slamming his joker down on the table. "If you're tired, baby, go grab a room upstairs. Didn't your man leave anyway?"

"He's not my man, but yes, he left."

"Take your pick of any room up there, Colie. Just like old times, you get to have whatever you want," he said after standing up and kissing me on the forehead.

I was happy to be with him again, and he was right. My father always gave me whatever I wanted. Taking his suggestion, I found a room upstairs then passed out on the bed.

I woke up a few hours later to use the bathroom. As I walked down the hall, I heard my father and a few other men laughing and talking. It had to be at least five or six in the morning. I couldn't believe they were still up. I walked to the room and peeped through the door. My father was sitting at a table with four other men and they were counting stacks of money, drinking, smoking weed and snorting cocaine. I was definitely in awe, but my suspicions of him not being a fucking crackhead were correct. He was obviously a drug dealer and that's when it hit me. That was how we lived so lavishly when I was younger. I was so caught up in my thoughts that I didn't see my father staring back at me. He smiled then winked, but I didn't smile back.

I jumped when I felt a hand on my ass then a man whispered in my ear, "You wanna party, sweet thing?"

"Hell no!" I screamed after shoving him off of me. I jumped again when the men who were at the table came rushing out the room. My dad soon followed.

"You alright, Colie?" my father asked.

"I...I'm fine," I answered a little shaken up.

"Did he touch you?"

"Yes, he touched my ass!"

My father walked up to the man while his friends had him hemmed up against the wall. "You do know this is my fucking daughter, right?" he said with gritted teeth.

"I didn't know, Bishop. I swear," the man pleaded.

It was dejavu all over again when Kingston killed Hummer for me. Well, at least that's what I thought. I wasn't ready to witness anything like that again.

"It's alright, daddy," I assured while rubbing his shoulder.

"You sure, Colie Cole?"

I quickly nodded my head 'yes'. I didn't need to witness anymore murders.

"Get this asshole out of my house," my father ordered to his friends. As they took the man and pushed him down the stairs, my father turned back to me as if nothing ever happened. "You need to go back to bed, Colie and sleep that alcohol off." Forgetting that I had to piss, I turned to go back to my bedroom. "My Colie Cole is back looking like yo mama," he said right before tapping me on my ass.

I blushed then went back to my room.

Chapter 21

After having lunch with my father, I halfheartedly went back to my hotel. I wasn't ready to go, but he had errands to run. He offered to let me stay at the house until he got back, but I had things to do as well. I was a little bothered when I walked into the room and didn't find Marko there. I imagined he was pissed off that I didn't answer or return his calls. He was probably even more pissed that I didn't return to the hotel the night before, but I couldn't babysit his feelings right now. Not only was I ecstatic about running into my father after all these years, but I also had a mission to complete. I showered and changed then headed to the nearest Walgreens with the SD card to develop the pictures of Jalisa fucking Marko. I would save the video if I needed to pull out the big guns.

I was so happy that there was a print your own station when I arrived at the drugstore because I really didn't feel like bribing the developer. I'd tried to develop nude and sexual pictures many times in the past, and always got a hard time. It wasn't like I was trying to develop pictures of child porno or some sick demented shit like that.

I printed about twenty-five pictures, then headed straight to Germaine's house with the evidence. This time when I got there, I didn't bother to park on the side of the road. Instead, I pulled right into the driveway right behind the Jaguar that I'd be driving soon. I grabbed the stack of photos from the passenger seat, then headed for the front door. After a few neighborly knocks, Jalisa answered the door with a baffled look on her face. The short Nikki Minaj bob wig she wore today was horrible. She looked horrible as well. It looked like she hadn't even taken a bath yet.

"You've got a lot of fucking nerves coming here!" she spat.

"Yeah, yeah, yeah! Whatever! Bitch, where's my husband?" I pushed her arm out of the way and stomped inside. "Germaine! Germaine!" I called out to him. He hurried from the back of the house moments later.

"Nikki, what the hell are you doing here?" he questioned with a confused look.

"Where are the boys?" I asked.

"They're at the babysitters. Why are you here?"

"We need to talk, Germaine."

"About what? More of your lies?" he responded. "Does A.J. know you're here?"

I decided to ignore his smart ass comment. "No, we need to discuss what Jalisa has been up to."

"What I've been up to?" Jalisa questioned.

"Yeah, what you've been up to, bitch," I smirked deceitfully, then handed Germaine the photos.

"What the fuck? How did you get these?" he asked studying each photo.

"They showed up at my hotel room door this morning," I replied. "I guess someone wanted me to know what your girl has been up to."

"When were these taken?" Germaine flipped the photos over to reveal the date. "Yesterday?"

Jalisa wanted to know what was going on so she snatched the photos from Germaine. "Oh my, God!" She covered her mouth with one hand.

"Yeah, bitch, that's you! Is this the kind of woman you want to be with, Germaine? Is this the kind of woman you want around our sons? She was with two men! Look at how she's enjoying them!" I poured more salt to the wound.

Jalisa looked at Germaine with tears in his eyes. "Germaine, I don't know anything about this! I swear!"

"Do you expect me to believe that when you staggered in here around three this morning?" Germaine questioned. "You told me you were going on a photo shoot. I thought you got paid to take pictures, not fuck niggas."

"Germaine, you've gotta believe me! You…" Jalisa tried to plead.

Germaine snatched the pictures back. "Look at these, Jalisa! You're all into this shit!"

Jalisa glanced at the smirk on my face. I could tell she knew I was behind it all. "She set me up, Germaine!"

"What?" I asked appalled. "I was with my father all day yesterday."

"Your father?" Germaine questioned curiously. Even Jalisa held a puzzled look.

"Yes, my father! I ran into him on Bourbon Street recently. I was with him all day yesterday, so he can vouch for my whereabouts."

It looked like Jalisa wanted to ask more questions about my dad, but remained focused. "She's lying, Germaine! Look at her! You can't believe anything she says. This is the same woman who kept a secret child away from you."

"Cierra was conceived before him so, don't use that as part of your defense," I blasted.

Suddenly, Jalisa ran over to me and threw a jab that landed right against my nose. Before I could retaliate, Germaine jumped between us. "Stop this shit!" he scolded. He turned to Jalisa. "I want you out of here." Her eyes widened in disbelief. "Yes, I want you out!"

When Germaine raced upstairs, Jalisa was right behind him. I could hear her begging him to stop. Wondering what he was doing, I soon got my answer when he came back downstairs with an arm full of clothes. I thought I'd destroyed all that bitches stuff, but it looked like the clothes were new. I saw tons of new price tags.

Jalisa was stunned as Germaine opened the front door and threw everything out. He ran back upstairs. Jalisa followed. Seconds later, the same thing happened. This time her shoes and some of her purses were included.

"Germaine, why are you doing this?" Jalisa cried.

"Because I want my life back."

Jalisa looked at me. "You don't even love him!"

"So," I replied defiantly. "One thing has nothing to do with the other. Now, you need to get your ass out of *my* house before I send the tape to your modeling agency." Again, her eyes widened in disbelief. "Oh, yeah, bitch. There was a tape outside my door, too"

Germaine walked over to the coffee table and handed Jalisa a key. "Get your Maxima off my street," he demanded. "The Jag and the Mercedes are both in my name, so those stay here."

"Germaine, please don't do this to me. I love you. I've always loved you," she dropped to her knees and begged. "Please! I think I was drugged."

Kicking her from his leg, Germaine stood by the door for her to leave. Her face was full of hurt, embarrassment and defeat while mine was framed with triumph. After looking at Germaine one last time, she finally ran out the door.

When he closed the door behind her, I immediately walked toward him and turned on the charm. "I'm so sorry about that."

"No, you're not, Nikki," he said after slowly removing my hands from his face. "I'm sure you had something to do with this."

I shook my head back and forth. "I promise you...not this time. Do you know how many people know you're married to me in New Orleans? Someone must've seen you two to-gether, then seen Jalisa up to no good. I don't know. However it happened, I wasn't involved."

Germaine didn't seem too convinced. "I need you to leave, too."

"What? You're kicking *me* out?"

"I'm not kicking you out, Nikki. I just need some time to think."

"What about the boys? Can I see them later?"

I could tell that he was battling with his answer. "Yes, you can see the boys later."

"How about if we go out for dinner like we used to?"

"Like when you could never find the time to do so?" he reminded.

"I deserved that, but things are different now, Germaine." This time, he allowed me to touch his face. "So, is it a yes?" I pecked his lips.

"Yeah, come back around six."

"Can I drive the Jaguar?"

"You're pushing it, Nikki."

"No further than I would usually do. Now, where are the keys?"

After moving my rental car out of the way, I stepped into the Jaguar, and decorated the driveway with Jalisa's choice of music. I flung all of the CDs out the window and adjusted the seat and mirrors to my comfort. Asking for the Jaguar had been a long shot, but I had to do it. I needed to see how much Germaine was still into me. When he handed me the keys, I knew that he was all in. The way he treated Jalisa was priceless. In my eyes, she had to know that he was *always* going to choose me over her. She knew how Germaine felt about me. He couldn't stop loving me in six short months.

I drove around the city for at least an hour basking in my newest victory. I smiled every time Jalisa's pitiful face popped into my head. She deserved what I did to her. Actually she deserved more. If I got the opportunity to fuck with her again, I would. To play mommy to my sons was a no-no, and hopefully this shit would teach her ass a lesson.

Maybe I will send the video to her agency, I thought

171

pulling up to my hotel.

I hoped that Marko wouldn't be in the room when I valet parked the car. As long as I'd been gone, I knew I'd be walking into an argument. It was probably best if he went back to Houston at this point anyway. His services weren't needed anymore. At least not now.

"Why'd you turn your phone off last night, Nikki, and where the hell have you been?" Marko asked as soon as I walked through the door. I hated that I allowed him to call me by my nick name. Now, I really wished his ass had gone back to Houston.

"Marko, I can't do this with you right now." I hurried over to my suitcase. "I've got to change to get ready to see my boys."

"And how do you plan on doing that?"

"My husband agreed to it when I went by his house to show him the pictures."

"So, you went without me?" he questioned.

"Marko, I didn't need you there for that. You served your purpose."

"Oh, I served my purpose?"

"Don't make this out to be anymore than it is, Marko," I replied.

"Were you with your husband last night? Is that why you turned off your fucking phone? Or did you sleep with one of the old niggas at the party?"

I swung around from my suitcase so that he could see the anger and insult on my face. "Are you fucking serious right now? How dare you say some shit like that? I got drunk, and my father wouldn't let me leave, so I stayed at his house. That's all you need to know."

"I'm going with you."

"No, you're not. I've got to do this on my own. My husband and I are taking the kids out to dinner."

"Out to dinner? I don't understand, Nikki. I thought the plan was to get rid of your husband not to be spending time with him."

"That's part of my plan, baby. I need to get him comfortable enough to tell me where my money is. That's all I'm doing. Don't you get it?"

"I don't like this. I feel like you're trying to get back with him."

"Believe me, I'm not."

Marko let out a huge sigh. "I know you think I'm acting a little crazy, but I'm doing all this because I like you...a lot." He walked up behind me, pushed my hair to the side and kissed my neck. His hand reached inside my pants.

"Marko, what are you doing?" I asked. I wasn't in the mood to fool around nor did I have the time. "I've got to change and need to run by the store to get my boys a few gifts."

"You'll have time for all of that. Right now, you've got to make time for me."

"Marko..."

"Shhhhhh. I'm showing you how much I like you. I'm showing you how much I want to be with you." His hands entered my panties then fingers inside my hot box. My eyes slowly began rolling into the back of my head. "That's right, baby. Show me who this pussy belongs to and make sure you remember that when you're with your husband."

He pulled my head back and kissed me. Our tongues danced and I rode his fingers even harder. I didn't have time for it, but I wanted more. Marko must've felt my need because within seconds he'd pushed my pants down, then bent me over the table.

"Ooooooh, Marko!" I called out when he pierced me.

"Are you going back to your husband, Nikki?" he asked while pounding me. "Are you gonna leave me?" He grabbed my hair and yanked my head back for an answer.

"No. I'm not going back to him. I'm not leaving you."

If Marko was trying to make sure that I stayed around, he was on the right track. I was on all fours and completely caught off guard when he suddenly pulled out of me, then stuck his tongue in my ass and his fingers back inside my honeycomb. "Oh shit, Marko!" The orgasm had come out of nowhere.

Marko stood over me stroking his dick. "You gonna help me out?" he asked.

I crawled over to him and finished him off. Minutes later, we both passed out from exhaustion on the floor. I woke up about an hour later and showered. When I came out of the bathroom to get dressed, Marko was lying in bed.

"You're so damn sexy," he said, watching me get dressed.

"I know," I giggled.

"How long do you think you'll be gone?"

"A few hours. Why?"

"Because I want you back in this bed with me tonight."

"I'll be here. I promise."

I grabbed my purse to walk out the door, but his words stopped me. "I think I love you, Nikki." I didn't need to hear that. "You don't have to say it back to me. I just wanted to tell you how I feel. Be careful and don't do anything stupid."

I knew what that meant, 'don't fuck my husband,' but if I had to do it to get what I wanted, I wouldn't hesitate.

"I'll be back soon, baby and I promise nothing is going to happen between me and Germaine."

Chapter 22

I pulled into Germaine's driveway, stepped out of the Jaguar and skipped toward the door. I got a little ahead of myself and turned the knob like it would be unlocked for me, but it wasn't. Germaine must've heard me because he opened the door a few seconds later. His eyes told me that I was stunning.

"Hey," I spoke first.

He had to gather his words. I made sure my body hugging Alexander Mcqueen dress would make him speechless.

"You look nice," he finally spoke. "Come on in. I'm still getting the boys ready. Jalisa used to…"

"No more Jalisa talk," I cut him off. "I'm here now. What do you need help with?"

After following Germaine upstairs, showering both my sons with tons of kisses, and getting them dressed, we finally headed out. We spent nearly two hours at a Mexican restaurant catching up. Germaine and I were talking so much that we didn't notice the boys going to sleep. We eventually carried them to the car, then went back to the house.

"Nathan is getting so heavy," I addressed Germaine as we walked up the stairs.

"I know. John John is, too. They're growing boys."

I watched Germaine disappear into Johnathan's room as I walked into Nathan's. I eased his shoes off his feet, then tucked him in. I kissed him on the cheek then walked toward Johnathan's room just as Germaine walked out. "Is John John still knocked out?"

"Yeah, are you about to leave?" he asked. I could tell in his voice that he didn't want me to.

"That's up to you. Do you want me to leave?" I shot back.

"No. Have a drink with me?"

"Sure. Do you have any champagne?"

He shook his head. "Actually I do."

"Then it's a date," I said followed by a devious smile. Men were so weak around me. Following him downstairs, I sat on the sofa as Germaine went into the kitchen. "Don't put any poison in there," I joked.

"I don't think that would kill you anyway," he laughed from the kitchen. A few moments later, he reentered the living room with a glass of champagne for me and a Heineken for him. "I remembered how much you loved Moscato," he said after handing me the glass.

"Well, I've been discriminating with my alcohol lately," I giggled.

"Now, that's a shocker."

"So, what else have you been up to?" I asked.

"Well, I've got a lot going on."

"Like what?"

"I'm trying to break back into the music business."

I tensed. "Oh really?"

"Yeah. I bought a small studio and I'm in the process of getting it furnished and getting some new equipment."

His words infuriated me, but I didn't let it show. *How in the hell can he sit up here and tell me how he's been spending my fucking money. He has a lot of nerve, like he worked hard for that shit.*

Suddenly, his phone rang.

"I'll be right back, Nikki."

Germaine set his beer down and retreated to the kitchen.

Now, I was mad as hell at him. Studios weren't cheap and the equipment for it wasn't either. I wanted to know more than ever how much money he had left. My eyes locked on his beer. I needed him to talk. I needed him to go deeper into what he'd done with my money and how much, if any, was left. I rummaged through my purse for the last ecstasy pill I'd planned on giving Jalisa in case the two we dropped in her water didn't work. After finding it, I dropped the pill in Germaine's beer. A minute later, he returned.

"Sorry about that," he apologized.

"It's okay. Did it have anything to do with your studio?" I pried.

He chugged his beer. "Somewhat. It was this producer that's thinking about going in with me on a second studio."

A second studio? It was hard for me to keep calm. As Germaine finished off the first beer, he went to the kitchen for another one.

"So, are you gonna be producing tracks like you did on my album?"

"Naw, I'm not interested in just being a producer this time. I'm trying to get a label started. I already have a name for it; Maine Street."

My blood boiled, but I wanted him to keep talking. "Maine Street, huh? Sounds cool," I lied. "Do you have your eye on any artists?"

"I got this one cat who seems a little hungry for it." He wiped his forehead. I knew the ecstasy was starting to work. The alcohol sped up the process.

I damn near regurgitated. "That sounds great, Germaine."

"I heard about your issues and how you had to sell Kingquole Records. You know we can always do something together," he suggested while rubbing my knee.

Was he serious? I had to drink the champagne to keep from laughing. "Thanks for the offer, but I'll pass."

"Why? I think we would work well together, Nikki. A husband and wife team." His hand inched closer to my thigh. I didn't stop him. I wore a dress just in case something like that would go down.

"I…I think I need to go, Germaine." I adjusted my purse on my shoulder and placed the glass on the table.

"Don't leave, Nikki."

"I think I need to," I poured it on even thicker.

"No, you don't. Everything that happened this past six months should've never gone down and I'm sorry for my part in any of it. I'm sorry for hitting you. You know I would never hit you, Nikki. I'm crazy about you. Always have been and I'm sure it will stay that way until the day I die."

Wow! He needed to be writing scripts for soap operas. "Germaine, there are a lot of things we haven't talked about."

"I know. I know. And we have all the time in the world to do that, Nikki, but right now, I'm about to do something crazy." I gave him a curious look as he dropped down on one knee.

OMG, I thought.

"When you left earlier, I thought about us and all that you did trying to get Jalisa away from me. I knew from that moment that you still love me, Nikki."

"Germaine, what in the hell are you doing?" I asked as he dug inside his pocket.

"Niquole Wright, let's start over. Will you marry me…again?"

The ring he presented nearly blinded me. I quickly sized it up. It was at least a four carat emerald cut with two side stones. Even more beautiful than my first ring.

"I know this is coming out of the blue, but it hurt like hell when I tried to make myself stop loving you."

"Germaine, this…this is too much." That wasn't a lie. It was too much especially since I knew he'd used my money to buy the damn ring. His actions came out of left field. He threw me off my game for a minute.

"I know it's a shocker, Nikki. You don't have to answer right now. We're still married. I just want to renew our vows. Just think about it."

"I will."

"In the meantime…"

Germaine removed my purse from my shoulder and tossed it on the floor. He then parted my legs. He didn't have to remove my panties because I didn't have any on. A trick I'd done when Marko wasn't watching.

"You just don't know how much I've missed this," Germaine moaned.

He pulled me to the edge of the sofa and dove in for his dessert. I knew I shouldn't have been taking it this far, but it was necessary to get what I wanted. The more he lapped, sucked, nibbled and tongued, the more I forgot about my original plan. When it came to oral, Germaine was the only man to make me cum simultaneously from a vaginal and clitoral orgasm. I wasn't going to deny myself that treat. I was on the brink of a tidal wave when the doorbell rang. Germaine lifted his head.

"Germaine, don't you fucking stop! Whoever the fuck that is can wait," I fussed, then pushed his head back down.

Following my demands, he went back to it, but the asshole at the door was relentless and kept ringing the bell. I clasped my hand on top of Germaine's head. I wasn't letting him up. Even if that was Jesus at the door giving us a free pass to the pearly gates, he was gonna have to wait. The ringing at the door continued.

"Shit!" Germaine said angrily after he hopped up.

"Why the fuck did you stop? They can wait."

"I gotta get the door, Nikki before they wake up the kids," he said, walking to the door. I hoped he cussed that bastard out for stopping this train from pulling into the station. "Jalisa?" I heard him gasp. I didn't bother to fix my clothes. I wanted that bitch to see my feet propped up on the table and my pussy hanging out. "Jalisa, no, you can't come in."

But she must've forced her way through. When she saw my legs spread wide open, she stopped. I could tell the bitch was drunk, and it looked like she'd been crying nonstop for hours. She turned to Germaine who was wiping my cream from his lips.

"So, you're in here eating this bitch's pussy, but you've never eaten mine?" she addressed him angrily.

"I told you. You're not me, so stop trying to be. You can't get the treatment I get, sweetie," I reminded her. I stood up and adjusted my dress not before giving her an eyeful of my plump ass.

Jalisa's eyes watered again. "This is fucked up, Germaine! I haven't been gone a whole damn day."

"You need to lower your voice before you wake my damn kids," I warned her.

"Bitch, I know you were behind those damn pictures. Did you think that I wouldn't check into that modeling job?"

I became a little nervous, but didn't let it show.

"What is she talking about, Nikki?" Germaine asked.

His ecstasy didn't seem to affect him the way Jalisa's did. *Shit, I probably needed more than one.*

"What is she talking about, Nikki?" Germaine repeated.

I didn't answer. Jalisa staggered closer to me. She was about to continue before something else caught her attention. I looked down to see what had her ass stuck. It was the ring. She picked it up from the table and huffed. "What's this, Germaine?" He didn't answer. "Did you ask this whore to marry you again? So, what was I to you?" she choked back tears.

"Jalisa, you're drunk. You need to sleep this off and we'll talk about it tomorrow," Germaine suggested.

"Where am I gonna go, Germaine? You kicked me out of our home...for this bitch! I never stood a chance with you. You just dragged me along until your *Nikki* came back, but your *Nikki* is never gonna change.

At that point, Jalisa picked up the ring and threw it across the room. The bitch better be glad I really didn't want that shit.

"Jalisa, you need to leave!" I was tired of her ass.

"You would want that wouldn't you, but I'm not done. I called THRONE about that modeling job. They never set anything up for me. In fact, they're shutting down their clothing line."

"What are you telling me this for?" I asked feeling a lot more nervous now.

"I spoke directly with A.J."

I needed to get the hell out of that house and quick. I grabbed my keys from the table. "Germaine, I'm leaving. As long as this trick keeps coming around, we're never gonna get anything accomplished."

"Don't go, Nikki. Stay. This is about to get interesting," Jalisa spat.

"Like I told you before, you need to lower your voice before you wake my kids," I warned again.

Jalisa laughed. "It's funny you should bring up the kids, dear sister. A.J. and I had a loooooong talk."

"I don't have to stay here for this shit."

Germaine blocked my way when I tried to leave. "Let's hear her out," he suggested eerily.

"Why? She's drunk! Whatever she's about to say is gonna be a lie anyway!" I belted.

"I don't think you should mention the word lie, bitch." Jalisa spat fire. "Niquole does Germaine know that one of his kids is not his?"

"You bitch!" I immediately charged her drunk ass and grabbed her neck. I squeezed as hard and tight as I could. "Stop fucking lying on me!" I thought that bitch was about to pass out before Germaine pulled me from her.

"Jalisa, get the hell out of here!" Germaine demanded.

"If you don't believe me, Germaine, ask A.J. for yourself!" Jalisa yelled.

I pulled away from Germaine. That bitch was not getting away that easily. When I reached her, I gave her a heavy-weight haymaker styled punch, which landed on her face. We both fell to the floor. She kept her hands over her face to protect it, but did manage to slap me a couple of times which only intensified my anger. My fingernails became knives as I clawed at her face.

Besides her hair, her face was precious to her as well. It was fucked up now. I wanted to make sure her modeling career was over.

"Damn it, Nikki!" Germaine yelled after scooping me from the floor.

"Oh my, God! You're crazy!" Jalisa screamed in terror as the blood dripped down her face.

I was a mad woman that was out for blood. I jumped out of Germaine's arms and socked that bitch in the face again. When she tripped over the area rug, I sat on her chest to finish what I'd started.

"Germaine, get this crazy bitch off of me!" she screamed for help.

When he snatched me up again, I had one more opportunity to let her know that I meant business. I kicked her in the mouth. Blood gushed. At that point, Jalisa scrambled to her feet then ran out of the house. I snatched up my purse from the floor and tried to hightail out myself, but Germaine grabbed my arm.

"What in the hell is wrong with you? Did you see what you did?"

"Of course I saw! I'm the one who did it!" I tried to rush out again. This time, he pulled me back even harder.

"What in the hell was she talking about, Nikki?"

"I don't know. The bitch was drunk." He squeezed my arm causing me to moan in pain. "You're hurting me!"

"She better be lying, Nikki."

"Is that a threat?" I yank my arm away.

"You can call it what you want, but she better be lying."

"Instead of handing out threats, you need to be handing me my fucking money."

Germaine stared at me. "I should've known that you were up to something."

"Yeah, you should've," I said before storming out only to find the tires on Jaguar slashed, now I had to take the Malibu rental again. "That bitch."

Chapter 23

"How's your food, Nikki?" Marko asked when we were in the hotel restaurant about to have lunch the following day.

Eating was the furthest thing from my mind. Marko and I needed to get this ball rolling and quick because Germaine was definitely going to find out about Johnathan. When he did, I would never get my damn money.

"Nikki, what's up? You've been acting kinda funky ever since you came back last night. What happened and don't lie to me?"

I stared into Marko's eyes and saw puppy love beaming from them. I hated corrupting him, but he'd signed his name on the dotted line when he agreed to help.

"Something happened last night, Marko and we need to speed this up with my husband," I whispered across the table.

He ate the shrimp from his fork, then placed it on the plate. "I'm listening," he said while chewing.

"I can't go into detail about what happened, but he needs to be gone."

"You want me to help you off a nigga and don't wanna tell me what happened when you went to see him last night?" he asked insulted and pissed.

I looked around to see if anyone had heard his dumb ass since he was so fucking loud. Luckily, there were only a handful of people in the restaurant with us, "Marko, it's just that he needs to be out of the picture before he finds out something important."

"Like what?" He wasn't going to let this go over smoothly.

"Look, all you need to know is that there is a lot of money involved, and when I get it you're not gonna have to worry about A.J. signing you to a new deal. I'll finance your project."

"Is this still about getting your kids, too?" Marko asked curiously as if all I was after was the money.

"Yes, Marko. So, we need to move in on him today," I replied trying to hide the panic in my voice.

"Today? How do you plan on that happening? We haven't even gone over any plans."

It sounded like he was trying to get out of it, but I wasn't having that. I needed this shit done. I was sure it would be easy to get a gun off the street and go cap Germaine, but I didn't want to be the one to pull the trigger. I wanted Marko to do it. My hands were already dirty enough.

"Marko, we can…"

"You vindictive, lying bitch!" My eyes widened with terror when I saw Germaine hovering over me. I was too engrossed in my conversation with Marko and didn't notice him coming our way.

"Germaine, h…h…how did you know where I was staying?" I panicked.

He held up my hotel room key. I wondered what had happened to it and so did Marko when I knocked on the door to get into the room. I watched Marko size Germaine up and vice versa.

"This key must've fallen out of your purse when I was eating your pussy," Germaine answered while still staring at Marko.

After his response, Marko turned to me. I wanted to grab the fork from my plate and stab Germaine in the jugular.

"Nikki, what the hell is going on?" Marko asked with a furious look on his face.

"Oh, he gets to call you, Nikki?" Germaine laughed. "What the hell did he do to earn that privilege?" I glared at Germaine. "How old is this dude anyway, Nikki? He looks kinda young."

Both me and Marko ignored Germaine's last comment.

"Nikki, when you came back to the room last night, you told me that nothing happened," Marko continued.

"My man, a lot happened," Germaine spoke for me. "You don't know what you're getting yourself into with this scandalous bitch."

"Germaine, will you…"

"Shut up! I'm talking!" Germaine barked at me. "I can't believe I fell for your shit again! And to think I proposed to your conniving ass again last night." From the look in Germaine's eyes, something told me he knew about Johnathan. I watched Marko try to slide out of the booth. I quickly reached over the table to stop him.

"Marko, please don't leave me," I begged. I didn't want to be around Germaine alone. If anything happened, Marko could serve as a witness.

"Yeah man, stick around for the grand finale. This is something that you should know about my dear wife. I'm sure she's kept you in the dark about a lot of shit, too." Marko sat back down and gave me a treacherous stare. I was up shit's creek without a paddle. "Nikki, after hearing Jalisa's story about Johnathan not being my son, I decided to call A.J. myself."

Knots formed in my stomach. "How did you contact A.J., Germaine?" I asked in an attempt to prolong his story so that I could figure out a way to get out of it.

"I'm buying one of his studios down here. Actually, it's the one that I was telling you about before you let me lick your clit," he smiled maliciously.

It felt like I'd been punched in the stomach.

"What the hell is he talking about, Nikki? And what does

A.J. have to do with any of this?" Marko asked after placing his hands on top of the table and slowly leaned forward. I never realized how big they were until that very moment. If he slapped someone with them, that victim would've surely taken flight.

"Marko, he's just mad because I wouldn't accept his proposal and…"

"I thought I told you to shut up," Germaine hissed at me. "A.J. has everything to do with this, main man. He wouldn't admit that Johnathan is his son, but he did say there was a strong possibility. So, my question to you, Nikki, is this… is there a *strong possibility* that Nathan could be his, too?"

The shit had hit the fan.

"What the fuck?" Marko gasped.

"Germaine, shut the hell up! You don't know what you're talking about!" I belted.

"He also told me something else, Nikki." It felt like I was about to have a panic attack. This was much worse than the Kingston drama. "He said that you tried to blackmail him in to getting your label back by using Johnathan as leverage," Germaine continued.

I needed to get out of that damn restaurant. There was too much animosity shooting my way. I didn't know what was going through Marko's head as he listened to Germaine's words. I didn't know what was going through Germaine's head as he spoke them. I was in the middle of a forest fire with no way out.

"Tell me the truth, Nikki. Are my sons really my sons?" Germaine asked. I couldn't answer him due to Marko peeling the skin from my body with his eyes. "Nikki, answer me! Are they my fucking sons?" Germaine screamed.

"No, Johnathan is not your son!" I yelled back. Surprisingly, I was happy to get that burden off my chest. He stared at me like I was diseased.

"What about Nathan?" I could tell in Germaine's voice that he was choking back tears but what I was about to say wasn't going to ease his pain.

"I…I…I don't know," I stuttered.

"What the fuck do you mean you don't know?" Germaine barked.

I'm sure this conversation made everyone's day in the restaurant. Wherever I went…drama followed.

"There's a fifty/fifty chance that he could be yours," I answered in a soft voice.

Germaine's eyes widened. "You have got to be fucking kidding me! So, I've been raising two kids that don't fucking belong to me?"

"Nathan is more than likely yours, Germaine."

"More than likely? How in the fuck is that suppose to help? He's probably not mine!" Suddenly, Germaine grabbed my hair and yanked me out of the booth. "All this fucking time, you've been lying to me and sneaking around with that nigga! Are you still fucking him?"

By this time, Marko had jumped up and pried himself between me and Germaine. "Get the fuck off of me!" Germaine spewed at Marko after pushing him. "Ask her! Ask her if she's still fucking A.J. since it's more than obvious that you know him."

Marko finally turned to me. "Nikki, are you still messing around with A.J?"

It didn't make any sense to continue the lie. "Sometimes," I answered softly.

Germaine pulled away from Marko.

"When was the last time?" Marko asked.

"Marko, let's not do this," I pleaded.

"Naw, we doing this. Answer the fucking question," Marko responded.

Where was a damn robber when you needed one? I needed something to happen to get me out of dodge. "The night before you met me," I answered softly.

"Speak up," Germaine demanded.

"The night before I met you, Marko," I answered a little louder.

"Now, ain't that some shit," Marko replied shockingly.

"You're a worthless mother," Germaine growled at me.

"Hey! Hey!" the manager shouted as he finally walked toward us. "Take that outside!" he ordered.

"Nikki, I'm making a promise to you today. You're never gonna see *my* boys again!" Germaine turned to Marko. "By the way, man, she has two *definite* kids by A.J. I just found out about an older one that they've been keeping secret. You better get out while you can."

Just like a time before when he was extremely pissed at me, Germaine spat in my face then walked out. Just when I thought it was over, Marko finished what Germaine had started.

"All this time, you and A.J." Marko started laughing. "Here you are fucking somebody who doesn't give a shit about you. Do you know A.J. asked me to get someone to take care of you the night of the THRONE party?"

My eyes increased by three sizes. "What?"

"Yeah, he didn't give me the reason, but he told me I could get a sweet record deal, if I took care of you." I was beyond shocked. "But you know what, I told him no. I told him I was falling in love with you, and could never hurt you."

Each word Marko spoke felt like a dagger going through my heart.

"A.J. called me stupid. That's when he warned me about you," Marko continued. "I'm just wondering if you ever planned on telling me about any of this…about you and *my boss* as you put it once. You know what? It doesn't even matter. The deal is off. Keep your money if you ever get it."

At that moment, he walked out, too. Surprisingly, I ran after him, and stopped him on the street.

"Marko, please, listen to me. None of this is my fault. You have to understand my position as to why I did the things that I did," I pleaded heavily.

"I do understand your position. It was on your back or on your knees making babies with A.J." Shaking his head, Marko walked off and never looked back.

I was a little embarrassed and pissed because a few passer-byers had overheard us. Germaine and A.J. had fucked me for the last time. I walked away from the loiterers who were standing around. When I was out of earshot from anyone, I pulled my cell phone from my purse and called my father, informing him of what happened. After being around him again and seeing how he rolled when the dude stepped out of line to me at the party, I quickly stored him in my mind as a backup plan. When he asked me how he could help, there was no hesitation in my response.

"I want you to off A.J. and Germaine. Just make sure my kids aren't around when it's Germaine's turn."

Chapter 24

The next morning, I burned rubber back to Houston. I was a little ticked off with myself for not getting a roundtrip flight when I flew in. With the Amex being on lockdown and Marko gone, I had just enough money to purchase gas for the drive. I would face the repercussions of taking the rental car to another state without informing Enterprise when the time came. Until then, I had to get the hell out of New Orleans.

As I drove back to Houston, I continued my calls from the night before to Marko. I didn't expect him to return to the room after my big bag of secrets were revealed, and I couldn't blame him. I sat up all night watching the door hoping he would walk through it. I needed to talk to him. I wanted him back on my side, but it was going to take an act from God for that to happen. In my heart, I truly felt something for Marko and I couldn't deny my feelings, which scared me. I didn't want this to be another Kingston situation. The only difference was that Marko actually gave a damn about me. He'd shown me that by choosing me over a record deal.

A few hours after arriving back at my mother's house, I called my father to see if Germaine had been taken care of yet. I tried to let him do his thing and wait for the confirmation call, but I was a nervous wreck. I needed to know something. I was tired of pacing the floor not knowing what was going on. When

I asked for his help and told him what I needed done, he assured me that it would be handled the following day. That was another reason why I got out of dodge so fast. I didn't want anything to be linked back to me. All I needed to do was sit back in Houston and wait for him to deliver my boys. I was so involved in my thoughts that I didn't hear Cliff walk in.

"So, you finally decided to come home?" Cliff tossed his keys on the table in the foyer. "Has your mama and the kid made it back yet?" he asked, then scanned the area.

"No one's here and I wish it would've stayed that way," I replied.

"Maxine said they had a lot of running around to do so I didn't expect them to be…"

"Cliff, I could care less about where they are. I've got a lot of things on my mind and I need you to leave me alone," I said, glancing at my phone to see if I'd missed a call or text while he was talking.

"Well, damn! It's nice to see you, too," he said sarcastically. I hoped my attitude would make him disappear into my mother's room, but that would've been too much. "So, your mama's not here. I've been missing you and I know you've missed me."

"Cliff, now is not the time," I replied irritably as I pushed him away from me.

"Are you on your monthly?"

"No!"

"Then this is the right time. I told you that your mama ain't been putting out so…"

"Look, I've got a lot of shit going on right now, Cliff, and I don't need you bothering me. I've had a long drive and I'm tired so leave me the hell alone."

"Baby, I'm just trying to show you that I miss you. What's the problem? Do you need more money?" He pulled his wallet from his back pocket, then handed me three hundred dollars. For once, I didn't want his money.

"Don't come in my fucking room Cliff, or you'll really

see how much of a bitch I can be," I threatened before disappearing in my room where I continued to stare at my phone.

I called Marko a few more times. I could tell that he was sending my calls to voicemail which gave me an inkling of hope. If he was truly done with me, he would've turned the phone off or disconnected it altogether. But obviously I'd spoke too soon. When I called back a few minutes later, he'd turned it off. Shit.

I didn't bother calling my father again. I was probably getting on his nerves or disturbing him from getting the job done. After thirty minutes of staring at the phone, I could neither ignore the yawns nor fight my closing eyes any longer. I fell asleep.

❖ ❖ ❖

"Auntie Nikki! Auntie Nikki!" I rolled over and slowly opened my eyes to find Cierra standing on the side of my bed smiling. "I bought this for you," she said cheerfully while handing me the wrapped box.

"What did I tell you about coming in my room without knocking?"

"Auntie Nikki, I did knock. Grandma told me to come in when you didn't say anything." Her smile slowly disappeared. "Are you gonna open your present?"

I stared at her wondering why I didn't name her Alphonsa. I had to giggle at that ugly ass name. I sat up in the bed and accepted the gift. As I was about to open it, I caught a glimpse of my phone next to my pillow. I dropped the present on the bed, which fell on the floor. I snatched up my phone to see if I'd missed any calls from my dad or Marko. No calls and it was almost six o'clock. I should've at least heard something from my father by now.

"This is ridiculous," I said after hopping off the bed and accidentally stepping on the present from Cierra.

I grabbed my purse and keys then flew out of the house. I

couldn't take not knowing what was going on and I damn sure couldn't take not talking to Marko. As I backed out of the driveway, I saw my mother swing the front door open. She was yelling all kinds of obscenities at me and I didn't know why until Cierra appeared from behind her. She was crying. Once again, I'd hurt her feelings, but this time, I really didn't mean to. It's just that I had way more important things on my mind that required my immediate attention. I needed to see Marko.

I drove away without looking back. When I made it to the stop sign at the end of the street, my phone rang. It was my father…finally.

"Dad, what's going on? I haven't heard from you and…" I ranted before being interrupted.

"Colie Cole, something happened," he said not sounding too pleased. I kept on driving.

"W…What happened?" My voice trembled. "Where are my boys?"

"Colie, we…"

"What the fuck?" I bellowed at the red light when my car was rear ended. "Shit…hold on, dad, some asshole just hit my car."

I glanced in my rearview mirror to see if the person had gotten out of their car. My eyes widened with terror when I saw Germaine jumping out of his truck. He was battered and bruised along with eyes that were swollen and a busted lip. I almost didn't recognize him.

"Dad, he's here! He's here!" I screamed before dropping the phone. Before I could lock the door, Germaine had yanked it open.

"You low down, evil bitch!" he yelled at me while viciously pulling my ass out of the car. He hemmed me up against the back door with his hands wrapped around my neck. "So, you gonna send some muthafuckas to try and kill me?"

"What…are…you…talking…about?" I struggled.

"You know damn well what I'm talking about! While them muthafuckas were jumping on me, all they kept saying was *this is from Niquole*! What the fuck is wrong with you? All I wanted to do was love you!" he yelled while choking me a little harder.

Thinking of what to do, something told me to knee him in the groin.

"Ahhhhhhhhh!" he screamed in pain then back handed me with a closed fist.

I hit his ass back. Cars passed by while we tussled. Some even slowed down to see what was going on. He was definitely getting the best of me, but I gave him a run for his money because I knew he was trying to kill me. I wasn't going to make it that easy for him. All of a sudden, Germaine lost his footing and staggered backwards. In the blink of an eye, he was out of my sight. I watched his body flip onto the hood of the black Ford Mustang then, topple to the asphalt. The driver couldn't hit his brakes fast enough. He drove over Germaine's body.

"Oh my God!" I yelled out when Germaine's body finally came to its resting place.

My feet were cemented to the ground. Part of me wanted to run to his aide, but the other part wanted to jump in my car and take off. A few cars stopped and a couple of the owners hurried to me to see if I was okay. I didn't want them near me. I just wanted to leave. I didn't want to be around the chaos. Although I wanted Germaine dead, I couldn't stand the sight of seeing his lifeless body. I dared myself to cry or show any emotions after what he'd put me through.

I watched all the onlookers as they snapped photos on their cell phones. Some even whispered and pointed at me. Suddenly, my eyes locked on Germaine's truck.

"My boys!" I panicked and ran as fast as I could to the truck hoping my sons were inside. "Johnathan? Nathan?" I called out to them after swinging open the driver's door. My heart sank when I learned they weren't inside. Oh my God, I hoped my father had them.

It wasn't long before sirens began blaring down the street. Two patrol cars, an ambulance and a fire truck soon surrounded the scene. One of the firemen walked over to the Mustang to check on the driver who was leaning against his car with his hands over his face. I could tell that he was in shock. The EMTs hurried to Germaine.

"Ma'am, are you okay?" one of the officers addressed me when he walked over. I wanted him to move out of my way so that I could see what the EMTs were doing. "Ma'am, do you need any help? A few bystanders told us that you were attacked."

Although it was music to my ears that I had witnesses for my defense, I still needed to see what was going on with Germaine.

"He has a pulse!" one of the EMTs yelled after administering CPR.

"No, no, no," I said softly as my heart sank. I needed him to be dead. I couldn't live the rest of my life knowing that he wouldn't stop coming after me until I was dead. "This can't be happening." I rocked back and forth like a mental patient as the EMTs placed Germaine on the gurney and wheeled him toward the ambulance.

"I've lost the pulse!" the EMT screamed. Seconds later, they quickly placed the gurney into the ambulance and started CPR again while the other prepared the defibrillator.

"Clear!" the other EMT yelled. I watched and waited impatiently for the outcome. Out of the corner of my eye, I saw the officers taking statements from the witnesses. I even saw one of them slap cuffs on the Mustang driver. He must've been intoxicated. "Clear!" the EMT yelled again.

"Please be dead. Please be dead," I mumbled. The officer cut a side eye at me.

"Let's go ahead and call it," one of the EMTs addressed the other. There was a straight line going across the defibrillator screen. Germaine had flatlined. I watched them cover him with a white sheet. With the officer still looking at me, I smiled.

Chapter 25

After nearly an hour of speaking with the police and denying his request to go downtown and give a statement of the events, I left. With the witness statements, he had more than enough evidence that I was attacked and there was no wrongdoing on my part. Although I wanted him dead, I still couldn't believe that Germaine was gone. Now, I had even bigger things to worry about. I needed to know where my sons were. The numerous calls to my father went unanswered. This only frightened me more.

"Dad, please have my boys," I prayed through tears. As I pulled into Marko's apartment complex, my father called back. "Dad, please tell me you have my boys?" I wasted no time.

"Colie, are you okay? I heard you say that he was there. Who were you talking about, Germaine?"

"Yeah, he was. He's dead now no thanks to you. You were supposed to handle things," I replied disappointedly. "Do you have my boys?"

"Colie, shit didn't go right."

"I know that much. Where are my boys? What happened?"

"I sent my crew to the house, but Germaine was coming out the house when they got there, so they beat him down right in the damn driveway. Someone must've called the cops. When my boys heard the sirens, they rolled out."

"Why didn't they just shoot his ass? Why do all of that outside?"

"Colie, I don't operate like that. I do things my way."

"Well, your way made Germaine drive all the way to Houston to come find me. Those dumb ass fools you sent told Germaine that I put them up to it. Was that your way, too?"

"None of that was supposed to happen, Colie. They weren't supposed to say anything."

"Well, they did!" I screamed looking at my bruises in the rearview mirror.

"Slow your roll, Colie Cole. I ain't the one to be yelling at," he chastised in a smooth manner.

"Where are my boys?" I wasn't trying to hear that daddy come late shit.

"I don't know. They didn't have time to check the house."

"What?" Now, I was really nervous.

"Don't worry. I keep my word. I'm gonna find 'em," he assured.

"How the hell are you gonna find them when you don't even know what they look like?" I hung up the phone. Talking to him was pointless. I tried to clean my face up before facing Marko, but my efforts didn't help much. I took a deep breath, then walked up to his apartment.

"Who is it?" he asked after I knocked.

"Marko, it's me…Nikki."

"What the fuck do you want?"

"Marko, please. Let me in. I need you," I pleaded while leaning against the door.

When tears dripped from my eyes, I knew that I really gave a damn about him. The tears were real and my heart ached. "Marko, I'm sorry. Please don't turn me away. Germaine just tried to kill me. I don't know where my boys are. Please, help me."

There was no response for several seconds. Just as I was

about to plead with him again, I finally heard the locks turn. When he opened the door and saw me, his eyes enlarged.

"Damn, Nikki." Marko sounded so sympathetic. He reached for my hand then gently pulled me inside. "What the hell happened to you?" Leading me to the bathroom, he wet a washcloth, then wiped my face. I felt safe and secure with him.

"It's a long story, but Germaine is dead." He gave me a questionable look. "I didn't do it. He came after me. We were fighting so hard, that he got hit by a car."

"Damn, that's fucked up." Marko continued to clean my wounds. "Are you okay?"

Tears streamed down my face. "Not really. I don't know where my kids are. I need you to help me find them."

"Nikki, this is some heavy shit to drop on me right now."

"You were willing to help me before you found out who their father was," I reminded.

"Nikki, this is different. A.J. is their father."

"Are you afraid of him or something?"

"Hell no! It's just that I'm trying to get re-signed and with me dealing with you, I know that ain't gonna happen."

I was furious. "Is that all you're worried about? A fucking record deal! What about me?"

"You hurt me, Niquole."

He hadn't called me that in a while. Maybe he was hurt. I had to calm down before things went the wrong way.

"Baby, I told you when I get this money I can finance your next project. Hell I'll even get a new label."

"That's very generous, Nikki but…"

"But nothing, Marko! You're either with me or you're not!" I was tired of this going back and forth with him. We were wasting precious time. I assumed my newly formed tears won him over because eventually he agreed.

"Do you even have an idea where your kids could be?" he asked.

"I have an idea. Let's go."

❅ ❅ ❅

I twiddled my fingers as we drove to Germaine's mother's house. That was the only place I knew my son's could possibly be.

"Slow down, Nikki." Marko said as I swerved around car after car.

"You don't understand. What if my son's aren't there?"

Deciding not to respond, Marko just sat in the passenger's seat allowing me to drive the way I wanted. Maybe he understood…maybe he didn't.

About twenty minutes later, I pulled into Glenda's driveway. The car had barely been placed in park, before I jumped out like the FEDS during a drug bust and ran up to the door, with Marko in tow. I banged on the door with both fists.

"You have a lot of nerve showing up here?" Glenda barked when she opened the door. It was dejavu all over again with me coming to take my kids from her. I hoped that was the case. "After all the trouble you've caused this family, you have…"

"Save that, Glenda! Do you have Johnathan and Nathan here?" I asked looking around her. It looked like she'd gained even more weight than I remembered.

"You need to leave, Niquole. You're trespassing on private property," she spat.

As calm as she was, it was obvious that she had no idea that her son was dead. I didn't want to be the one to give her the news until my sons were in my possession.

"Do you think I give a damn about that when it comes to my sons, Glenda?"

"Germaine told me what you did in New Orleans," she said.

"I'm sure he did. Now, where are my boys?" I replied.

"They're safe," Glenda answered. "Now leave."

I looked back at Marko. His facial expression told me that he knew what I was about to do. I pushed Glenda so hard that she fell on her fat, wide ass.

"Marko, come and help me find my sons!" I barked when I saw him trying to help Glenda up. "Leave her ass down there where she belongs."

"Nikki, you're out of line," he scolded after grabbing my arm. I yanked away. "This is not the right way to do things."

"Fuck her! You don't know what she has put me through!" I lashed back. "Once you really get to know me, you'll find out that I play by my own damn rules!"

Before he could reply, Johnathan came running from the back of the house. When he saw me, he stood still. I could tell that he wanted to run to me. "You see what I'm talking about, Marko? They've brainwashed my kids and turned them against me," I sniffled. Johnathan proved that statement wrong when he ran into my arms. All I could do was cry. Nathan toddled from the back soon after. "Get him! Get him!" I spoke frantically to Marko as my trembling finger pointed at Nathan.

"Shit!" Marko yelled as if he thought what we were doing was wrong.

Nathan was a little resistant, but Marko did a little cooing at him to calm him down. After both kids were secure in our arms, we headed for the door only to find Jalisa standing in the threshold. Her wig looked tangled and her face was in desperate need of makeup, but that wouldn't have helped with the bandages on her face. By that time, Glenda was at the coffee table talking to the police on the phone.

"What in the hell are you doing here?" I snapped. I quickly handed Johnathan to Marko and told him to put them in the car.

"I followed Germaine here from New Orleans. I saw what happened to him." Tears formed in her eyes. "I knew he'd lead me to you."

"What? What happened to my son?" Glenda asked.

"Ask your daughter-in-law," Jalisa answered.

"You two bitches can chit chat. I'm leaving," I said. However, before I could walk out the door, Jalisa pulled out a gun from behind her back.

My heart instantly started to race. "Are you crazy?" I yelled at her.

"You're damn right I'm crazy! You and our devil ass daddy have ruined my fucking life! You took the one man from me that I ever loved! You ruined my fucking career! You fucked up my face! Did you think I was gonna let you get away with this shit?"

I couldn't help but wonder what our father had to do with this. She couldn't have been talking about what he did to Germaine.

"Jalisa, just put the gun down, baby," Glenda coaxed. "She's not worth it. She's about to go to jail anyway for kidnapping as soon as the cops get here."

"You don't get it, Mrs. Evans. She's not gonna stop." If Jalisa was going to shoot me, she would hear my last words.

"You're damn right I'm not gonna stop until I get what I want. I told you that it's all about me…not you. You've known that from the jump. You were always in my fucking shadow. I carried your ass. If it wasn't for me, you wouldn't be shit!"

"You're right. I wouldn't be. I'll never be you. You win!"

My mouth hit the floor when Jalisa stuck the barrel of the gun in her mouth and blew her brains out. Glenda immediately started screaming to the top of her lungs. I probably would've screamed if something would come out, but I was speechless. Jalisa had taken the most awful way to part this world, and I couldn't believe she'd decided to do that shit directly in front of me. I wondered what was going through her head before she pulled the trigger. I hoped she didn't think that her suicide would make me change. If she did, she was more stupid than I thought.

"Oh my, God!" Glenda continued to scream before dropping to her knees in shock.

All I could do was stare at Jalisa's stupid, insecure ass.

She was the sister with the real issues. I stepped over her ass like she didn't mean shit to me because she didn't. Before I walked out the door, I turned to Glenda who was crying uncontrollably.

"I wouldn't worry about her, Glenda. I'm sure she and Germaine are together in hell. That's what she wanted anyway for her and Germaine to be together."

"You're so damn evil! You're just plain evil!" she cried louder. "Where is my son? Where is my damn son? What did you do to him?"

"Don't expect your son to come back looking for my boys. He's dead right along with her," I said before looking down at Jalisa's body one last time and walking out.

Chapter 26

A week and a half later, I was laying in the twin size bed in my mother's house with Nathan locked in my arms while Johnathan and Cierra were laying on the air mattress on the floor. They were all sound asleep and looked so peaceful. They played together so well when I brought the boys home. It warmed my heart to have them all together, even Cierra. I couldn't continue mistreating her. None of this was her fault. My mother was right, she needed to know her cousins. I just wasn't able or ready to let them know that they were brothers and sisters. Cierra would probably need counseling for that, which I wasn't ready to deal with since I'd probably need counseling, too.

"Nikki?" I heard my mom whisper from the door.

When I looked up, I saw a huge smile on her face. She was happy to have the boys back, too. I'm sure she'd never admit it, but she was happy. We all were. Our relationship was even improving…just a little.

"I'm going to the store to get some things for dinner, but I'll be back in time to keep Cierra so that you and the boys can go to Germaine's funeral. It starts at noon, right?"

Like I said…just a little. She'd lost her mind if she thought I was going to that bastard's funeral. "Mama, you know I'm not going to that funeral. Even if Germaine's family hadn't threatened me if I showed up, I still wasn't going."

"Nikki, that's not right. He was still your husband. You missed Jalisa's funeral yesterday in New Orleans and…"

"Your words are falling on deaf ears." I put Nathan down, then slipped out of bed to continue this conversation in the living room because I knew it was about to get heated. "Mama, I don't owe either one of their asses a damn thing after they kept my kids away from me."

She shook her head. "This isn't right. Those boys need to pay their final respects to their father. Germaine loved them, Nikki."

"Well, you go for them then because we're not going. And when you walk in that church, watch how fast you get kicked out because you're my mother."

"Nikki, Germaine's family knows you didn't have anything to do with his death. It was all over the news that it was an accident. The guy who hit him is facing charges."

"Mama, do you think they give a damn about that? All they know is that *I* was there. They don't give a shit that he beat the hell out of me on the street right before it happened. In their eyes, I killed him."

"What about Jalisa? What was your excuse for not attending hers? She was your sister," she said as if my response would be any different.

"She's a fucking coward for killing herself and just like Germaine, she didn't deserve any final respects from me either. Good fucking riddance to them both."

"This is unreal." My mother continued to shake her head from side to side.

"Please don't act like this is a shock to you."

"You're right, it's not."

"Besides, I have other plans for today."

"Like what?"

"I'm taking the kids to the Houston Aquarium."

"Wow…goodbye, Nikki," she pouted while grabbing her purse and keys then walking out the door.

I chuckled before going back to my room. With the kids still asleep, I retrieved my phone from the nightstand to call Chase Bank. When my lawyers learned about Germaine's death, they quickly got to work making sure I had access to his bank account in New Orleans. Being his wife, all the money Germaine stole and hadn't spent was coming right back to me. The crazy thing was, for now I could only see what the balance was. It was gonna take ten to fourteen business days from the date of his death for the money to be transferred back to me. I hated dumb ass bank policies. It took him minutes to take my shit, but it was gonna take days for me to get it back. That's why I hadn't left my mother's house yet. But as soon as my money came, my kids and I were out of the house. I still hadn't decided if I was gonna take Cierra yet.

Speaking of money, that was another thing Germaine's family was so pissed off about. I hadn't offered to pay one dime toward burying him, and wasn't going to. That money in his bank account was for me and my kids to start over. If they knew about the insurance policy I had on him, they would really be pissed. Shit, Glenda should've been grateful. The police told me several times where Germaine's Mercedes truck had been impounded, but I never bothered to pick it up. Instead, I gave them her number, so she would at least have that piece of him.

For the past two days, I'd been calling Germaine's account to hear the balance over and over again to make sure nothing had changed. As soon as I dialed the 1-800 number, then put in the right information, the automated machine brought a smile to my face. Five hundred, ninety-two thousand and thirteen cents is what was in the account. I had no idea all the things Germaine had spent the other three hundred and fifty-eight grand on, but I was so grateful that he hadn't spent it all. That money was going to be a new beginning for me and my family.

"Mommy?" Johnathan yawned breaking my train of thought.

I glanced at him. He was rubbing his eyes with the back of his hand. He could still pass for Germaine's son although he wasn't. I guess the saying was true; *if you feed them long enough, they will look like you.* I used to hear my mother's friends saying that all the time. Nathan, on the other hand, I was really unsure about because he looked just like me. But at the end of the day it didn't matter who their father was because they were *my* kids.

"Hey, sweetie," I grinned before leaning down to kiss Johnathan's cheek.

"Where's daddy and Auntie Jalisa?" he asked. My insides turned at the mention of those two.

"They went out of town," I lied.

"When are they coming back?"

I wasn't up for the questions because I couldn't tell him the truth. "Hey, let's wake up your brother and cousin and go to the aquarium and see the big fish. How does that sound?"

"Yaaaaaaaaaay," he said, jumping out of bed.

Again, my mother was right. Eventually I was gonna have to tell my boys something, but for now, we were going to have some fun.

❁ ❁ ❁

After an exhausting five hours at the Houston Aquarium, we were back my mother's house. Luckily the kids had fallen asleep because right along with them, I was completely exhausted. Marko also joined us which made the day even more fun. He was very good with the kids and they quickly attached to him as well. Cierra and I walked around taking turns pushing Nathan in the stroller while Marko and Johnathan ran amuck admiring all the aquatic animals. I enjoyed every minute with them. Those five hours showed me what I'd been missing when I was too busy running my label and running behind Kingston.

I had to carry the kids in the house one by one even the older two. They were too tired and stuffed with junk food and could hardly move. After putting them to bed, I found a note stuck to the dresser mirror.

Nikki, I put the air mattress in Cierra's room so you can have more space. We can talk about beds for the boys when I get back from the casino.

See you guys later,

Mom.

I balled up the note and tossed it in the trash. I couldn't believe that she was finally acting like a decent grandmother. I wondered how she was going to feel whenever I broke the news about us leaving.

"How was your day?" I turned to Cliff standing at the door.

"This room is off limits to you, Cliff," I warned him.

"I'm sorry," he apologized but continued inside. I felt a little eerie with him being in there with my kids. He seductively grabbed my hips. "You look so sexy standing up here. I just couldn't resist you," he whispered in my ear.

Immediately, I grabbed his hand and pulled him out of the room.

"Don't you ever pull no shit like that again with my kids around," I scolded.

"Baby, I'm sorry. It's just so hard to contain myself when I'm around you. The kids are asleep so…"

"You need to slow your role, Cliff."

"I'll pay you," he bribed.

I laughed at his sad attempt. "I don't need your money, sweetie."

"Then let me have you. Let me just taste you," he begged.

He walked up to me and slipped his hand inside my pants. My pussy clenched when his fingers glided inside. I couldn't resist. I rolled on his fingers. When he saw that I was a willing partner, he removed his hand, then my pants. With me still standing, he dropped to his knees, tossed my leg over his shoulder then his head disappeared between my thighs. Even though it felt good, there was no way I was gonna continue standing the way my thigh was trembling. I fell onto the sofa and he followed suit.

"Auntie Nikki?"

When I heard Cierra's voice, I shoved Cliff and covered myself with one of the throw pillows. Luckily, she didn't see anything because when I looked up, she was just appearing from around the corner.

"Auntie Nikki, my stomach hurts," she whined all the way over to me. She glanced at my leggings on the floor then back at me. I watched her stare at my bare legs. I knew she was wondering what was going on. Cliff had scurried out of the living room leaving me to handle the situation. "Why don't you have on your pants? Why did Uncle Cliff run away?"

"I thought you said that your stomach was hurting?" I hoped to redirect her thoughts. She rubbed her stomach then just like that, she threw up on the floor.

I frowned. "You couldn't make it to the bathroom?"

She gave me a pathetic, helpless look that I couldn't ignore. Butt ass naked, I got up from the sofa and started toward her until I heard my mother at the door. I snatched my pants off the floor and darted to my room to find Johnathan lying in a pool of vomit and tears scurrying down his cheeks. They'd both gotten sick from something. I hurried back into my pants and lifted him off the bed. With him in my arms, I walked back to the living room to find my mother tending to Cierra.

"Did you know she was in here like this?" she blasted.

"Yes, I knew but when I heard Johnathan crying, I ran to see what was wrong," I lied. I caught a glimpse of Cliff peeking around the corner. "Asshole," I mumbled hoping he could read lips. "Do we need to take them to the hospital?" I questioned my mother. It had been a while since I was in mommy mode.

"What did they eat?" she asked, then walked into the kitchen and pulled out a bottle of Pepto-Bismol from the refrigerator. I set Johnathan down when my mother reached for him.

"Is it safe to give them Pepto-Bismol?" I questioned.

"You got any better ideas," she said, giving Cierra her

dose.

I hated my mother's smart ass mouth sometimes. *Why didn't her ass stay at the casino?* "They had hot dogs, candy, ice cream and a little popcorn, at the aquarium."

"Why did you give these kids all that crap?"

I shrugged my shoulders. "They wanted it so I gave it to them."

"Look, I know you haven't had much experience being a mother, but you've gottta learn to…"

I cut her off. "What do you mean I don't have much experience being a mother?" I asked in a tone to let her know I was offended.

"Nikki it's self explanatory. Cierra has been with Adrienne and Germaine basically raised John John and Nathan."

"I know how to be a mother!" I yelled.

"Well, if you did, you would've known not to give them all that shit. You're thirty-two years old with three kids and you don't even know the basic stuff. You were so quick to take them to the hospital. Some things don't require a hospital, Nikki. These kids just have upset stomachs and…"

"Okay! Okay! I've got a lot of shit to learn, but I don't appreciate you belittling me in front of them either. I'm not dumb or stupid."

"I'm not saying that."

"It doesn't matter anyway because we'll be out of this shithole as soon as I get my money and find a house."

"Nikki, you don't have to leave. I can help you with the kids."

"Oh, you want to help me now?" I laughed. "I do recall that you were trying to help Germaine keep the boys away from me."

"Don't do this in front of them," my mother suggested.

I looked at Cierra and Johnathan who were both staring down my throat.

"You're right. I won't do this in front of them."

"Where are you going?" she asked when I walked off.

Instead of answering, I went into my room, packed an overnight back filled with necessities for all four of us, retrieved my purse and then loaded Nathan in my arms. I returned to the kitchen. "What are you doing, Nikki?" my mother asked when I waved for Cierra and Johnathan to follow me. "Those kids are sick. Don't take them out of this house," she practically begged.

I couldn't be around her at the moment. I had to leave. The kids followed me to the door. When Cierra and Johnathan stepped outside, I turned to my mother before I followed behind them.

"If I'd had a better fucking mother, maybe I would stand a chance at being a better mother, too."

Chapter 27

When I walked out of my mother's house, my first instinct was to go to a hotel. That was a normal thing for me to do when I ran from life, but something drove me to Marko's apartment. When he saw me and the kids, he gladly invited us inside. When he learned of Cierra and Johnathan's ailments, he even went out and bought them some bubble gum flavored chewable Mylanta along with some Pedialyte. I wondered how he knew so much about kids. Everything he did reminded me of Germaine. The only difference was that I enjoyed sharing the moments with Marko much better.

I spent the next day house hunting. But I had to admit, having three kids with me made the task a little difficult so I swallowed my pride and took them back to my mother's. She was more than happy to keep them while I continued my search, but I made it clear that I would be back to get them when I finished.

After being out all day and not finding exactly what I wanted, I went back to pick the kids up at my mother's. However instead of walking into a peaceful environment, I immediately heard yelling and screaming when I stepped inside the front door. At first I thought the male voice belonged to Cliff. But the more I listened the more I realized that the voice didn't belong to Cliff at all. It belonged to my father. I rushed into the living room.

"What's going on in here?" That question was directed right at my mother. "Why are you yelling at him?"

"Why did you tell him where I lived?" she scolded. Her face was fire red and so were her eyes. Snot dripped from her nose and tears poured from her eyes.

"Because he's my father! He wanted to know!"

My father walked over to me with his arms spread apart. "Hey, Colie, Cole."

I returned the hug. "Hey, dad."

"Hey, I took care of that for you. No problems this time," he replied.

My eyes enlarged. Was that confirmation that A.J. was gone?

"What is he talking about, Niquole? What did you have him do?" my mother questioned.

"That's none of your business, Maxine. That's between me and Colie," my father had put his foot down like he used to do when I was younger. I could tell that my mother was a little tense with him being in the house.

"None of my business?" she questioned. "I don't care how fucked up my relationship is with her, Niquole is still *my* daughter."

"And he's still my father. If it wasn't for you, he would've never left me." I stepped in to defend.

"Bishop, it's time for you to tell her the truth. Tell her why I kicked you out. I can't take the lies anymore," my mother cried.

"I already know why. You kicked him out because you found out about Jalisa," I said.

"I didn't give a damn about him having another child, Nikki. Jalisa was one of three that I found out about. I just used her because she was the easiest lie. I loved your dad more than life itself and the fucked up part about this entire situation is, after all the shit that he put me through, I still love him."

Her tears and cries went into overdrive. For once, she had me speechless. I'd never seen my mother break down like that. Emotionally, she was just as fucked up as I was. I turned to my father who had a stupid, guilty look on his face. There was definitely more to this story.

My father turned to me, then held my hand. "Look, I didn't come here for this. Colie, Cole. I came to see about you and my grandbabies since we never talked about that again, and to tell you what I'd taken care of. Now, since all that's done, I'm out. You know where I am if you ever need me again."

"Oh, hell, no! You stand your ass right there and tell her the truth, Bishop!" my mother shouted to the top of her lungs.

Something was wrong. I turned to my father again hoping he would tell me what was going on. But his facial expression told me that he wasn't saying a thing.

"Mama, if this is about him being a drug dealer, I don't care about that. I…"

"Nikki your father is not only a drug dealer, but he's a damn pimp."

My eyes bulged. After looking back and forth between my two parents, I finally processed what she'd said. I wasn't there to judge him.

"Okay, so what he's a pimp, too. Big deal. He's still my father and you kicked him out! I needed him!" I yelled.

"Bishop, tell her the truth!" my mother belted. When he still refused to say anything, she continued. "You didn't need him, Nikki! He tried to pimp you out when you were *fifteen years old*! That's why I kicked his ass out! I kicked him out to save you! He tried to do the same thing to Adrienne and that's why I sent her away to her father!"

It felt like I was about to pass out. "What?" I gasped. "You're lying! Tell her she's lying, daddy!" When he refused to say a word, his silence confirmed my mother's accusations.

"I used to be one of his girls, Nikki," my mother added. "And one day he came to me and told me that I was getting old and he needed young meat. He was saying that as he was staring at you sleeping."

"I didn't see a fucking problem with it," my father finally jumped in. "She was a fast ass anyway. When Milwaukee told me that he fucked her, I knew it was time."

All this shit felt like a dream This couldn't be happening.

"Jalisa did it so I figured Niquole would, too since they were so tight," he spoke.

"Jalisa?" I gasped again.

"Model by day, high priced whore by night. She took my operation to the next level with her going to other countries and shit," he stated boldly.

Now, I knew what Jalisa meant by saying our father had screwed up her life and what Adrienne meant by her words. I wondered if anybody else's family was as fucked up as mine. Before any of us could say another word, Cliff walked in. My father looked like he'd just seen a long lost friend.

"Cliff, man, what the fuck you doing here?" my father asked making me realize that the two of them knew each other.

Cliff glanced back and forth from me to my mother. I was curious to know how he and my father knew each other.

"I'm getting what you promised me seventeen years ago," Cliff answered. His eyes locked on me when he spoke those words.

What the hell? I felt cheap and played. I think I stopped breathing.

"Well, nigga, you owe me and if you were fucking Max-ine, too, you owe me double," my father addressed him defiantly. I stood and listened to them speak of me as if I were a piece of meat.

"Bishop, I paid her. So…"

"So nothing, nigga! You pay me!" my father yelled.

"Look, she's not fifteen anymore and Maxine is not one of your girls anymore either!" Cliff defended himself.

This had to have been some kind of sick joke. Did they even forget that I was in the room?

"Niquole, did you sleep with Cliff?" my mother asked

through tears. When I didn't respond, I believe she already knew the answer. She looked back at Cliff. "How could you?"

Cliff didn't say anything, but I did. I could no longer hold my tongue.

"You piece of shit!" I addressed my father viciously. "I'm your fucking daughter! I loved you! I defended you! You tried to pimp me out!"

"Look, you were a high commodity back then. Well, seems like you still are since Cliff has pierced that ass," my father responded.

Cliff chuckled.

"And you!" I addressed Cliff. "You played me from the beginning with that innocent act like what we were doing was wrong when all along that was part of your plan. You worthless old fuck!"

"You didn't mind taking my money, did you?" Cliff shot back.

At that moment, I picked up the cordless phone from the table I was standing next to and threw it at his head. He ducked. My mother eventually pulled me away when she saw me walking toward my father next.

"I'm your daughter!" my voice trembled. "All this time, I didn't mean shit to you!"

"You did mean something to me, but business is business, Colie," he replied coldly.

I could speak no longer. For once, I needed my mother's help. I turned to her and hoped she saw the pain and hurt in my eyes. She did.

"Both of you get the fuck out of my house! Bishop, if you ever show your face around here again, the cops will get some incriminating evidence against you," my mother roared.

"What evidence?" he laughed. "You ain't got shit on me."

"Keep thinking that, asshole. Remember, I was with you ever since I was seventeen-years-old. I really hope that you're not still riding your girlfriends around in the car with you when you do your dirty business." I could tell that my mother had him by the balls. "If anything ever happens to me or Niquole, the right people will know what to do with the evidence I have on you." She turned to Cliff. "And you piece of shit. The only reason you found me was to get to my daughter."

Cliff shook his head. "I didn't even know she was here, Maxine. I was here for you, but…"

"If you don't get your sad, pathetic ass out of my house, I'll kill both of you! Both of you decrepit fuckas get the hell out! Get out!" My mother shoved me out of the way and jumped in their faces like a woman pumped up on heroin. They actually looked afraid.

"I need my clothes, Maxine," Cliff spoke like a scolded child.

"They pick up the garbage tomorrow morning so I suggest you beat them here before they arrive asshole. Until then, get the fuck out!" my mother roared.

They both walked out with their dicks between their legs. My mother and I stared at each other and waited for the other to speak. I couldn't figure out what words to possibly say to her after that performance. After all this time, I was pissed off at the wrong person.

"I'm so sorry, Nikki. I'm happy you finally heard the truth." I didn't know how to accept her apology even after learning what she did to protect me. "I hope you'll find it in your heart one day to forgive me."

How could I not, but I struggled to do so. I couldn't just turn if off like that.

"Thanks," was all I could come up with. She would have to accept that until the time came for me to show my appreciation…if it ever came.

"Oh my God. Why did you sleep with Cliff?" she questioned.

"Does it even matter now? He's gone. You don't have to worry about me doing it again." That was a start to an apology.

"Grandma, can we have some popcorn?" We both turned

to Cierra.

"Where were they during all of this?" I questioned my mother.

"I'm sure they didn't hear any of this, Nikki. When I saw Bishop, I put the kids in the back room and turned the TV up loud because I knew he and I would be arguing."

"Hey, that's Uncle A.J. on TV," Cierra spoke as she walked closer to the television.

Turning my attention toward the flat screen, my mouth dropped when a photo of A.J. flashed across the screen. My mother quickly turned up the volume as the news caster spoke.

"THRONE Records CEO, Alphonso "A.J." Townes, was found murdered two days ago in a Hyatt hotel room," the woman stated. I blocked out anything else she said, since I couldn't get over the fact that Cierra knew who he was.

How in the hell did she know him? I turned to my mother for answers.

"Grandma, is Uncle A.J. dead?" Cierra was on the brink of tears.

Someone needed to start talking.

Chapter 28

After learning of A.J.'s death and Cierra's unknown involvement with him, I turned the T.V. off. Desperately trying to calm her down, my mother sent Cierra to her room to go lay down when she saw the expression on my face.

"How does she know A.J.?" I questioned as soon as Cierra was out of earshot.

"I swear, I have no idea."

"Please don't lie to me."

"After what just happened with me, you, your dad and Cliff, I think I'm past lying, Nikki. I don't know and actually, I'd like to know myself, but I have a question for you." I should've known she wasn't going to let it slide. "Did Bishop do something to A.J. for you?" Once again my silence answered her question. She paused for a while. "Why did you do that, Nikki?"

"Because it needed to be done."

"What in the hell did he do to you?"

More secrets were about to be revealed.

"He should've kept his mouth shut about Johnathan that's what he did."

My mother looked confused. "What about Johnathan?"

"Johnathan is A.J.'s son, Mama and if he'd have kept his mouth shut about it, he'd still be alive."

She placed her hand across her heart like it would keep her from having a heart attack. "I can't believe this."

"Well, I guess the saying is true; like father, like daughter." My stomach twisted in knots at my words because they were true. I was just like my dad.

"I…I think I'm gonna go check on Cierra, then lay down myself. This is all too much," my mother said before disappearing in the back.

A few minutes later, I grabbed my phone from out my purse and called the person who really should've been able to answer my question. She was the only other person who had to know how Cierra knew A.J., and why she referred to him as her uncle.

"Hello," Adrienne answered on the third ring.

"How in the hell does Cierra know A.J. and why is she calling him Uncle A.J.?"

She paused for a moment. "What are you talking about, Nikki?" Her delayed response was a sure sign of guilt to me. That bitch knew something.

"Don't play fucking games, Adrienne. You better start talking," I warned.

I listened to her take a deep breath. "Nikki, A.J. has been in Cierra's life since she was a baby. He made me promise to never tell you."

"What? Since she was a baby? That bastard told me that he didn't want anything to do with her."

"There's something else."

I was actually nervous to hear what else she had to say. "What other secret could you possibly be keeping from me?"

"I'm in Georgia."

"Georgia? I thought you were *overseas*. What are you doing there?"

"I've been seeing A.J. for a while. He's leaving his wife. I'm in Georgia getting things prepared for us and once we're settled, we're coming back for Cierra." I stared at my I-phone in disbelief. I couldn't believe my ears. All I could do was burst out into a roar of uncontrollable laughter. "I didn't want you to find out like this, Nikki. Mama doesn't know, so please don't tell her. I'll tell her when the time is right."

"So, you've been seeing my child's fa…"

"She's not your child, remember?" Adrienne reminded.

"After hearing this bullshit, she *is* mine. And what I was saying before you interrupted was how in the hell do you expect me to keep your secret when you've been lying to me all this time? That shit sounds real stupid right now."

"What can I say other than I'm sorry, Nikki."

"Just like Jalisa, you've always been jealous of me. What the fuck is it about me that makes y'all wanna be me? Why the fuck do y'all always want what's mine?"

"I'm not trying to be you, Niquole and A.J. doesn't belong to you." I could hear the anger in my sister's voice.

"He's my child's father so that makes him off limits."

"Cierra is my daughter."

I could tell Adrienne was getting a little concerned since she knew legally she couldn't take Cierra away from me. She'd never legally adopted her. I made sure that didn't happen. I decided to toy with her a little more.

"Okay, I'll give you that much, but when you and A.J. come back for her, are you going to take his other child, too?"

"What are you talking about? He and his wife don't have any kids."

"Yeah, but I have his other child. Johnathan is his son, Adrienne."

You could hear an ant piss due to the silence.

"You're lying. A.J. never told me that Johnathan was his son. You never told anyone for that matter!" Adrienne's voice cracked at every word.

"He just found out. I never told anyone until recently."

"You're lying! You're lying!" Adrienne repeated.

"There's a possibility that Nathan may be his, too." I could sense her anger through the phone, so it was only fair that I poured the heat on a little thicker. "You see, big sister, A.J. and

I never stopped fucking around. In fact, we were together about a month ago."

"You're lying!" she sniffled.

"What reason would I have to lie to you?"

"Because you don't want me to have him, that's why!"

"Bitch, you should've picked another man!" Her sniffles increased. "Are you crying?" I giggled. "Well, let me bring more tears to your eyes. I hope you enjoy being in Georgia alone because A.J. ain't coming!"

"He is coming! I know he is!" she cried. "He loves me! You just don't want me to be happy! You want everything and everyone to yourself." I was sick of the pity party.

"Bitch, A.J. is dead! And as far as Cierra goes, she's dead to you, too!" I hung up.

Chapter 29

Three weeks after all the chaos. I was sitting down with a realtor signing the papers to my new, five bedroom, three and a half bathroom home. Marko called me for the tenth time within thirty minutes. I assumed he didn't take the hint that I couldn't talk to him when I ignored his previous calls. Although Marko and I had become close, I still wasn't ready to let him completely inside my world. I didn't even wanna tell him about my new purchase. For the first time, I had my guard up when it came to a man since every last one of them in my life had ended up hurting me. It was best that way until I felt more comfortable. When he wasn't letting up on his phone calls, I put my pen down.

"Excuse me, Martin," I addressed the realtor. "I need to take this call. I'll be right back."

"Sure, take your time, Ms. Wright. These papers aren't going anywhere."

"I'm sure the

y're not," I smiled back, then walked out of his office. "What is it, Marko? I'm busy."

"I've been calling you over and over. What are you doing that you can't take my call? You're so fucking secretive."

"I'm not being secretive. I'm taking care of business. What is it?"

"You need to get down to THRONE quick!" he demanded hastily.

He'd also lost his mind. I'd be a fool to show my face in there after all of the tension and hateful stares that I received at A.J.'s funeral. Even Tara had a few unkind words to say to me that I let roll off my shoulder. I was a bold bitch to show up at his funeral being that I was the one responsible for his death, but I had to say my goodbyes to my children's father. My mother thought it was odd that I would attend A.J.'s funeral and not Germaine's, but what she didn't understand was that I cared a lot more about A.J. than I did Germaine. Yeah, they'd both hurt and deceived me, but for some strange reason, A.J. held a more special place in my heart.

"Nikki, did you hear me?"

"Yes, Marko, I heard you, but I'm not coming down there. I'm handling some important business right now."

"What kind of business?"

"I can't tell you. Not now anyway."

"See! There you go with them fucking secrets. If we're gonna be together then you gotta stop with that shit, Nikki." That was going to be hard for me to do since I was so used to keeping secrets. "Well whatever the fuck you're during needs to be put on hold. Trust me, you need to get down here quick. Hurry up," he said just before hanging up.

"No his ass didn't just hang up in my face."

But I had to admit, I was more than curious as to why he wanted me at THRONE. After quickly signing the rest of the paperwork for the house, I told Martin I would call him with any questions, then rushed to my car.

Arriving at the label about twenty minutes later, when I

walked inside there still seemed to be a lot of mourning in the air. I ignored it all. I was too busy making mental notes as to how I was going to remodel everything. I knew it was going to be a fight to buy the label back since Tara owned it now. However, I figured if I tossed enough money in her face, she'd give it to me. I pulled my cell phone from my purse to call Marko.

"I'm here," I stated when he answered.

"Come down to A.J.'s old office."

"For what, Marko? What's going…" He hung up again. *We're definitely gonna talk about that hanging up shit when I see him*, I thought. *I don't roll like that.* As I neared A.J.'s office, I could hear Tara yelling and screaming to the top of her lungs. "What the hell is going on?" I mumbled. When I made it to the door, Marko yanked it open.

"Get in here," he ordered a little gentler this time.

When I walked inside, I saw A.J.'s two lawyers who were present when I signed my label over to him and Tara who was pointing and shouting in their faces.

"Ms. Wright, please come in," one of the lawyers addressed me. Still clueless as to what was going on, I walked a little further inside. When Tara heard my name, she jerked her head around like the chick in *The Exorcist* movie.

"What the fuck is she doing here?" Tara barked at me. "Bitch, get out! I'm handling business with my husband's label! You have no fucking right to be here! Marko, you called this trifling bitch, didn't you?" she stabbed Marko with her eyes.

"Actually, Mrs. Townes, we asked Mr. Pendleton to contact Ms. Wright because she has every right to be here. We can't get these proceedings going without her," one of the lawyer's spoke.

"Why does she need to be here?" Tara asked nastily.

Hell, I was wondering the same thing.

"Because a lot of Mr. Townes' will has something to do with her."

My eyes widened. "What will?" I asked.

"Mr. Townes states in his will that in the event of his

death, his two million dollar life insurance policy goes to his daughter Cierra."

. "Whaaaaaaaaaaaaaaaaaaaat?" Tara screamed. "What the fuck are you talking about? What does this bitch have to do with Cierra?"

"You know about Cierra?" I questioned her.

"Yes, I know about her! I'm not stupid! I know her mother's name is Adrienne and she lives in Chicago! So, what the hell do you have to do with it Niquole?"

This was hilarious and it was about to get even funnier.

"Well, Tara, sorry to say this, but you are stupid. You should've investigated a little more. Adrienne is *my* sister and Cierra is *my* daughter," I answered.

Tara looked like she was seconds from blowing up. "What the hell do you mean your daughter?"

"I gave birth to her, but my sister raised her."

"You shady bitch! I knew about your rendezvous with A.J. back in the day, but this takes the fucking cake."

"Well, let me give you another slice. My oldest son is A.J.'s son, too and there's a strong possibility that my youngest son is his as well."

Tara was stunned and finally speechless.

"Umm...there's more," the lawyer interjected. I could tell that he wanted to get this over with so that he could leave before the bullets started spraying.

"More? There can't be any more after this shit," Tara voiced her anger. "I get the label so there can't be anything else."

"Mrs. Townes, I'm sorry, but THRONE goes to Niquole Wright. Mr. Townes words state that in the event of his death, THRONE goes to Niquole Wright. His final words were *she deserves it*."

Shock was an understatement and my mouth hit the floor. After all he and I had gone through, A.J. had finally done right by me. Maybe he really did love me. Suddenly, I started feeling like shit for being the cause of his death.

"Are you serious?" Tara yelled. "What do I get? What am I entitled to?" She started crying.

"Don't y'all have a couple of houses and a few cars? You still have those. Be happy with what you got left," I poured more salt on the new wound.

"Bitch, shut up! Just shut the fuck up!" Tara screamed while stomping her four inch heel into the floor.

"Mrs. Townes, don't forget you'll still be entitled to Mr. Townes other label in New Orleans," the lawyer informed.

"What about his studios?" Marko finally got in on the action.

"Well, his studio in New Orleans was purchased by Germaine Evans, which I'm sure Ms. Wright is entitled to," the lawyer said looking at me. "However, Mr. Townes' additional studios in Memphis, Houston and Atlanta are to be run by Marko Deante' Pendleton," the lawyer read off the paper.

Marko and I turned to each other. We couldn't fight back the smiles.

"Ms. Wright, please stop by our offices at any time to take care of the paperwork for all that we discussed today," the same lawyer stated before putting some paperwork in his briefcase.

"You assholes. I can't believe this. I was supposed to get everything!" Tara screamed at the lawyers then glared at Marko. "You were sniffing up A.J.'s ass all this time to make sure you got those damn studios, weren't you?" When Marko grinned, I was next on Tara's shit list. "You're a slick bitch. I wanted kids! He told me that he wasn't ready for kids yet!"

"Maybe he just didn't want any with you," I smirked wickedly.

"You bitch! I hope you choke on that fucking money," Tara spat.

I started coughing as a joke.

"You two shady, sneaky bastards deserve each other!" She said right before storming out and leaving a trail of tears in the wind. The lawyers soon followed.

I turned to Marko. "Was what she said true?"

"Yep. All those times I was putting you off for A.J., I was making my mark with him. Sometimes, it pays to kiss a little ass. Look at us now. We both got what we wanted."

Epilogue

6 Months Later

I sat at the studio mixer board and listened to Marko spit his rhymes into the microphone for his debut album, *Mind Games*. For once, I kept to my word. I signed him on my new label. I would've been a fool not to. Since he was indeed a conscious rapper and could also sing, Marko was a wanted man. He looked so passionate and sexy standing up there in his black Armani shirt, baggy jeans and Pittsburg Steelers ball cap. If the three producers and two of his friends weren't in the studio with us, I would've run inside the booth and ravaged his ass. Seconds after my naughty thoughts, the song was over and he stepped out.

"Man, that shit was hot!" One of his friends stepped to him and gave him a manly hug.

"Thanks, Jig," Marko said, then walked over to me. He swallowed a gulp of water from the Kentwood bottle. "Baby, what time is your appointment?" he asked.

"In an hour then after that, I have to head over to the florist to check on the arrangements for the wedding and reception." He knelt down and kissed me on the lips then kissed my stomach. "You're already spoiling them," I giggled.

"In two and a half months Marquole and Niqo will be

here."

I laughed. "Oh hell naw! You're crazy if you think I'm naming our babies that ghetto shit. If we spell it Niko, that name for our baby boy isn't too bad, but that Marquole shit has gotta go."

"Whatever you say, baby? So, are you sure you don't want me to go to this appointment with you?"

"It's just another routine appointment. Just make sure you pick up the kids from school and daycare then take them to my mom so that you can meet me at the florist."

Marko shook his head. "Baby, I'm happy to do the cake thing with you, but that flower shit just ain't for me."

"Well, all of that came with the package when you put this ring on my finger, and asked me to marry you," I said staring at the 3-karat, princess cut diamond that sparkled on my finger.

"I'm sick of this wedding shit already. I would've kept the kids and you and your mom could've done that. Isn't that a girl thing anyway?"

"You better be there at five Marko or there will be no more of what we did to make Niqo and Markaya."

"See ya' at five," he smiled before helping my wobbly ass out of the chair.

I kissed him goodbye and left. The babies tumbled around in my swollen stomach as I walked to my new Audi A8. I couldn't wipe the smile off my face as I thought about how good my life had turned out despite all the drama. Yes, I was paid again, but for once in my life it wasn't money that made me happy. It was love. I was in love with my life, in love with my kids and in love with a man who truly loved me. A man who'd accepted all my baggage and never ending issues. He deserved an award for putting up with me. It was only right if I married him, and had his kids before some other woman came along and stole him.

My phone rang inside my Tory Burch tote that accidentally slipped off my arm when I reached inside to retrieve the phone. I slowly eased down to pick it up. When I was back in the upright position, I couldn't help but smile again at my new marquise that read: *JNCM Entertainment*. Kingquole Records was no more and THRONE was definitely out of the picture. It was time for a new start with everything. The first initials of my children's names were perfect for the name of my label since they were truly the reason I got it back.

The kids had transitioned well in our new home, but I was still doing everything I could to keep Germaine and A.J. out of their minds. I even went as far as to say they'd joined the circus. That only stirred the pot because they were anxious to see them perform. My mother offered on several occasions to sit down with me and help tell them the truth, but I still couldn't do it yet, especially since my relationship with them was going so well. Cierra often brought up Adrienne and I would tell her that she was overseas and couldn't make phone calls or send emails. I was sure that lie would eventually blow up in my face, but that was a chance I was willing to take right now. Adrienne had agreed to stay in Georgia and away from us. Hell, with me paying her to stay out of our lives, I'm sure that shit wasn't gonna be too hard. My relationship with my mom was piecing together slowly as well. It was all about forgiveness between us. I even bought her a new house so that she could get away from the awful memories that I'd left inside the old one.

After picking up the tote, I retrieved the phone only to find out that I'd missed the call. Knowing whoever it was would call back or leave a message I continued toward my car. However, I made an abrupt stop when I felt a sharp pain in my abdomen.

"Two and half more months," I spoke to my babies. "Y'all got to stay in there until then," I said, rubbing my stomach.

Just as I was about to say something else, I heard a noise. Turning to my left and right, I scoped the parking lot looking to see what the noise could've been, but didn't notice anything.

"Maybe I'm tripping," I said, when nothing seemed out

of the norm.

Continuing to my car, I'd just unlocked the driver's side door, when someone grabbed the back of my hair. My first instinct was to protect my babies so I immediately placed my hands on my stomach.

"Is that A.J.'s baby?"

I couldn't believe my ears. It was Tara.

"Tara? What the hell is wrong with you? Let me go!"

She released her hold, but made sure to push me up against the car. "Turn around!" she yelled. "Turn around!"

"Okay!"

As soon as I followed her demands, she stared at me, then shook her head. "Did you really think I was going to let this shit go?"

"Tara please. Don't do anything stupid. I didn't know A.J. had a will that included me and our daugh…." I suddenly stopped talking when the sharp pain struck again. I bent over slightly then applied pressure to my abdomen hoping that would ease the pain. "Not now," I breathed through the pain. "Please not now."

"You took everything away from me!"

"Tara, I swear to you…I didn't know," I pleaded again. The sharp pain returned, this time it was even more intense. "I think I'm going into labor."

"Too bad for you. If that's A.J.'s baby, he or she is about to meet their father."

"These are not A.J.'s babies!" I yelled. "Marko is the father."

"Babies? Well, it doesn't even fucking matter. You'll never live to see either of them! Remember…you picked the wrong man, bitch!"

All of a sudden, Tara pulled out a hammer and hit me in my stomach. The pain was so excruciating, I immediately fell to the ground. I didn't even have time to yell out before she hit me in the stomach once again. I couldn't believe this was happening as Tara landed several more blows to my chest, neck and face.

Suddenly visions of my family skipped around in my head. I could see everyone so clearly. Johnathan, Nathan, Cierra, Marko, my mother and even my two new babies were right in front of me. I wanted to cry out. I wanted to tell them how much I loved them, but nothing would come out. Too bad I couldn't touch them. All I could do was wave goodbye as I knew I was about to die. After all the shit I'd done, I guess that saying was true, karma truly was a bitch. When Tara landed one last final blow to my head, I let the devil have me. It was probably for the best anyway since I really didn't know if the twins belonged to Marko or Cliff.

The King of Erotica is back!!!!

A NOVEL BY BEST SELLING AUTHOR

J. TREMBLE

Bedroom
GANGSTA

COMING SOON

COMING SOON

218077735

MAIL TO:
PO Box 423
Brandywine, MD 20613
301-362-6508

FAX TO:
301-579-9913

ORDER FORM

Ship to:	
Address:	

Date:	Phone:
Email:	

City & State:	Zip:

Make all money orders and cashiers checks payable to: **Life Changing Books**

Qty.	ISBN	Title	Release Date	Price
	0-9741394-2-4	Bruised by Azarel	Jul-05	$ 15.00
	0-9741394-7-5	Bruised 2: The Ultimate Revenge by Azarel	Oct-06	$ 15.00
	0-9741394-3-2	Secrets of a Housewife by J. Tremble	Feb-06	$ 15.00
	0-9741394-6-7	The Millionaire Mistress by Tiphani	Nov-06	$ 15.00
	1-934230-99-5	More Secrets More Lies by J. Tremble	Feb-07	$ 15.00
	1-934230-95-2	A Private Affair by Mike Warren	May-07	$ 15.00
	1-934230-93-6	Deep by Danette Majette	Jul-07	$ 15.00
	1-934230-96-0	Flexin & Sexin Volume 1	Jun-07	$ 15.00
	1-934230-92-8	Talk of the Town by Tonya Ridley	Jul-07	$ 15.00
	1-934230-89-8	Still a Mistress by Tiphani	Nov-07	$ 15.00
	1-934230-91-X	Daddy's House by Azarel	Nov-07	$ 15.00
	1-934230-88-X	Naughty Little Angel by J. Tremble	Feb-08	$ 15.00
	1-934230847	In Those Jeans by Chantel Jolie	Jun-08	$ 15.00
	1-934230820	Rich Girls by Kendall Banks	Oct-08	$ 15.00
	1-934230839	Expensive Taste by Tiphani	Nov-08	$ 15.00
	1-934230782	Brooklyn Brothel by C. Stecko	Jan-09	$ 15.00
	1-934230669	Good Girl Gone bad by Danette Majette	Mar-09	$ 15.00
	1-934230804	From Hood to Hollywood by Sasha Raye	Mar-09	$ 15.00
	1-934230707	Sweet Swagger by Mike Warren	Jun-09	$ 15.00
	1-934230677	Carbon Copy by Azarel	Jul-09	$ 15.00
	1-934230723	Millionaire Mistress 3 by Tiphani	Nov-09	$ 15.00
	1-934230715	A Woman Scorned by Ericka Williams	Nov-09	$ 15.00
	1-934230685	My Man Her Son by J. Tremble	Feb-10	$ 15.00
	1-924230731	Love Heist by Jackie D.	Mar-10	$ 15.00
	1-934230812	Flexin & Sexin Volume 2	Apr-10	$ 15.00
	1-934230748	The Dirty Divorce by Miss KP	May-10	$ 15.00
	1-934230758	Chedda Boyz by CJ Hudson	Jul-10	$ 15.00
	1-934230766	Snitch by VegasClarke	Oct-10	$ 15.00
	1-934230693	Money Maker by Tonya Ridley	Oct-10	$ 15.00
	1-934230774	The Dirty Divorce Part 2 by Miss KP	Nov-10	$ 15.00
	1-934230170	The Available Wife by Carla Pennington	Jan-11	$ 15.00
	1-934230774	One Night Stand by Kendall Banks	Feb-11	$ 15.00
	1-934230278	Bitter by Danette Majette	Feb-11	$ 15.00
	1-934230299	Married to a Balla by Jackie D.	May-11	$ 15.00
	1-934230308	The Dirty Divorce Part 3 by Miss KP	Jun-11	$ 15.00
	1-934230316	Next Door Nympho By CJ Hudson	Jun-11	$ 15.00
	1-934230286	Bedroom Gangsta by J. Tremble	Sep-11	$ 15.00

			Total for Books	$

	Shipping Charges (add $4.95 for 1-4 books*)	$
	Total Enclosed (add lines)	$

* Prison Orders- Please allow up to three (3) weeks for delivery.

Please Note: We are not held responsible for returned prison orders. Make sure the facility will receive books before ordering.

*Shipping and Handling of 5-10 books is $6.95, please contact us if your order is more than 10 books.
(301)362-8508